FR.
THE S. ... ISLAND

Francis Vivian was born Arthur Ernest Ashley in 1906 at East Retford, Nottinghamshire. He was the younger brother of noted photographer Hallam Ashley. Vivian laboured for a decade as a painter and decorator before becoming an author of popular fiction in 1932. In 1940 he married schoolteacher Dorothy Wallwork, and the couple had a daughter.

After the Second World War he became assistant editor at the Nottinghamshire Free Press and circuit lecturer on many subjects, ranging from crime to bee-keeping (the latter forming a major theme in the Inspector Knollis mystery *The Singing Masons*). A founding member of the Nottingham Writers' Club, Vivian once awarded first prize in a writing competition to a young Alan Sillitoe, the future bestselling author.

The ten Inspector Knollis mysteries were published between 1941 and 1956. In the novels, ingenious plotting and fair play are paramount. A colleague recalled that 'the reader could always arrive at a correct solution from the given data. Inspector Knollis never picked up an undisclosed clue which, it was later revealed, held the solution to the mystery all along.'

Francis Vivian died on April 2, 1979 at the age of 73.

THE INSPECTOR KNOLLIS MYSTERIES
Available from Dean Street Press

FRANCIS VIVIAN

THE SLEEPING ISLAND

With an introduction by Curtis Evans

DEAN STREET PRESS

INTRODUCTION

SHORTLY BEFORE his death in 1951, American agriculturalist and scholar Everett Franklin Phillips, then Professor Emeritus of Apiculture (beekeeping) at Cornell University, wrote British newspaperman Arthur Ernest Ashley (1906-1979), author of detective novels under the pseudonym Francis Vivian, requesting a copy of his beekeeping mystery *The Singing Masons*, the sixth Inspector Gordon Knollis investigation, which had been published the previous year in the United Kingdom. The eminent professor wanted the book for Cornell's Everett F. Phillips Beekeeping Collection, "one of the largest and most complete apiculture libraries in the world" (currently in the process of digitization at Cornell's The Hive and the Honeybee website). Sixteen years later Ernest Ashely, or Francis Vivian as I shall henceforward name him, to an American fan requesting an autograph ("Why anyone in the United States, where I am not known," he self-deprecatingly observed, "should want my autograph I cannot imagine, but I am flattered by your request and return your card, duly signed.") declared that fulfilling Professor Phillip's donation request was his "greatest satisfaction as a writer." With ghoulish relish he added, "I believe there was some objection by the Librarian, but the good doctor insisted, and so in it went! It was probably destroyed after Dr. Phillips died. Stung to death."

After investigation I have found no indication that the August 1951 death of Professor Phillips, who was 73 years old at the time, was due to anything other than natural causes. One assumes that what would have been the painfully ironic demise of the American nation's most distinguished apiculturist from bee stings would have merited some mention in his death notices. Yet Francis Vivian's fabulistic claim otherwise provides us with a glimpse of that mordant sense of humor and storytelling relish which glint throughout the eighteen mystery novels Vivian published between 1937 and 1959.

Ten of these mysteries were tales of the ingenious sleuthing exploits of series detective Inspector Gordon Knollis, head of the Burnham C.I.D. in the first novel in the series and a Scotland Yard detective in the rest. (Knollis returns to Burnham in later novels.) The debut Inspector Knollis mystery, *The Death of Mr. Lomas*, which was published in 1941, is actually the seventh Francis Vivian detective novel. However, after the Second World War, when the author belatedly returned to his vocation of mystery writing, all of the remaining detective novels he published, with two exceptions, chronicle the criminal cases of the keen and clever Knollis. These other Inspector Knollis tales are: *Sable Messenger* (1947), *The Threefold Cord* (1947), *The Ninth Enemy* (1948), *The Laughing Dog* (1949), *The Singing Masons* (1950), *The Elusive Bowman* (1951), *The Sleeping Island* (1951), *The Ladies of Locksley* (1953) and *Darkling Death* (1956). (Inspector Knollis also is passingly mentioned in Francis Vivian's final mystery, published in 1959, *Dead Opposite the Church*.) By the late Forties and early Fifties, when Hodder & Stoughton, one of England's most important purveyors of crime and mystery fiction, was publishing the Francis Vivian novels, the Inspector Knollis mysteries had achieved wide popularity in the UK, where "according to the booksellers and librarians," the author's newspaper colleague John Hall later recalled in the *Guardian* (possibly with some exaggeration), "Francis Vivian was neck and neck with Ngaio Marsh in second place after Agatha Christie." (Hardcover sales and penny library rentals must be meant here, as with one exception--a paperback original--Francis Vivian, in great contrast with Crime Queens Marsh and Christie, both mainstays of Penguin Books in the UK, was never published in softcover.)

John Hall asserted that in Francis Vivian's native coal and iron county of Nottinghamshire, where Vivian from the 1940s through the 1960s was an assistant editor and "colour man" (writer of local color stories) on the Nottingham, or Notts, *Free Press*, the detective novelist "through a large stretch of the coalfield is reckoned the best local author after Byron and D. H. Lawrence." Hall added that "People who wouldn't know Alan

Sillitoe from George Eliot will stop Ernest in the street and tell him they solved his last detective story." Somewhat ironically, given this assertion, Vivian in his capacity as a founding member of the Nottingham Writers Club awarded first prize in a 1950 Nottingham writing competition to no other than 22-year-old local aspirant Alan Sillitoe, future "angry young man" author of *Saturday Night and Sunday Morning* (1958) and *The Loneliness of the Long Distance Runner* (1959). In his 1995 autobiography Sillitoe recollected that Vivian, "a crime novelist who earned his living by writing . . . gave [my story] first prize, telling me it was so well written and original that nothing further need be done, and that I should try to get it published." This was "The General's Dilemma," which Sillitoe later expanded into his second novel, *The General* (1960).

While never himself an angry young man (he was, rather, a "ragged-trousered" philosopher), Francis Vivian came from fairly humble origins in life and well knew how to wield both the hammer and the pen. Born on March 23, 1906, Vivian was one of two children of Arthur Ernest Ashley, Sr., a photographer and picture framer in East Retford, Nottinghamshire, and Elizabeth Hallam. His elder brother, Hallam Ashley (1900-1987), moved to Norwich and became a freelance photographer. Today he is known for his photographs, taken from the 1940s through the 1960s, chronicling rural labor in East Anglia (many of which were collected in the 2010 book *Traditional Crafts and Industries in East Anglia: The Photographs of Hallam Ashley*). For his part, Francis Vivian started working at age 15 as a gas meter emptier, then labored for 11 years as a housepainter and decorator before successfully establishing himself in 1932 as a writer of short fiction for newspapers and general magazines. In 1937, he published his first detective novel, *Death at the Salutation*. Three years later, he wed schoolteacher Dorothy Wallwork, with whom he had one daughter.

After the Second World War Francis Vivian's work with the Notts *Free Press* consumed much of his time, yet he was still able for the next half-dozen years to publish annually a detective novel (or two), as well as to give popular lectures on a plethora of intriguing subjects, including, naturally enough, crime, but also fiction writing (he published two guidebooks on that subject), psychic forces (he believed himself to be psychic), black magic, Greek civilization, drama, psychology and beekeeping. The latter occupation he himself took up as a hobby, following in the path of Sherlock Holmes. Vivian's fascination with such esoterica invariably found its way into his detective novels, much to the delight of his loyal readership.

As a detective novelist, John Hall recalled, Francis Vivian "took great pride in the fact that the reader could always arrive at a correct solution from the given data. His Inspector never picked up an undisclosed clue which, it was later revealed, held the solution to the mystery all along." Vivian died on April 2, 1979, at the respectable if not quite venerable age of 73, just like Professor Everett Franklin Phillips. To my knowledge the late mystery writer had not been stung to death by bees.

Curtis Evans

Pt. Ailaimo — Pt Grecale

Lighthouse

Creta Bay

poor roads

Salina Bay

Town

Palma Bay

Guitgia Bay

LAMPEDUSA ISLAND
(Eastern end)

Chapter I
THE NIGHT IN QUESTION

Brenda Murray knew what was coming as soon as Paul came down from the bathroom. It had been coming for two hours, ever since he got home from the bank at half-past five. He'd been watching her closely over tea, and twice he'd opened his mouth as if to say something and then closed it again very tightly, so that his flat-chinned and pock-marked little face looked flatter than ever and more like that of a frog. His bulging eyes were focused on her with an unblinking fixity as he entered the room, and that was an infallible sign. Another row was on the way.

She shrank deeper into the fireside chair, almost crouching among the cushions, and forced her eyes to meet the pages of the library book and wander along the lines of print. The words ebbed and flowed erratically in her consciousness, and made little sense. She knew what the novel was about, of course. It was the usual love-story, laced with troubles and complications and misunderstandings which all came right in the end. Just like life, said the descriptive paragraph on the highly coloured jacket, and that wasn't true. Life wasn't even a little bit like that. Once things took a wrong turn . . .

"It's the twelfth of February," said Paul, his thin and high-pitched voice superimposing itself on her thoughts and the drifting sense of the story. "The twelfth of February, and you're in mourning again!"

She said nothing. There was nothing to be said. Neither did she look up, because she knew what she would see, and it would be hateful. She would see Paul standing in the middle of the carpet, his shoulders hunched, his bloodless and pitted face sneering at her, and a cigarette, sodden at the end, hanging from the extreme corner of his thin lips.

"The twelfth of August, nineteen-forty-three, was the day Dennis Palmer died. I married you six weeks later, and thought you'd forget him, and we'd be happy together. First you started celebrating the anniversary of his death, and then his birthday.

Not satisfied with those, you started sorrowing on the dates when he took you here, and there, and somewhere else. And now you've established a half-yearly wake during which you can wallow in a bath of self-pity and sentimentality! I'm sick of it, Brenda! You hear me! Sick of it! And I won't have it! It's only a matter of time before you introduce quarterly celebrations—Hilary, Easter, Trinity, and Michaelmas. For God's sake, pull yourself together and learn to live like a normal human being!"

She bent her head lower over the book, bit her lip, and tried to stem the tide of tears that was gathering behind her blue eyes.

"If you'd ever been married to him it might have been understandable!" Paul went on in a biting tone. "I could have put up with the ghost of a first husband, but when a first fiancé starts haunting the dining-room, the lounge, and the bedrooms, then I put my foot down!"

She put her finger in the book as a marker, and closed it. When she looked up at him there was fire in her eyes, and her oval features were so tense that her cheeks were hollow and her lips shapeless.

"I'd remind you, Paul," she said in a coldly calm voice, "that the house was bought with Dennis's money, and that he does not haunt the bedrooms! You're coarse! So utterly coarse! And he was your friend!" she added bitterly.

Paul nodded casually, and without removing the cigarette blew the ash to the carpet. "He was a decent bloke, and the last thing he'd have asked of you would have been this senseless series of wakes. You're neurotic, that's your trouble! There are better-balanced people in nursing-homes and mental hospitals!"

His voice took on a falsetto tone, intended to be a mockery of her own. "It's five and a half years since my poor darling Dennis died! Five and a half years and six minutes by the clock! Oh dear me! Give me a dozen nice clean hankies for me to weep into!"

Brenda jumped up and threw the book at his squat head. "You—you rotter! I hate you! God, how I loathe you, Paul!"

Paul moved his head with the skill of a trained boxer, so that the book flew over his shoulder to sprawl on the carpet behind him. He stood looking at her for a few seconds, his hands twitching in his pockets. Then he gave a deep sigh, and relaxed.

"Funny that, Bren!" he said in a mild voice. "I don't hate you—and I should do, shouldn't I? Queer, when you come to think about it. There are only the two of us, and we should have been able to make a go of it! Two of us with nobody else left in the world, and we can't agree and stick together. I sometimes wonder if things would have been different if there'd been a baby."

He paused for a moment, and shook his head. "No, you didn't want a baby unless it could have been Dennis's. I was never good enough to be the father of any child of yours. We should never have married, really. You married me because you so urgently wanted the love that Dennis could no longer give you—and then that wasn't right, and you've lived with a dream ever since. Dennis has always been between us."

Brenda shook her head slowly. "No, Paul, it isn't that!"

"Then what on earth is it?" he asked. He laughed bitterly. "What else could it be?"

"Marriage should be give and take, Paul!"

"Isn't it here? Haven't I done my best?"

Brenda sighed deeply, regretfully. "I've given, and you've taken—ever since our wedding-day. You've never been satisfied with what I've done for you. A woman will give everything and anything to the man she loves, but in her own time and according to her moods. You've never been content to wait on my moods. You've only ever wanted but one thing from me—money, and there's been no end to your demands."

She gave him a puzzled look.

"What have you done with it, Paul? What *have* you done with it? I bought the house and gave you the deeds. I put a thousand pounds into your bank account. You've spent that, and all your salary as it's been paid to you, and now—"

"Now what?" he asked irritably.

"I didn't mean telling you this," she said slowly. She lifted an eyebrow and smiled cynically. "You've mortgaged the house behind my back to raise yet more money!"

He started, and avoided her eyes.

"You didn't think I knew that, did you, Paul? We used to boast that this was the only house in the Avenue that didn't owe a lifetime's savings to the building societies. And then I came across a paying-in book for the East Courtney Building Society the other day. You're rotten, Paul! Absolutely rotten!"

"I—" he began.

She cut him short. "You can't explain! It would be all lies, anyway. But you're finished, you know! You'll get no more out of me. Morgan's drafting a new will, and when I die every penny will go back to the Palmers."

"That's all right by me," said Paul. "The money's been nothing but a curse from the beginning."

Brenda glanced at the oak presentation clock on the mantelpiece, the clock given to them at their wedding by the staff of the bank in which Paul worked.

"If you're going to see Benson about the hedge you'd better be going, hadn't you?"

With a peculiar mental detachment which was characteristic of him, Paul replied: "Fairfax says *cupressus* won't grow in this soil. Too much lime. I'll ask Benson for what he considers to be the next best thing. I rang him this afternoon and fixed up to see him at eight. Dunno what it'll cost. Shouldn't run you more than a pound or two."

"I pay again?" Brenda inquired mildly. "Oh well, I don't mind that. We need the windbreak. The crocuses didn't last a week last year, and the daffs. were beaten flat before they had a chance to bloom."

Paul walked to the door, and stood uncertainly for a few moments, his flat face twisted as his tongue explored the inside of his cheek. "Bren! What are we going to do? We can't go on like this!"

"I'll think about it," she said, and bent to pick up the library book.

Paul took a step into the hall.

"Paul!"

"Er—yes?"

"How much did you raise on the house?"

"You saw the book!"

"I didn't look in it. I couldn't!"

"Well, five hundred, if you want to know," he replied surlily.

"I'll pay it off. The house can remain in your name, but the deeds go into my safe deposit!"

He went into the entrance hall without making any reply. Shuffling noises sounded as he crammed his squat body into his greatcoat.

"I'll be back about half-past eight to nine!" he called.

"Then go on to the club?"

"Well, I don't know!"

"I'd prefer you to do so, Paul. I want to think, and I can't do it when you're fidgeting about the room. It isn't as if you could sit and read. You—you wander about until you *irritate* me!"

There was a short pause, a clucking sound, and then he called through: "All right, but I'll drop in and tell you what Benson says. What about Fluff? Want me to call him in?"

"No, I'll do it myself, later. He's busy courting Moresby's Julia at present, so I suppose they'll be giving kittens away again shortly."

The front door closed, and she sighed her relief. She sought the sanctuary of the chair and glanced at the vivid book-jacket. Paradox of paradoxes! That a book dealing with other people's troubles could take one away from one's own for a short spell!

Her head jerked into attention as a faint tapping came on the back door. She laid her book aside, went through to the kitchen, switched on the outside light, and opened the door.

A tall, thin-faced man of about thirty years of age stood smiling at her, and swaying uncertainly on his feet.

"Evening, Bren!"

"Roy Palmer!" she exclaimed. "But Paul's only just gone out. It's a wonder you didn't meet him in the Avenue!"

He pushed her back and walked indoors, closing the door behind him. "Didn't want to meet him. I was waiting for him to get clear. Great row you had, wasn't it? I was listening under the window. Nice little man! Great little guy! If Den was alive he'd wring the ugly little head from his shoulders. Might do it myself yet. But I haven't called to talk about him."

He looked round the kitchen. "Not very warm, is it? Do we have to talk here, Brenda?"

She led him into the dining-room and threw a careless hand towards a chair. "Sit down, Roy—before you fall down!"

She backed up to the fireplace, opened a silver case, threw him a cigarette, and placed one between her own lips. "What do you want?" she asked bluntly as she lit her cigarette and threw the lighter across to him.

He grinned up at her, and twisted his hands together in a gesture of pitiful supplication. "Alms, for the love of Allah! Baksheesh! Charity!"

"Money!" Brenda said with a nod.

"In the name of Allah, the Merciful, the Compassionate, for the poor and distressed, lady!"

"Cut it out!"

He did so, and his manner changed suddenly. He looked earnestly into her oval face, framed by a wealth of chestnut-brown hair.

"Mother's ill, Brenda—very ill!"

"Nothing really serious, I hope?" she replied conventionally.

Roy Palmer's features twitched. He looked weary and ill himself. "Euphemistically described by the medicine men as an incurable disease—carcinoma."

"But that's cancer!" she said in an awed whisper.

"Cancer, Brenda. She's had all the exams and tests at the hospital. They can give her a few more years of life—life in comparative comfort—if she can have an immediate operation."

Brenda wrinkled her forehead. "Can't they operate? Is that what you mean?"

Roy Palmer shrugged. "They can, but they are short of beds—or staff to look after them. Under this present system she'll have to queue up for months outside the theatre door—and by then it might be too late. She's having a rotten time, Brenda. Myself and the old fellow are taking turns sitting up o' nights with her. She's under morphia."

"There must be an alternative to the queue!"

"There is—a nursing-home!"

Brenda nodded as she looked down at his bent head and his twitching hands. "I see! You've come to me for the money!"

He looked up then. "Brenda, we've known each other for a long time now. I was in love with you once, but you never knew it. I'm not asking for money for myself, but for my mother—Dennis's mother. If you can't help her, then one night when I'm nursing her she'll make a mistake and take an overdose of morphia—"

"Roy!" Brenda said sharply, "That's—murder!"

"In the eyes of the law, yes."

"In the eyes of God, Roy!"

His lips twisted. "The eyes of God . . . !"

"They'll hang you!"

"Oh no, they won't!" he replied with a short laugh. "I've got it all worked out. She'll apparently take the tablets herself while I'm downstairs getting a warm drink in the middle of the night, and when I get back I obviously won't know. I shall think she's dropped off into a sound sleep—and no one will be more upset than me when she doesn't wake, and when the truth is known!"

"How much do you want?" Brenda cut in. "Minimum of two-fifty, Bren. That will allow for post-operative treatment and convalescence."

"Two-fifty!"

"Why not?" he snapped. "It's Dennis's money!"

"My money, you mean!"

He got out of the chair, grasped her by the shoulders, and forced her into the opposite one. "*Dennis's* money, see! He didn't will it to you. He left it in your care, and you knew all the time it wasn't for yourself. He intended you to share it out if anything happened to him!"

Brenda got up and slipped past him. "You reek of beer! Now listen, Roy! You can have the two-fifty, and as much more as your mother may need, but do remember this: it is my money. It was a gift!"

"It had to be a gift to dodge the law, didn't it?" Roy Palmer stormed. "Dennis told you; *You'll know what to do if the time should come.* That's what he said! Those were his very words. Grandfather gave it to him to cut out complications with probate and death duties. He had no education, but he knew Den had, and he knew Den would play the game. Den got the premonition about not coming back from the war, and handed the trust to you. And what have you done with it? Let that pockmarked little rat get his hands on it!"

Brenda bridled. "Roy! That's enough!"

He sneered, and shook his head. "Oh no, you're going to get it now! I've been wanting to tell you for a long time. Don't like hearing the truth, do you? He wants the money, and you're denying him, and he'll murder you for it in the end—just as he murdered Dennis for it!"

Brenda stepped back, and the poker went rolling noisily across the tiled hearth. "Roy! You don't know what you're saying!"

He gave a dry laugh. "I don't, eh? I can't prove it, but I know he murdered Dennis! Peter Fairfax knows it, because he was on the island with them, and he can't prove it, either. Your little rat is a clever rat! What rat isn't?" he asked the room.

Brenda stood with one hand over her heart, her blue eyes wide with horror. Roy Palmer grabbed her by the arm and marched her to the sideboard, over which hung a framed aerial photographic map of an island, a long narrow island.

"Lampedusa Island, Brenda. I know it off by heart now, because I've asked so many questions about it. That bit sticking up there is Point Ailaimo, and at the bottom of the cliffs down which he'd climbed my brother Dennis was found drowned. Paul was over here on the east coast, bathing in Creta Bay—but he killed Dennis as surely as if he'd held him down under the water! How did he do it? That's what we all want to know, but he did! Even Fairfax thinks he did, and Peter Fairfax was in charge of their radio crew. Fairfax was on the inquiry, but neither Fairfax, nor the Wing-Commander, nor anybody else could prove it was anything else but death by misadventure. Paul Murray was within a few weeks of blighty leave, Brenda, and he knew about Dennis's money, and what he'd done with it, and he came home, Brenda, and married Dennis's girl—you!—and took Dennis's money. And," Palmer said heavily, "I'll tell you another person in East Courtney who knows!"

Brenda stood before the map of the island. In the corner of the frame was a snapshot of a grave, a grave set under a twisted and gnarled fig-tree, and there was a plain wooden cross set over it.

"Who else, Roy?" she asked. The panic was leaving her. Her soul was quiet, her mind and body relaxed.

Roy Palmer gave a queer little laugh. "Drunk, aren't I? Drunk enough to know what I'm saying, and not sober enough to stop my tongue from saying what my mind has wanted to say for five long years! Jennings knows! Jennings at the top of the Avenue. Jennings, the local editor, who also writes books about crimes of the past. He knows a lot about crime, and one night I put the whole thing to him, and then asked him a question. He never answered me, Bren, but the answer was *in his eyes.* He knows that Paul Murray is a murderer!"

With a deal of dramatic gesture he ticked off the fingers of his left hand. "There's Fairfax, and Jennings, and me—and now you. That makes four of us!"

He suddenly remembered. "Hey! That money for my mother! Do I get it, or do I go home and get the morphia tablets out? It's for you to decide."

"You shall have it, Roy."

"Y'see, Bren, I want to get hold of it before your little rat murders you."

"Roy," Brenda said calmly. "I'm leaving my money to your family. You must know that if you listened under the window."

"That's right! You did say so. It'll be nice for mother—providing you hurry up and die first!"

"Why not race Paul for it," Brenda said wryly. "Murder me before he persuades me to tear up the new will, and the whole lot's yours without any further trouble!"

She pulled open a drawer in the sideboard, and took out her pen and cheque-book. She looked at the photograph of the grave, and then wrote rapidly. "Three hundred pounds, Roy, and I pray God the remaining years of her life may be more free of pain than mine."

"They will be, Bren," Palmer said muzzily. "They will be, because you're doin' the right thing!"

With her back still towards him she asked: "Roy, what does he do with all the money?"

"You don't know?"

"I asked you a question, Roy!"

"You can't see under your nose?"

"A woman?"

"What else?"

She was so calm that he stared at her in surprise. "Funny, that," she said. "Paul with a woman."

Palmer shrugged. "Some women go for the fascination of ugly little blokes. You did, for one!"

"There was something nice about him then," she said reminiscently. "You know who she is?"

He tapped his pocket, and the cheque that now lay within his wallet. "It's Friday night, and I can't get to the bank before Monday morning. I don't suppose you'd think of anything like stopping the cheque when you'd thought about it a bit longer?"

Brenda dragged the sideboard from the wall, revealing a small wall-safe. She opened it with a key from the drawer and took out a handful of notes.

"Three hundred pounds, Roy. Every cent in the house apart from my housekeeping money. What's her name?"

"That as well as the cheque?" he asked with his brows lifted in amazement.

"Her name, Roy!"

"Dickinson. Gloria Dickinson, Number Four, Dale Road. She's known about town as Glorious Dickinson because of her painted glamour."

"Two more questions," Brenda said firmly. "Who else knows?"

"All the blessed town!" said Palmer with an expansive and all-embracing gesture.

Brenda nodded. "I'm being laughed at, eh? Second question, Roy. How long has it been going on?"

"But it never stopped!" Palmer blurted out in astonishment. "You surely knew that!"

"Never stopped?" she asked quickly. "What do you mean, Roy?"

"Oh lord, I know I'm wuzzy, Bren, but this's too much to push across a bloke! Oh lord! He was engaged to her before he married you. He never dropped her. I didn't know for two years after you married him, but as soon as he got hold of the first lot of your money he pushed her into the flat in Dale Road, and it's just kept going on. Oh lord, I don't like this!"

"Then it wasn't *since* . . ." murmured Brenda, and took her lip between her teeth. "He married me for—for—"

"Den's money. We tried to tell you, Bren, but you wouldn't listen! It wasn't just the money we were bothered about—it was you! Our house was your home! You were one of us! Dad and Mum loved you as their own. So did I, but you were Den's girl—"

She suddenly thrust the wad of notes into his hands. "Get out, Roy! I can stand no more! No, put your pen away! I don't want any receipt from you. The money's yours!"

She stood between the sideboard and the wall, her fingers locked tightly together, her blue eyes fixed on him as he hesitated at going and leaving her.

"You may not get the rest of the money, Roy! It's brought me nothing but unhappiness, and if I left it to him—and her! You see what I mean?"

"Nearly eight thousand pounds—or what's left of it," said Roy Palmer.

"Please go now, Roy!"

"Sorry, Bren! I didn't intend this happening. Honest, I didn't! I wouldn't hurt you deliberately."

"Please, Roy!"

He stumbled from the room. She heard the back door close behind him, but did not move for some minutes. Leave the money to him and his girl. That was the solution. Let the curse go to them. Upstairs in the wardrobe was a revolver, an Italian revolver, a souvenir of the war. Paul could have everything she possessed—and much good may it do him! No, he couldn't have Fluffy! Fluffy was the only thing on earth she still loved. Queer, to find one's solace in a half-Persian cat which had a penchant for philandering—like Paul! One bullet for Fluffy, and one for herself. . . .

She pushed the sideboard back to the wall, and went to the back door. The lamp that hung over it was still switched on, and beyond the boundary of the yellow arc all was black with the intensity of a cold and cloudy February night.

"Fluffy! Flu-uffy!"

A shriek of animal pain came from the far end of the garden.

"Fluffy!"

Again the agonised scream, from beyond the lily pool and the fence of chestnut palings.

She clutched her heart. Her own darling Fluffy was in trouble, and she must find him! She sped through the garden, sensing rather than seeing her way round the lily pond. The rest was a series of blurred impressions, of tripping, of falling into the pool, of something sharp hurting her neck, of water entering her lungs with every despairing breath, and finally of a deep and abiding darkness overtaking her.

CHAPTER II
THE EVIDENCE OF THE WIDOWER

FRANK JENNINGS, the editor of the *East Courtney Weekly News*, was a keen murder-mystery fan, but no one was more surprised than he, as he wrote in his Random Notes column, to find himself mixed up in a murder mystery in real life, and in his own town, and that the mystery surrounded the murder of the wife of one of his own neighbours.

The Jennings and the Murrays lived in the same Brandon Avenue, which was about three-quarters of a mile from the town centre, and regarded as residential. The Avenue was originally intended to be the beginning of a private housing scheme on the Courtney-Debenham road—until the builder went bankrupt, when it resulted in twenty neat and well-built houses, a few heaps of sand and bricks, a derelict wooden hut, and several acres of open grassland.

There were ten houses on each side. The Jennings lived in Number Three, the second house on the left going down. The Murrays were at Number Ten, also known as Avalon, halfway down on the opposite side. The houses were all detached ones, all built from the same plan, but with alternate ones reversed; each had a garage at the side of the house, the front wall of which was parallel with the rear wall of the house. There was a small plot of garden in front of each house, and a long rambling garden at the back which had been dealt with in varying ways by the individual occupiers.

The Murrays moved into Avalon early in nineteen-forty-six, and the Jennings into Number Three about a month earlier. Most of the houses in the Avenue were purchased through the local building society, and although everyone in the Avenue knew the truth, it was both convenient and conventional for a pretence to be kept up, and it was allowed that each occupier had bought the little place, you know!

Number Two, across the way from the Jennings's home, was a private club, the Brandon Club. A nice little place where the members could go of an evening for a quiet and genteel drink; everything in Brandon Avenue and on the ribbon-built main road was genteel if nothing else of note. The club was select, described as progressive, and prospective candidates were vetted by the committee before being allowed to pay the annual subscription of two guineas plus the ten and sixpence for a share. And it was in the club, as Jennings told Detective-Inspector Barnard of the East Courtney C.I.D., that the Murray case was first brought to his attention. He regarded this as a poor show, since he'd always been ambitious to discover a real-life murder for himself.

It was exactly a quarter of a minute to nine on the night of the twelfth of February. Jennings was standing at the long bar with

Holmes, the lawyer from Number Seven, doing three things: waiting for the nine o'clock news, drinking Bass, and discussing Jennings's main hobby, which was the writing-up of famous murder cases into popular form and publishing them six to a volume, complete with his own observations on the rights and wrongs of each individual case.

It was a hobby that added considerably to his income. He'd already written-up a volume of unsolved cases, a volume of cases in which the issue had been in doubt but in which the accused had been hanged, and a volume in which the issue had been in doubt but in which the accused had been acquitted. The latter had been tricky to handle, but as a journalist he knew the libel laws, and had skilfully skidded round the more awkward corners without crashing into trouble.

He was a bird-like little man with sparse brown hair and eager eyes, a few years on the wrong side of forty. He invariably wore a blue suit with a faint chalk-stripe, and the inevitable Brandon Avenue bowler hat. He was about five feet six and a half, carried a confident pleased-with-my-little-self smile on thickish lips, and always had an array of pens and coloured pencils poking above the top of the outside breast pocket of his double-breasted jacket.

Holmes was tall, and inclined to be both dignified and absent-minded, one of those people whose eyes are always searching the heavens for the solutions to other people's troubles, a hatchet-faced man who occasionally tripped over kerbs and upsticking water-hydrant covers because he was not looking where he was going. He generally did a share of his wife's shopping while in town, and was regarded by the few unscrupulous tradesmen who disgraced the Thursday market as fair game for quickly marked-up prices.

". . . and so, as I see it," Jennings was saying, "someone gets away with the perfect murder every week of the year—"

The swing doors were flung wide, and Paul Murray almost fell into the room in his haste. He raced across the room and grabbed Jennings by the arm, spilling his beer. "Quick, Jennings! It's my wife—Brenda!"

Jennings blinked, and looked him up and down. He'd seen him many times before, of course; a flat faced fellow with a pock-marked skin and projecting lobeless ears. Jennings was interested in ears, having lately dipped into the last-century researches of Lombroso. Murray had a thick neck which never seemed to emerge from his soft collars, and short-cut mousy hair which was well-oiled and brushed straight back over his oval head. Jennings had seen all this before, but he hadn't seen Murray excited, and so he was interested.

"What is it that's wrong?" he asked in the tone he used to his staff on making-up night.

"Brenda," Murray said quickly. "You've got to come! She—she's had an accident!"

There were only the three of them in the bar, the other members being in the billiards room, or the card room, or the dominoes room. Jennings turned to the steward. "Don't tell anyone else yet. We don't want a circus!"

He and Holmes looked at each other, pushed their tankards on the counter, and followed Murray outside. Once clear of the double sets of swing doors, he broke into a run towards his home. Jennings and Holmes had no choice but to forget their ages, jettison their dignity, and do the same.

Jennings, being trained in the art of observation, noticed several things as they approached Avalon. The front gate was wide open, and the front door was wide open; the hall light was switched on. At the far end of the passage which was graced with the name of entrance hall he saw into the kitchen, and that also was lighted.

Murray led them through the house and out into the open air again via the back door. The grill-protected lamp over the back door was switched on, sending an exploratory yellow light over the lawn and the narrow path that ran alongside it.

Murray reached the far side of the lily pool and stood pointing into the water. The pool was a superior one for the class of house, about twelve feet long and seven wide. It had a causeway round it of three-by-two paving-stones, and in the middle was a pedestal with a statue mounted on it, the statue of a nude girl;

she was bending forward, her hands on her knees, as if watching the nine ornamental fish which served, together with five water-lilies, to decorate the pool.

Jennings and Holmes came up to Murray. His hands and face were all they could make out of him in the now starlit night.

Jennings struck a match, while Holmes played in-effectually with his cigarette-lighter. They made little enough illumination between them, but enough for Jennings to see Brenda Murray lying face down in the pool, and below the surface of the water.

Jennings said: "Oh!"

Holmes said: "Oh, my God!"

Murray stood, helpless, his still-pointing finger tremulous.

Jennings hitched his trousers, a creature of habit even in such circumstances, and knelt while he fumbled to take hold of the belt at the dead woman's waist. Holmes shook the paralysis from his mind and bent down to help. Between them they got her out of the pool and carried her back to the house, Murray fretting around and getting in the way, one knuckled hand pressed tight to his thin lips.

They found cushions, and laid her on them across the hearth, taking it in turns to apply artificial respiration. After his second turn Jennings went, white-faced, to the telephone in the hall, closing the kitchen door behind him. He dialled Courtney 432, and asked for Detective-Inspector Barnard. The officer on duty put him through to Sergeant Scroggey, to whom he told his tale. "And I'm thinking you'd better come round, Scroggey!" he said in conclusion.

"If it's accident or suicide, you want the uniformed jobs," Scroggey replied. "We've enough breaking-and-enterings and robberies-with-violence to keep us busy without having to go out on accident cases!"

"I think you should come round," said Jennings persistently, "and I can't say more over the blower!"

Scroggey swore. "You blankety amateurs! Okay!"

As Jennings went back he met Murray in the door-way, twisting his hands together as if trying to wring his fingers from the palms. "She's dead, Jennings! Holmes says she's dead!"

"I know, old man," Jennings said softly. "I've sent for the police."

The remark shook Murray back to some semblance of normality. He stopped keening, and thrust his nose into Jennings's face. "The police!"

"Of course," said Jennings, laying a sympathetic hand on Murray's arm. "That's the routine, you know."

"But it must have been an accident," Murray pleaded. "We don't want the police round here! She—she didn't—"

"I know," replied Jennings, "but it's still a job for the police. They have to make a report to the coroner. Sorry, old man, but that's the way of things. Why not sit somewhere and take it quietly?"

Murray wandered into the dining-room without a word. It was obvious to Jennings that he was barely conscious of what was going on around him.

Holmes was still in the kitchen. He'd put a cushion-cover over her face, and done his best to pull her skirt down over her knees.

"Hadn't we better try to get her upstairs to a bed?" he murmured in a hushed voice. "Y'know, before she starts to go stiff."

They got her upstairs with difficulty. Her body was limp, and awkward to manoeuvre, but eventually they laid her on her own bed and did their best, in a clumsy masculine way, to straighten her out.

"Lying there," said Holmes, "she doesn't look as if she's come to a tragic end, does she? She might be asleep, and dreaming. See the smile playing round the corners of her lips?"

Jennings grimaced.

"I feel somewhat embarrassed," said Holmes, "as if I'd unsuspectingly walked into her room while she was dressing—as if I'd caught her *en dishabille*—and didn't quite know how to get out again with a satisfactory apology. It isn't right for her to be dead, anyway! She was so vitally alive when she was alive. Often used to see her in town, dashing about as if constantly determined to keep a full diary of appointments. Always smart, too! Favoured colours off the red, which suited her—tans, and browns, and gingers. I can't remember seeing her with a hat, and the dark-brown hair used to dance on her shoulders. I've seen worse faces on magazine covers; far worse, because she didn't seem to rely a great deal on cosmetics, did she? No need to do so, of course. And now she's dead! It isn't right, Jennings!"

Jennings gave the briefest of nods. "If you've finished Hamlet's soliloquy over Yorick's skull," he said, and drew a sheet over Brenda Murray's body.

They went downstairs. Murray was in the dining room, sitting despondently in a fireside chair, his elbows on his knees, his flat chin resting on clenched fists. He was a bent-shouldered fellow at the best, and now he looked like a Notre Dame gargoyle brooding over the miseries of the whole of mankind.

Jennings hunted round and found a bottle of whisky and three glasses. He was pretty liberal with it considering it wasn't his own property. He pushed a half-glass under Murray's nose, and poured good three-finger glasses for himself and Holmes.

"We need it," he said, as if subconsciously aware of the need for some form of apology.

A sound in the Avenue caught his ear. With a warning wink at Holmes he put his glass down and went out to meet Scroggey as he thrust a long leg from a police car.

Scroggey was a big man, with a square face, the most vivid of blue eyes, and sandy hair and eyebrows. He was capable of humour, and possessed an unfortunate knack of bringing it into play in the wrong places and at the wrong times. Twice in three months he'd been pulled up by the coroner for unnecessary and unseemly levity when giving evidence. Bodies were bodies to Scroggey, and not the vacated temples of human souls. "Once I leave this hulk behind," he said, "you can use it for fertilising the rhubarb for all I care. I'll have finished with it!"

Now he was all question marks and suspicion.

"I hope it's something good, Mr. Jennings," he said in a warning voice. "What's it all about, anyway?"

Jennings led him round the side of the house to the lily pool, meanwhile telling how Murray had fetched him and Holmes from the club.

"You two the only witnesses?"

"So far as we know," said Jennings.

"Suicide job, or have you got another idea in your skull?"

Jennings shrugged. "I only report deaths. You people decide the cause. It was so unusual that I felt a bit—well—uneasy about it. I thought you should see things straight away."

Scroggey's long and powerful torch-beam scudded across the surface of the water, round the paving, and at last came to rest on the ground between them.

"It was just here," said Jennings.

"I see that by the wetness," Scroggey said shortly. "Face downwards, you said? Were there any marks on the stones before you pulled her out?"

Jennings puckered his forehead. "No-o, I don't think so. I can't remember seeing any."

Scroggey nodded. "We'll take it there weren't any."

"What kind of marks are you thinking about?"

"Slipping-in marks. There's neither slime nor moss on these pavers, so it couldn't be an accident of that kind."

"And the stones are well-laid," added Jennings. "Smooth stones laid flush, and no edges sticking up."

"Any bruises on the body?"

"There again," Jennings said apologetically, "I can only say I didn't notice any. We were too busy trying to revive her."

"Artificial respiration, of course. Much water in her?"

"Look at the hearthrug when you get indoors," said Jennings, and shivered in the cold night breeze.

"Face clear of cuts and bruises, eh?" murmured Scroggey. "Yes, Mr. Jennings, I think you were right in sending for us. It may be all right, but you never know. Anyone would have the deuce of a job doing suicide in such a shallow pool. It can't be more than two feet deep. Notice anything else that might be useful?"

"The front gate, front door, and back door were all wide open, and lights on straight through the house."

"Where's the husband?"

"In the dining-room in a bit of a trance. I gave him a glass of whisky. He was all in—seemed mentally numbed."

Scroggey grinned in the pale light reflected from the paving-stones. "Whose whisky? His own?"

"Oh yes, it was in the sideboard."

"You know the house so well?"

Jennings shrugged. "All the houses in the Avenue are built to the same design. We live in pretty much the same fashion. I'd a pretty good idea I'd find it in the spot where I keep my own."

"Logic!" sighed Scroggey. "It's hanged many an innocent man. Let's go indoors and see him, shall we? It might be a bit warmer in there."

Holmes had fetched Desmond, the doctor who lived at the bottom of the Avenue. Jennings was annoyed with himself for neglecting that elementary action.

"Somehow," he excused himself, "the first word that came into my head was *police*—probably due to my preoccupation with police matters in my spare time. Queer how our minds become conditioned. . . ."

The doctor was still upstairs, examining the body. Murray was in the dining-room, his whisky barely touched. He was staring into the fire.

"Tell him who I am," whispered Scroggey.

"Murray," said Jennings, aware that he was speaking far too loudly owing to his nervous state; "Sergeant Scroggey would like a word with you!"

Murray looked up, dull-eyed and slack-jawed. "Well?" he said listlessly.

"Sorry to bother you with questions," Scroggey said in a gentle voice, "but at what time did you find your wife?"

Murray's eyes were as vacant as deserted snail-shells. "Find her? At what time? I don't know! I didn't look. It was just before I went to the club for Mr. Jennings."

"Obviously," said Scroggey. "How did you find her?"

"I'd been out, you see," Murray said. "When I got back the gate was open—and I remembered closing it when I went out. I let myself in at the front door with my own key. A draught hit me, and I knew the back door was open. I went to the door and called my wife, then called upstairs. There was no reply, so I went round the house and then out into the garden. I remembered the cat. . . ."

"You remembered the cat," said Scroggey in a non-committal manner.

"Blue Persian—or half-Persian," Jennings whispered.

"We've no children, and she was fond of it," said Murray, obviously straining to keep his mind on the matter in hand. "She didn't like it to be out after dark, so she went out most evenings to coax it in. Its fur takes a lot of keeping right," he added irrelevantly.

"Yes?" said Scroggey.

"It can squeeze through the chestnut palings at the end of the garden, so I wondered if she was up there, and went out to look for her. That's how I found her."

"In pitch darkness?"

"I had a torch."

"Where is it now?"

"Somewhere in the kitchen. I flung it down when I ran through the house to fetch Mr. Jennings."

"It's immaterial," said Scroggey. "When you found her, what did you do? Try to get her out of the pool?"

Murray shook his head. "I ran for help. I never thought of anything else. I didn't know what to do."

Scroggey turned to Jennings. "You at the club every night, and at the same time, Mr. Jennings?"

"Most nights, but it doesn't run to a schedule."

"Still, it was a fairly safe bet he'd find you there tonight?"

Jennings pulled a face. "Oh, fifty-fifty! I'm mostly there between nine and ten. Depends whether I've any functions to attend."

Dr. Desmond appeared in the doorway, signalling to Scroggey. Jennings nudged him with his elbow to attract his attention.

"Thanks," Scroggey said to Murray, and sauntered into the entrance hall. Jennings and Holmes followed, the latter closing the door behind him.

"There are two incised bruises on the nape of her neck, about four inches apart," said the doctor.

Scroggey scowled at Jennings, and made his way up the stairs. The doctor went with him. Jennings followed, since nobody seemed to object. He was getting a good story. Apart from being editor of the local weekly, he had lineage as district correspondent for a national daily, and up to now he had no competition in this affair. It was a first-class scoop, as he whispered to Holmes on the way up the stairs.

Dr. Desmond unsheeted the body and rolled it over. "See?" he said.

Scroggey bent over the limp remains of Brenda Murray. "Those marks remind me of something."

"Snake-bites," said Jennings.

Scroggey snapped his thick fingers. "Snake-bites, my foot!"

"Punctures with bruises round them," said Jennings.

"Horribly unprofessional description," murmured Dr. Desmond.

"Afraid of handling a cadaver?" Scroggey asked Jennings.

"Holmes and I fished her out, carried her in, and then brought her upstairs!"

"Fair enough," said Scroggey. "Arrange her exactly as you found her in the pool. Pity you pulled her out. Photographs help enormously. Handle her, man! She can't bite you! She's dead."

Jennings and Holmes arranged her so that she was lying on her stomach, with her right hand and arm stretched out beyond her head, and her left hand and wrist doubled under her left breast.

"I see it," said Scroggey. He made a vee of his first and second fingers and held them over the incised bruises. "Better have her taken to the mortuary. It's murder."

"Murder!" exclaimed Jennings.

"Not accident nor suicide?" murmured Holmes.

"Not unless she held herself down in the pool," Scroggey said sarcastically. "Can I step across and use your 'phone, Mr. Jennings? I prefer some of my calls to be private."

"The wife's home, and knows you," said Jennings.

Scroggey went down the stairs lightly for a heavy man, and to ease the uncomfortable silence left in the room Jennings coughed loudly, and then murmured an apology, as if he'd dropped the collection plate in a church of praying people.

The doctor looked down at Brenda Murray. "The sergeant's quite right. She was murdered. I wonder . . ."

He ran his tongue over his lips. "Perhaps better wait until we have her in the mortuary."

"For what?" Jennings asked curiously.

"You hadn't noticed?" the doctor asked. "The back of her right stocking is torn, as is the front of her left one—over the ankle. It is reasonable to expect scratches on the corresponding parts of the flesh."

He drew the sheet over her and led the way down-stairs. They waited in the kitchen, leaving Murray alone with his sorrow. Scroggey came back in due course, and jabbed a finger in Jennings's chest. "You and Mr. Holmes are policemen for the time being."

At the far end of the garden he said: "All got torches? I want a long piece of wood with a forked end like a catapult."

It was Duggan, the driver of the police car, who found it, a fairly straight branch of sycamore about six feet long, lying on the opposite side of the fence in the long grass.

The doctor mentioned the torn stockings to Scroggey, who nodded scornfully. "Think I didn't notice 'em?"

He swept the beam of his torch in a path leading from the fence to the edge of the pool. "Tripped up with the branch, pushed into the water, and held down with this forked end. She hadn't a chance. Chummy certainly has original ideas. It should be an interesting case!"

"Chummy?" murmured Holmes.

"The name of the guy we don't know, or the name of the guy we suspect and don't care to name," said Scroggey laconically. "The Old Man's going to like this—unless they call in the Yard. That's the sensible thing to do. It's going to be a teaser, and the county can't really spare the money."

"See," said Dr. Desmond, "you only pay if you send to the Yard when the thing has beaten you local fellows. Isn't that it?"

"Right," said Scroggey. "I think I'll advise the Old Man to send for the Yard."

Jennings smiled to himself. Inspector Barnard was about the last person in the world to be influenced by the opinions of one of his sergeants. Still, that was Scroggey all over—loads of talk.

Scroggey handed the branch back to Duggan to take charge of, and went back to the house to interview Murray once more. There was nothing private about the interview. Jennings and Holmes and the doctor stood in or around the doorway and heard it all.

Murray's story was as wide open as a barn door. He'd gone into town to see a nurseryman about a hedge for the line along which the chestnut palings ran. Some friend had put him off *cupressus macrocarpa*, telling him it wouldn't grow in limy soil, so he'd been to ask for professional advice. The nurseryman wasn't at his place of business, so he'd come straight home, intending to tell his wife, and then go to the Brandon Club for an hour. He'd missed the bus, and sooner than wait twenty minutes for the next on a cold February night, well, he'd walked. Just that, and no more.

Where was the cat? He didn't know. Despite its aristocratic pedigree, or because of it, it was no more than an old roué and was probably having a night on the tiles.

And then in walked Duggan, carrying the limp body of the cat over his left arm. "Dead," he said shortly. "Neck pulled out. Also its throat squashed in. Somebody round here doesn't like cats!"

Murray sat and stared open-mouthed.

"Where was it?" asked Scroggey.

"About six yards from the fence, as the crow flies."

Paul Murray got up and walked across to Duggan, to stroke the cold fur with a white and pock-marked hand. "Poor little devil!" he said.

Scroggey was standing behind him, waiting. He saw Murray's shoulders sag, and caught him as he collapsed in a dead faint. He balanced him on powerful arms, as easily as if he had been nursing a baby. "You take him, Doc. Share and share alike. You take the living, and I'll take the dead."

"What a crude man!" Holmes said in a shocked voice.

CHAPTER III
THE EVIDENCE OF PETER FAIRFAX

NANCY FAIRFAX fetched the morning paper from the mat, and glanced over the front page while the porridge boiled in the porringer. She read the headlines, and the first paragraph of the centre column. Then she read the centre column again, blinked, shook her head as if to clear the mist away, and ran to the foot of the stairs.

"Peter! Oh, Peter!"

"Coming, darling," replied a casual voice, and her husband appeared on the landing, grinning over the banisters at her, a tall, black-haired, black-browed, black-moustached fellow with deep-blue eyes.

"Bags of usual panic," he murmured as he came down the stairs. "Porridge going cold, kippers spoiling, and tea stewed beyond drinkability. The way of a wife with a feckless husband is hard. All that, despite the fact that I thought up the kippers myself, and brought them home like any member of the proletariat, wrapped in a newspaper—yes, I say, despite all that, I show no appreciation for my wife's cooking of them—"

"Peter!" Nancy almost screamed. "Will you please listen! Brenda Murray's dead—murdered!"

He came down the last few stairs and took her hands in his own, nodding solemnly. "I know, darling. I knew last night."

"You knew? How could you? Why didn't you tell me?"

"I wanted you to sleep, my sweet, and one doesn't sleep after such news."

"Who told you, Peter? How did you get to know? Was that why you were late home?"

"That was it," sighed Fairfax. "Barnard came in very late, looking for someone. I think it was me."

"Barnard?" Nancy Fairfax asked, her brows creased with puzzlement.

"The detective fellow, the inspector down at the local C.I.D."

"Looking for you. Why for you, Peter?" she asked quickly.

She stared into his bold and now expressionless eyes. She was five feet seven, two inches shorter than her husband; a slim, good-looking woman of thirty-one with light-brown hair, and the knack of looking well-dressed even in her plain deep-gold morning-dress with its protecting blue apron.

"What did he tell you, Peter? How did it happen? Who did it?"

"The kippers," he said gravely. "Suppose we adjourn to the diner, and I'll tell you about it over brekker. The kippers, the porridge, the tea. . . ."

Nancy shrugged, and went back to the kitchen. Peter followed her, clasped her shoulders in firm hands, and kissed her behind each ear. "I'll help with the carrying and serving, darling. You take the teapot, and I'll follow up with the porridge."

He let her go first, and then leaned over the table and quickly scanned the centre column of the *Argus*. He learned that the East Courtney police and the county authorities had decided to call in the Yard, and that Mr. Frank Jennings, editor of the *East Courtney Weekly News*, was an important witness. "Peter! The porridge, darling!"

"Coming, ma'am," he replied lightly, but the grimness of his expression did not match the casual tone of his voice.

"Now then," said Nancy, when the tea was poured.

"It was probably about half-past ten, darling. I was trying to wangle another tankard out of Jonesey and he wouldn't come clean. Barnard came in, looked round, and came straight over to me. He wanted to talk to me. Made me go all gooseflesh, having a 'tec walk up like that. Thought he was going to arrest me for something!"

"Peter! Please get on with the story!"

"Wanted to know if I knew the Murrays of Brandon Avenue—which meant he knew jolly well that I did. I admitted that I did know them, and that we'd swopped tea and buns on odd occasions. What did I know about them? Awkward question, that. I mean, one knows a lot about people, and it depended on what he wanted to know, as I pointed out to him."

Nancy shook her head sadly. "You can be an irritating person, Peter. I bet the Inspector was itching to kick you! It means you were stalling him, of course. Why?"

"Somewhat direct question, darling," Peter murmured. "One doesn't go exposing the love-lives and financial-statuses—or stati—of one's friends just as soon as the questions are popped. The man was far too eager for information. He wanted to know whether Brenda and Paul got on well together, and I started slipping in odd questions that he couldn't dodge, and so slowly got the whole story. Very cute of me, I must say," he added modestly.

"What—was the story, Peter?"

"Bluntly, darling, someone tripped her into the lily pool, and—er—held her head under water with a forked stick until she drowned."

"Poor, poor Brenda!"

After a minute she looked over her handkerchief, and asked: "Paul? Where was he at the time?"

"That," Peter replied slowly, "was apparently what Barnard was trying to find out—among a lot of other things. They'd interviewed him, y'see, and he'd brought in my name."

"Your name?" Nancy asked vaguely.

Peter dabbed the surface of the untouched porridge with his spoon. "Mm! Unfortunate, in a way. You see, I ran into Paul in town yesterday noon, and for want of something to say we started talking about gardens. He wanted to shove a hedge along the back fence, to act as a windbreak, and was going to order about four or five dozen cupressus until I put him off the stuff and suggested he had a pow-wow with Benson. So he told Barnard he'd been to see Benson, and the chappie wasn't in—well, he told Barnard's man, which is the same thing. Point seems to be that he hadn't an alibi for the vital time, and Barnard was fishing to see if he had any motive for doing her in himself—Paul, I mean, not Barnard."

Nancy pushed the porridge away. "I wonder if he did, Peter? He was rotten to her, you know. That night when she had a broken shoulder-strap. . . ."

"There were lots of nights, darling. I wouldn't have lost an hour's sleep if it had been Paul. He's a louse. Bein' Brenda makes it different."

Nancy reached a hand across the table to him. "You had a bad night, darling?"

"Not too good," he said crisply, pushing back his chair. "I'll fetch the kippers."

Brenda shuddered. "Don't bring mine! I couldn't face it!"

"They were well washed! I did them myself!"

"What's that got to do with it?"

Peter hurried towards the doorway. "Dunno," he muttered. "One has to say something."

"It's a horrible thing!" said Nancy.

"I prefer haddock myself," said Peter, "but it's Hobson's choice."

On his return he neatly slipped the point of the fish-knife under the backbone of the kipper and removed it in one piece. "The old hand loseth not its touch. I once won a mess competition for kipper and sardine filleting. That was down at Tangmere, I think. Yes, it was when old Dogsbody was the O.C. He said it was the neatest job he'd seen, and promoted me to Official Fish Filleter for Royal Occasions—job apparently was to fillet His Majesty's kipper if he ever dined in our mess. I remember I also won a threepenny sweepstake on the result."

"What will happen now?" Nancy asked absently.

"I'll eat the remainder, barring the head and tail, which aren't cooked, anyway."

"Peter! Will you stop fooling! I know you're trying to keep my mind off the affair, but I'm not in the mood this morning. What really will happen now?"

"Yours truly has the morning off. Barnard wants to have a run round here about ten-thirty to see if there's anything you can tell him, so I stay home as moral support and witness to the interview. You won't mind, will you?"

"I wouldn't have slept if I'd known," Nancy said with a light shudder.

"That's why I said nothing last night," Peter nodded wisely.

Nancy asked for his empty cup and refilled that and her own. "I'm worried, Peter."

"So's Barnard. I think they'll call in the Yard."

"The morning paper says so."

"Does it?" Peter asked in an innocent tone.

"Does that mean they've no idea who—killed her?"

"Not a clue last night, according to Barnard. I'm afraid Courtney's going to be front-page news for a day or two, darling. I suggest you hop off to your mother's for a time. As we were acquainted with the Murrays, we'll have reporters on the doorstep from morning till night."

Nancy shook her head. "Won't do, Peter! I'll stick it. If there's anything I can do to help poor Bren, even now she's dead, then I'll do it. It's all I can do—and you wouldn't run away!"

"Faithful unto death, that's me," Peter said lightly. "I'd stay until the lava covered me up and turned me into a statue like the centenarian they found at Pompeii."

"Centurion," Nancy corrected him absently. She stared into her cup, at a lone leaf sailing round its circumference. "Think of it, Peter! There's some poor woman, sitting at breakfast, as I am now, facing a murderer and not aware of it!"

"Thanks!" Peter said in a dry tone.

Nancy pushed the remark away impatiently. "You know what I mean!"

"Socking the husband by comparing him with a murderer," replied Peter. "On the other hand, you know, the bloke may be single, or could even be a woman!"

"Peter!"

"Sweetheart?"

"Who could have murdered her?"

"Lots of people," Peter answered her. "What you mean to ask is, Who did it? Murray himself, or young Palmer, or somebody out of her past about whom we know nothing. The motive is the thing to look for, according to Barnard. Ask yourself why she was done in, and why she was murdered in such an unusual manner. Ask yourself who benefits by her death—either from a psychological or emotional or monetary point of view. He explained quite a lot about these jobs, all about the psychology of murderers, and so on. Interesting bloke, really, although I don't go abundance on bobbies as a rule. . . ."

He played with the ruins of the kipper for a few moments, and then added: "Paul found her, and that seems to stink in Barnard's nostrils. Says—or hinted—that it's a highly suspicious factor, especially as he can't satisfactorily account for the hour or so between leaving home and getting back again. Barnard can't challenge his statement that he walked back from town, and Murray can't prove it. Barnard says it's what they call a useful alibi, one that can flummox the police, and one that the most competent K.G. jibs at trying to break down. Anyway, seems to me that whether he did it or not they'll be watching him closely for a long time—until they line somebody else up for the job, if you'll pardon my grammar."

"I could almost feel sorry for Paul," said Nancy reflectively.

"Almost!" Peter echoed caustically.

It was eleven o'clock when Inspector Barnard arrived. He was a sparely-built man with a fresh complexion and light hair, a pleasant man who went about his work competently and yet without any air of officialdom surrounding him.

With him was a lean man dressed in a grey suit, a solemn man with keen grey eyes, a long thin nose, high cheek-bones, and a chin that was lifted just half an inch too high, giving him the appearance of a person with too good an opinion of himself. His eyelids fell far over the grey eyes, as if he was habitually anxious to conceal his thoughts. Peter Fairfax later described him as a chartered accountant who was also either a Pilgrim Father or an Eastern ascetic. "The bloke looked as if he spent all his time contemplating his umbilicus, and had never had a day's fun in his life. Lord!"

Barnard made the introductions. His companion was Detective-Inspector Gordon Knollis, of the Yard, now in charge of the investigation into the death of Mrs. Brenda Murray. "The Yard are specialists, you know," Barnard added modestly.

Surprisingly, Knollis's severe features relaxed, and he smiled in a friendly manner. "He hopes we are," he said lightly.

"Anyway," said Barnard, "we'd like to ask your wife a few questions about the Murray *ménage*."

Nancy Fairfax had coffee waiting, and they seated themselves in the lounge, the watery February sun adding its feeble warmth to the efforts of the electric fire.

"You knew the Murrays pretty well?" Knollis asked, to open the inquisition.

"Pretty well, yes," Peter replied.

"How and when did you first meet them, Mr. Fairfax?"

Peter grimaced. "This is going to be a long story, Inspector! It goes back some years."

"We've time!" Knollis replied with a smile.

"Well, I first dropped across Paul Murray in the R.A.F. during the war. I was signals officer with a unit that went to Lampedusa—"

"There's a composite photographic map of it over the sideboard in Murray's dining-room," Barnard offered gratuitously.

Peter nodded. "That's correct. I've a similar one upstairs. I got them from the Imperial War Museum—official war photographs, you know. Five all told. There's the map, two aerial shots of the town and harbour, a photo of two Guards raising the flag over the Governor's house, and one of wrecked Junkers on the airfield."

"You met Murray on the island?" Knollis asked quickly, stalling Peter on further irrelevant details.

"He was one of the bods on the V.H.F. site up by the lighthouse."

Knollis blinked. "Sorry, Mr. Fairfax, but you are speaking a language strange to me!"

Nancy intervened.

"It's Raffese, Inspector. Bods are birds or men. V.H.F. means Very High Frequency."

"Good for you," smiled Peter. "Murray was one of my crew. They were working two radio outfits, one for D/F or direction finding, and the other for Air Sea Rescue, working on different frequencies—or wavelengths if you like it better that way round. I got to know he came from Courtney, and had quite a few chats with him about the old town."

"There was also Dennis Palmer," Barnard said in a quiet voice.

Peter looked at his fingers, and nodded. "Yes, there was also Dennis Palmer!"

"Palmer met his death there," Barnard said to Knollis. "He was engaged to the late Mrs. Murray at the time."

"I'm interested in Palmer," said Knollis, leaning forward and interlacing his fingers.

"He also was a Courtney man," said Peter. "Both being erks—rankers—he and Murray were thrown together pretty much, and seemed to get on well together. We heard—but I'm going too fast for you! We left the island the day after Palmer's death. The outfit went back to the mainland to be dispersed, and I lost sight of Murray, who was posted to another outfit. I heard later that he was almost due for home leave at that time, and later still heard that he'd married Palmer's girl while on leave. Bit of a shaker, was that! I mean, you don't do these things!"

"But Murray did," Knollis said blandly. "How did Palmer die, Mr. Fairfax?"

"By drowning. Seemed he couldn't swim very well, and went off for a spot of solo practice. Nobody knows what happened to him, but his body was found by the island fishermen. We held an inquiry, and he was buried next day, an hour before we embarked for the trip back to the Tunisian mainland."

"Accident, of course?"

Peter shrugged. "Death by misadventure, we decided. He'd climbed down the cliff to this spot. It wasn't really a cove, but a wide shelf sheltered by the jutting cliff to the west. The water was about seven fathoms deep just there—that's about forty-two feet, isn't it? The tide's negligible in the Med., of course, but there were tricky in-shore currents on the north side of the island—"

"The north side, Mr. Fairfax?"

"Chock under the eastern face of Point Ailaimo."

Knollis chewed his lip. "Tell me, Mr. Fairfax; were the signals units established on the northern coast of the island?"

"Well, no, not actually. The radio tenders or vans were on the north-east corner, almost on Cape Grecale, but the billet was on the south side of Creta Bay."

Knollis smiled. "I wonder if we could have your photographic map of the island for a few minutes. I'm lost, not knowing the island."

"Is it so important?" Peter asked as he rose and went towards the door.

"Probably not," replied Knollis, "but the Palmer story fills in the background of the present affair."

While Peter was away, Knollis turned to Nancy Fairfax, neat in a plain frock of spring green with emerald-green cuffs and collar. "You knew the Murrays well, it would seem, Mrs. Fairfax. Did they get on well together? Was Mr. Murray—shall we say—kind to his wife?"

She hesitated for a moment before answering, and then her features hardened. "No, he was not!"

"Tell me something about him, please."

"They came over for dinner one evening last August," she said slowly. "She broke a shoulder-strap, and we went to my room to sew it. She had to remove her frock, of course. . . ."

"Yes?" Knollis murmured patiently.

"There—there was a horrible bruise between her breasts, and a similar one on her back."

"He knocked her about," Knollis remarked unnecessarily.

"It was the anniversary of Dennis's death," Nancy Fairfax explained. "She had a weep on my shoulder and told me all about it. She'd felt a bit sad, and Paul had told her to forget Dennis once and for all. She said she couldn't, and it was no use trying. He lashed out at her with his fist. She turned her back in self-protection, and he hit her again, and told her he was only sparing her face because they were coming out that evening."

"It had happened before, Mrs. Fairfax?"

"I don't know for sure, Inspector, but something similar has happened since then. She 'fell against the bureau' early in January, or perhaps it was late December, and had an awful eye."

"Money—" began Knollis.

"I'll answer that for you, Inspector," Peter said as he re-entered the room. "Palmer gave his money, a matter of several thousands of pounds, to Brenda. Murray came on leave, as I've told you, after Palmer's death, and married it."

"It? Married it?" Knollis queried.

"The money. He's chiselled her ever since."

"The photographic map," said Knollis eagerly.

Peter laid it on the table, and pointed to the spots to which he had referred. "The radio tenders were about here, the billet was here—a dug-out affair on Creta Bay—and this is where Palmer was found, chock at the foot of Point Ailaimo."

"Where was Murray that afternoon?"

The black moustache wriggled as Peter Fairfax grimaced. "Murray? Lord, you aren't thinking that, are you? He was bathing with other bods in Creta Bay. We checked on that at the inquiry, of course, because so far as we could discover he was the last person known to see or speak to Palmer."

"The natives? The islanders?" Knollis murmured.

"Not so," said Peter. "Most of them are concentrated in the one town, Lampedusa itself. There are odd hovels scattered over the island, but they were all friendly folk, only too pleased to see the 'brave and noble English soldiers' there. And Palmer was the type who could get on with anybody. Charmin' type, he was. No, nothing doing in that respect, sir!"

"He'd neither towel nor bathing-trunks?"

Peter laughed loudly. "In the Med.? You needed neither, sir. One bathed in the raw, and the sun dried the old body satisfactorily in a matter of minutes. An uncomplicated life, and an uninhibited one. In fact, it was an uninhibited island," he said with a bright smile.

"Very humorous remark," Knollis said gravely. "What I'm getting at is whether there was any reason why this Palmer might have put an end to his own life?"

"Why should he?" Peter protested. "He was worth about eight thousand pounds, for a guess. He had a good job here in Courtney to pass away the time, and that was ready and waiting for him whenever he was released from the Service. He had Brenda waiting for him, and, believe me, she was fair to look upon, and worshipped the ground he rode over on his bicycle!"

He shook his head vigorously.

"No, Inspector! Everything was in his favour. The gods must have loved him too much. In any case, he wasn't the type for self-destruction, being one of the frank ones of the earth who tell everybody their business. I mean, if he'd had trouble he'd have unloaded on somebody—and you don't have troubles when you put half of them on somebody else's back, do you?"

"I see," said Knollis. "Now, Inspector Barnard tells me that you and the Murrays exchanged visits on occasion?"

Nancy Fairfax answered the question. "Yes, but it was a one-sided arrangement. I'd meet Brenda in town, invite her to tea—"

"In such a manner that she couldn't refuse," interrupted Peter, "and later she'd ring through to say she'd forgotten a previous engagement."

"Peter! They came twice! But we were only asked back once."

"Once too often," Peter said in a solemn tone. "Visiting Murray was like visiting a suffragan bishop when he was suffering because he'd just found out his wife was unfaithful to him. A horrible atmosphere of restraint. He wouldn't talk, and it seemed as if she daren't, so I had to jabber like a kookaburra for two hours to cover the silence until we could get out."

"I always felt sorry for her," sighed Nancy.

"It was a peculiar mode of murder," Knollis said, more to himself than to his companions. "A lily pool, populated by ornamental goldfish. Why was such a mode chosen? Where lies the significance? Lilies? Water? Fish? Know anything about fish, Mr. Fairfax?"

"We had kippers for breakfast," Peter said brightly.

Barnard smiled. "Then you got them home safely. You should have seen him nursing them, Mrs. Fairfax. He looked as if he'd never carried a parcel in his life!"

"He hasn't," Nancy laughed. "He hates them. I was shaken when he produced them. He said he fancied one for breakfast, and that was that. He does go off at tangents!"

"The point is that both Dennis Palmer and his one-time fiancée met their deaths by drowning," murmured Knollis.

"And Murray was nowhere near on either occasion," Peter said thoughtfully. "Peculiar coincidence. . . ."

"You know the town well," said Knollis. "Would you say it was possible for anyone to walk from the town centre to Brandon Avenue without being seen?"

Peter thought about it for a moment. "Not without being seen, but perhaps without being noticed," he eventually replied. "There's a lot of difference, really. The road's lighted by those ghastly orange efforts slung out over the middle on wire, and I've noticed that they tend to make people look like warmed-up corpses, and virtually unrecognisable."

"You've walked it at night, Mr. Fairfax?"

"When he leaves the club late and misses the bus," Nancy said with mock severity.

Knollis gave one of his rare smiles. "You also do that, eh?"

Peter nodded. "And I can't say I've been out on a case. If I offered that excuse she'd turn witty and want to know how many bottles were in it—y'know, the old corny joke. Oh, I'm no Trappist, but certainly one of the Trapped. Home by half-past ten or up before the Inquisition!"

"Can't you find a few conferences?" Knollis asked.

"Only junior partner at present, and technical side at that," replied Peter. "Not trusted with such important doings yet. But the day will come! Oh yes, the day will come, and then there'll be conferences every second evening!"

"You try it!" warned Nancy.

"Well," said Knollis, "we must be getting along to jog Murray's memory once more. Peculiar business, you know! We go about our daily lives, satisfied that we're fully awake and observant, and yet if asked what we did or what we saw at a certain time, we find ourselves floundering."

Peter looked up with wide eyes and arched black brows. "Suppose that's true!"

"When did you last see Murray, for instance?" asked Knollis.

Peter laughed. "Thought for the moment you were going to quote the title under the old picture and ask me when I last saw my father. Murray? Yesterday noon as ever was. I ran across him when going to lunch."

"Who was going to lunch?"

"Both of us—he to a café, me to home."

"He usually lunched in town?"

"Can't really say, Inspector."

"You had a chat?"

"I told Inspector Barnard all that last night, sir, but the whole thing was cussedness on my part, because he don't like talking if he can avoid it. Probably got one of those inferiority what's-its, and may resent the fact that he was under my command at one time."

"You told him *cupressus* wouldn't grow, according to Inspector Barnard?"

"Neither will it. You are a gardener, sir?"

"In an amateurish way," said Knollis.

"*Cupressus* won't have it, and that's certain," said Peter conversationally. "Neither will laurels, nor rhododendrons. Another thing we tried to grow was Rose of Sharon—y'know, St. John's Wort. Remember that, Nance? The leaves came on, lasted a day, turned brown, and dropped off. It was like having browned-off creeping paralysis in the garden. It just went along on hands and knees, despondently."

"Murray thank you for the information?"

Peter grimaced, and then grinned. "I wouldn't say that. He sort of acknowledged it with a nod. I suggested he pop in to see Benson, and he said he'd better do that, Brenda being keen on a windbreak to protect the borders."

"He said anything about seeing him last night?"

Peter hesitated. "I won't be definite about that, because he was moving away then. He may have done, or may not. I dunno. Just shows the uncertainty of impressions, doesn't it?"

Knollis rose and moved towards the door leading to the entrance hall. "I'm grateful for the way in which you've helped me to sketch in the Murray background. I'm sure it will all prove useful."

When the car drove away, Peter took Nancy's hand and led her indoors.

"Poor old Paul!" he said. "Looks as if he's in the soup, doesn't it?"

"Shows how easily one can get mixed up in such a horrible affair, and how suspicious one's simplest actions can appear," said Nancy. "Peter, do *you* think Paul killed Brenda?"

"Candidly, darling," replied Peter, brushing his black moustache away from his mouth; "candidly, I don't, but I do hope he hangs for it. It would be poetic justice and all that."

She turned her face up to look into the expressionless blue eyes. "What on earth do you mean, darling?"

He put his hands on her shoulders and sighed. "I've never told you before, sweetheart, and I can't prove it, but I know in my old heart that Paul murdered Dennis for his money."

"What! Peter!"

Peter gave a wry smile. "Brenda learned the truth last night, too. She had a visitor, and he told her all he knew. Quarter of an hour later she was dead."

Nancy backed him to the stairs, and forced him to sit on the third step. Then she sat on the bottom one and stared up at him. "How—how do you know all this, darling?" she asked suspiciously.

"Because, darling," Peter replied in a casual voice, "I was listening under the dining-room window!"

Her fingers gripped his legs and dug into them like claws. "Peter! What were you doing there? Who was in the house with her? What did he tell her?"

"Hm?" Peter murmured absently. "I went to tell her something. The visitor was Roy Palmer. I *think* it was Roy who done her in, but I ain't sure, darlin', and so I'm keepin' quiet. You see, darling, Mrs. P. is dying of cancer, and Roy wanted money very badly."

He looked down at her with a serio-quizzical manner she had never before seen on his face. "One word more, and the subject is then taboo unto time eternal. If it was Roy, he was justified. I don't intend to see him hanged for the job if I can help it, but I do intend to flummox up the evidence so thoroughly that Paul hasn't anything to stand on but a trapdoor in an execution-cell. That shocks you, of course, but then you don't really know me, even after all these years of married life. I have a code, darling, that means a great deal to me! Anyway, I've eaten half the evidence, and the other can go on the fire!"

"Eaten the evidence?" Nancy asked curiously.

"The kippers," he said, and bent to kiss the top of her head.

Chapter IV
THE FRANKNESS OF MURRAY

Sergeant Scroggey was in an expansive mood with Jennings when he called at police headquarters that morning. He threw a hand towards a square of green baize on a side-table. "One Persian pussy. The decoy. Somebody had caught it and was waiting by the pool, somebody who knew she went out round a certain time to call it in. He started to strangle it, and its yelling took her to the fence in double-quick time. He was waiting, as I said. Must have been somebody who didn't like cats, too."

"Oh?" said Jennings, raising his brows. "Murray?"

Scroggey threw a square of chewing-gum into his mouth. "Didn't Murray like cats?"

"I saw him kick it across the lawn not many weeks ago."

Scroggey nodded. "Wife not present?"

"She was going up to the street to the bus. I was following her. Murray was at the gate, with the cat rubbing round his legs. I won't say he actually kicked it, being fair to him, but sort of turfed it across the lawn."

"Doesn't indicate habitual cruelty," Scroggey remarked casually. "More like temporary annoyance with his wife."

"You lean towards him?" queried Jennings.

Scroggey scowled. "As much as I would towards a rattlesnake. Me, I don't like him, whether he did her in or not. A nasty slinking little man with deep thoughts! Anyway, what have you brought us, Mr. Jennings?"

"I haven't brought anything. I dropped in on the way to the office to see if you'd anything for me."

Scroggey stared fixedly at the ceiling. "You may say that the police have the matter in hand, and an arrest is expected shortly."

"That's not true!" complained Jennings. "It's a hoary old cliché!"

Scroggey looked down at Jennings's perky bird-like face. "Maybe it isn't true, but it's all you're going to use. I know it's the old stuff, but it always serves to give Chummy the jitters, and the more jitters he has the quicker he'll give himself away—or run away."

"It's hackneyed," Jennings continued to protest.

"So's everything in the *East Courtney Weekly News*," Scroggey retorted rudely. "If you cut out the weddings and funerals, you've nothing left but adverts—and the writing up of those events stinks! Right down all the columns, week in and week out, we read about a pretty wedding, or a pretty bride, or a pretty scene in church, and everybody that dies is well-known, respected, and much-lamented—while the truth is that more than half of them have had trouble with us in their time! And you accuse us of using hackneyed stuff!"

"You deliberately trying to be rude?" Jennings asked.

"It comes natural," grinned Scroggey. "Forget it. I have read a worse local rag than yours, only I can't remember where it was because it was so long ago! Anyway, an arrest is imminent—and the good Lord protect you if you go any farther."

Jennings refused to take umbrage. He looked cautiously and wonderingly at Scroggey, and meanwhile played with the pens and pencils sticking from his breast-pocket. "Pity you're not more co-operative, Scroggey. I mean, you can't expect us to work with you, can you?"

"What do you know?" asked Scroggey, switching the gum to the other cheek. "I knew you'd something on your mind when you walked in."

"I live in Brandon Avenue."

"That's true. Most interesting piece of news!"

"So does my wife," said Jennings.

Scroggey's mouth twisted. "Now there's a thing! East Courtney is getting back to normal. Banner for the front page of your paper. *Local Man Lives With Wife!* It should send your circulation up to two hundred—or your pulse up to a hundred!"

Jennings gripped the edge of the table with both hands. "My wife went into the front room last night," he went on persistently. "She went to fetch her library book. It was lying on the settee in the bay."

Scroggey planted his great hands flat down on the table and pushed his large head under Jennings's nose.

"Okay, Mr. Jennings, whether it was the window bay or Galway Bay doesn't matter. What did she see through the window?"

"You know Mr. Peter Fairfax?"

"The Old Man and Inspector Knollis are out there now, getting Murray's background."

Jennings's smile was a superior and knowing one as he said: "Fairfax was standing under the lamp outside Number Five, looking towards Murray's house. He was walking towards it just as she was coming out of the room."

"I take it she hadn't switched on the light?"

"No, she knew where the book was, and there's a certain glow from the other room, of course."

"Time?"

"She isn't sure."

Scroggey stood upright, and relaxed. "That's been worth listening to. We're a long way ahead now!"

"And still no more than the cliché for my paper, Sergeant?" Jennings asked stiffly.

"You know the game as well as I do," Scroggey pointed out.

Jennings polished his nails on the lapel of his blue suit. "Yes, of course. I was only leg-pulling, you know! Well, I must be off now. I've a pretty wedding to attend in a pretty church in my private capacity at noon—you'll see it reported next week!"

"Not unless my fish and chips happen to be wrapped in the thing," said Scroggey. "That's the only time I read the *Weekly News*. By the way, Mr. Jennings, can't you use better paper? The vinegar soaks through!"

Jennings walked to the door. "I know the answer to that, but I'm too much of a gentleman to use it."

Scroggey grinned as the door closed, and threw himself into a chair and put his long legs up on the desk. He took them down a minute later as Barnard and Knollis walked in.

"Met Jennings on the street," said Barnard. "He says he's left some vital evidence with you."

Scroggey gave a scornful laugh. "His wife saw Mr. Fairfax loitering in the Avenue at some unspecified time last night."

Knollis unclothed his eyes and looked interested. "Fairfax, eh? That is interesting!"

"And Jennings gave me a point about the cat, sir," said Scroggey. He repeated Jennings's story, and his own interpretation.

"I'm with you there, Scroggey," said Knollis. "In all probability he was using the cat as a scapegoat for his wife—kicking her by proxy. The odds are that he was really quite fond of the animal. People without children mostly are."

"Well, the sight of it dead certainly turned him over last night, sir," said Scroggey. "It seemed to be the last straw."

"And if there were differences between Murray and his wife, it's on the cards that he thought a great deal of the animal."

"That's a point for him," grumbled Barnard.

"We're out to discover the truth, not condemn a man because we don't particularly like him!" said Knollis.

"Well, look," Barnard said in an uneasy voice; "you agree that the person who mauled the cat must have killed Mrs. Murray?"

"It would be a most unusual case if he didn't," said Knollis. "In fact, it would be a remarkable coincidence, and I don't believe in such things."

"What are we going to do with Fairfax?"

"Check on him first. That's obvious. Now I'd like to have a look at Brandon Avenue again. Can I take Scroggey while you get on with the office work?"

Barnard nodded. "Any jobs need organising?"

"Check on the time Fairfax got to the club, and then ask him where he was before that time. Don't let him know we're aware he was in the Avenue."

Murray was apparently turning the dining-room inside out when Knollis and Scroggey got there. He had no alternative but to take them into the room, and Knollis nodded towards the confusion and the opened bureau. "These jobs have to be done, don't they?" he said in a sympathetic voice.

Murray hunched his shoulders. "I'm looking for my wife's will. Oh, and there's another thing. Somebody called on her after I went out last night."

"How do you know that, Mr. Murray?"

Murray went across the room and drew the side-board from the wall, revealing the safe. "There was a matter of three hundred pounds in there, and it isn't there now!"

"Sure it was there when you went out?"

Murray hesitated. "It was there yesterday morning, and as my wife hadn't been farther than the shop round the corner I can't see any reason why it shouldn't be there now!"

"Have you handled the safe a great deal?" asked Knollis.

"Just opened it, looked inside, and closed it again," Murray replied. "Why?"

"Well, if we can assume there shouldn't be any prints other than your own and your wife's! You wouldn't mind having your prints taken?"

"Naturally not."

Knollis turned to Scroggey, instructing him to fetch the bag from the car.

"Anything handy that your wife used regularly, Mr. Murray? Dressing-set is usually prolific. . . ."

"I'll go up to the bedroom and find something," said Murray, making for the door.

Knollis put out a hand to stay him. "I'd rather the sergeant did that. He's trained to handle things without confusing existing prints. You won't object to him going upstairs?"

"Half of East Courtney seemed to be tramping up and down last night," Murray said sarcastically, "so I don't suppose one more or less will make any difference."

Scroggey went to work while Knollis watched. Twenty minutes later Knollis looked round at the interested Murray. "Only your wife and yourself handled the safe. That's definite!"

"Then that means she gave the money to someone!"

"It means she took the money out of the safe," said Knollis, correcting him. "Unless you did so yourself."

"I didn't! Why should I mention it if I'd done it myself?"

"That's quite a point," Knollis smiled. "Were you and your wife on good terms, Mr. Murray? It's a question I came to ask you."

Murray flashed him a quick glance, and his flat chin went down on his chest. "No," he said slowly. "We weren't."

"How bad was it?" Knollis asked him.

"Just a matter of time before one of us got fed up and cleared out. The money was the trouble right from the beginning—that and the fellow she was engaged to before she met me. You see, this fellow gave her all his money. I was on the same unit when he was accidentally drowned. I came on leave shortly afterwards, and living in the same town I naturally came to see her—went to see her at her mother's home. I—well—I fell in love with her. We were married before I went back to the Med."

"Yes?" Knollis coaxed him quietly.

"The truth is that she wasn't in love with me—although she thought she was at the time. Oh, I don't blame her, and I should have had more sense myself. I can see it all now. She was left stranded with Palmer's death and needed someone to comfort her, and I just happened to turn up. She thought it was love she felt for me, and wrote most passionate letters while I was away.

It was a different story when I got back. She was comparing me with Palmer all the while, and I apparently didn't measure up to his standard in her opinion. Then again, she wanted to live well, and it couldn't be done on my salary, and she thought I was trying to chisel her when I asked for money to spend on her or the house. That idea got in, stayed in, and developed. On top of all this she went into perpetual mourning for Palmer, and it was like living with a ghost in the house. I could see she was thinking about him all the time—or with an idealised vision of him. It was an uncomfortable life for both of us."

"I see," said Knollis. "Now at what time did you leave the house last evening?"

Murray scratched his ear, and screwed his pock-marked face in thought. "Something before eight, and I'm not at all sure to ten minutes. It might have been about ten minutes to—and that's probably the best guess."

"Surely you can remember the time you went out!" Knollis protested. "Hadn't you an appointment with a Mr. Benson?"

"Not actually an appointment," said Murray. "I rang him during the afternoon and he said he'd see me about eight one night if I cared to call round, so it seemed reasonable to suppose I could find him in at that time last night."

"He lives—where?"

"In Croxton Street, behind his shop."

"Middle-aged bachelor," interrupted Scroggey. "Has a woman and a girl looking after him and the house during the day-time, but won't have either on the premises after nightfall because of the gossip. His nurseries are on the other side of the town."

"There's another thing," said Murray. "We'd had a row and I more or less slammed my way out of the house without bothering to look at the clock."

"A row, Mr. Murray? What about?"

Murray gave a weary sigh. "Palmer again. He died on the twelfth of August, nineteen-forty-three, and she not only kept that anniversary and his birthday as sacred days, but had started keeping a half-yearly wake as well."

"It was the twelfth of February yesterday," said Knollis, snapping his fingers. "See, didn't Inspector Barnard tell me that Palmer met his death on Lampedusa?" He cast a glance at the framed photograph over the sideboard.

A gleam came into Murray's eyes. "You're thinking about her being found in the pool—in water!"

"I was, yes," Knollis admitted.

"Then *you* think it more than a coincidence!"

Knollis smiled dryly. "I don't believe in that so-called unnatural collision of similar events. Neither do you, apparently."

"The connection was bound to occur to me."

Knollis looked hard at him, narrowing his eyes. "Well, and what do you think, Mr. Murray?"

"Dennis Palmer was drowned. He gave his money to Brenda—my wife—instead of to his family. They resented it, regarding it as treachery. Neither did they want her to marry me, but seemingly wanted her to embrace a life of spinsterhood."

Knollis wagged a long forefinger. "Look, Mr. Murray, you're accusing the Palmer family of murdering your wife. Now in what way would they benefit? In what way can they benefit?"

Murray's reply was blunt. "That's why I'm looking for her will!"

"You're afraid lest she's made one in their favour?"

"Well," said Murray with a shrug, "I've told you how things stood between us. She might have decided to cut me out and make sure the money went to the Palmers when she died."

"You're suggesting the Palmers would know of the will? That your line of reasoning, Mr. Murray?"

"Somebody called after I went out last night," Murray said stubbornly.

"You're reducing the problem to its simplest terms," said Knollis. "Suppose your wife didn't make a will in favour of the Palmer family, and that no member of the family called last night? What then?"

Murray raised his flat face and looked Knollis squarely. "Then I'm stuck!"

"There's always a motive, Mr. Murray," Knollis said softly. "Always a motive. Someone always benefits in some way when a murder is committed. Someone gains something, whether it be money, revenge, or relief. That is what we look for in these cases, someone who *benefits*. And if the Palmers don't benefit—who does?"

"Me," Murray said with a twisted smile. "The money will come to me."

"Her own people?"

"Both died since the war. She's no surviving relative at all."

"Taking into account this incompatibility of temperament," said Knollis; "do you think she'd be likely to leave the money to a charity, or a home, or some society?"

Murray shook his head. "Not Brenda. She'd no pity or charity to spare for anything but her own bereaved soul. That sounds callous, but it's the truth."

"I think we'd better have a look round outside."

Murray led them to the garden, and then turned to point to the lamp over the back door. "That was switched on when I came home last night."

A white Sealyham terrier came trotting round the side of the house, sniffing hard at the ground. It went to the back door, swung away, came straight past their feet without looking up, and made for the boundary fence.

"Police dog," Knollis said humorously.

"Lives just below," explained Murray. "My wife used to put scraps out for it."

"I wonder . . ." murmured Knollis, and followed the little dog up the garden, just in time to see it squeeze through the chestnut railing into the field. It made for a point about six yards from the fence, circled anxiously, looked up as if surprised, sniffed a flattened patch of coarse grass, and then seemed to shrug its shoulders and pad away down the field.

"That's where they found Fluffy," said Murray as he stood beside Knollis. "Probably looking for him. They were good friends, and used to play together as if they were both cats, or both dogs."

Scroggey was missing when Knollis turned his back on the field to look into the pool. He joined him a few minutes later.

"When were the windows last cleaned outside, Mr. Murray?" he asked, with a significant glance at Knollis.

Murray put a hand to his forehead. "Not yesterday, and not the day before. Oh, I don't know—probably early in the week. I seem to remember seeing his handcart standing in the street when I came home to lunch either Wednesday or Thursday."

"You come home to lunch every day?" asked Knollis.

"Mostly, yes. I stayed in town yesterday, being fed up with my wife's mourning bout."

"Why the query about the ladder, Scroggey?" asked Knollis.

"Somebody's been listening under the dining-room window, sir. There are prints."

"Let's go," said Knollis.

Scroggey pointed out the obvious; two footprints in the narrow flower-border under the window, between the house wall and the concrete path.

"Crouching, too," said Knollis.

"How do you make that out?" asked Murray keenly.

Knollis pointed. "No heel marks, and only the front third of the soles in contact with the soil. When did it last rain?"

Murray shook his head. Scroggey had been out on Tuesday night, and could say that there was a very sharp and very short shower just after midnight.

Knollis examined the window, and then went round the house looking at all the others, and the doors. "No signs of any unorthodox entry, Mr. Murray. I'm inclined to agree that your wife might have let someone in? Any guesses yet?"

"Afraid not," replied Murray. "We'd few friends—we were trying to show a good face to the world, and it's difficult if you have intimate friends."

"The Palmers?" asked Knollis. "How many of them are there?"

"The old couple—both hitting it up into the sixty-five region for a guess, and then Roy. Roy will be about thirty-one."

"He knew your wife?"

"Of course."

"I expected that answer," said Knollis, "but wondered if he might have been overseas with one of the Services at the time his brother was courting your wife, as she became."

"He knew her," said Murray.

"Has he made himself at all objectionable over the money business?" Knollis asked.

Murray nodded slowly. "He's the one who fought Brenda. She used to run into him in town, and he was always horrible to her, always giving her cracks about her having a good time on his brother's money, and asking if the odd shilling that was left was quite safe, and so on. He was getting on her nerves at one time. He used to tell her that Dennis was like King Arthur, and would come back one day and want an account of her stewardship."

An idea occurred to Knollis. "The house-name on your gate . . ."

"Avalon? One of Brenda's ideas. As she bought the house I let her call it what the devil she liked. It didn't matter to me—there was a number to it, anyway, so the postman couldn't get lost!"

"Know what the name means?"

Murray shrugged. "Some classical reference, isn't it? I suppose I should know, but I don't. A friend of hers suggested it."

"It means the Island of the Blessed, or, alternatively, the Island of Sleep—where your King Arthur is supposed to be sleeping until he is recalled to save England from an invader."

Murray glanced up sharply. "The Island of Sleep?"

"Who was the friend who suggested the name to her?" asked Knollis.

"Chap by the name of Fairfax. As a matter of fact, he was our signals officer when Dennis Palmer went west," said Murray. Then he paused and glanced sharply at Knollis. "Doesn't it sound as if he and Palmer had got together, sir? Palmer rubbing her about King Arthur, and Fairfax suggesting the name of the house?"

"It does, doesn't it?" Knollis replied in a non-committal manner. "Don't disturb those prints, please. I'm sending a man to make casts of them."

CHAPTER V
THE EVIDENCE OF THE CHART

KNOLLIS AND SCROGGEY went back to see Fairfax after lunch, and the first thing Knollis did was look at the shoes Fairfax was wearing. They were narrow-toed tan ones with derby fronts. The prints under the window at Murray's house were those of medium-toed shoes. Knollis clicked his tongue with annoyance. Another good idea had gone wrong.

"Soon back!" Fairfax greeted them, his dark eyes bulging under the heavy black brows. He satisfactorily filled the doorway, and stood with his legs apart, his hands in his jacket pockets, obviously defending his castle.

"An item of information reached us," said Knollis. "We thought you should have the chance to clarify it."

"We are slowly turning into an information bureau, aren't we?" Fairfax murmured smoothly. "What is it this time? Where can you get a ticket for the Cup Final?"

Knollis ignored his sarcasm. "You were seen in Brandon Avenue last night, Mr. Fairfax."

Fairfax's bristly moustache was thrust out. "Pity!" he said. "I think you'd better come inside. Not exactly warm on the step, is it?"

He took them to the dining-room, where Nancy Fairfax was pretending to relax with a cup of tea and a book. If the book hadn't been upside down, she might have convinced Knollis that she hadn't been listening at the door.

"You were in Brandon Avenue," said Knollis when he had greeted Nancy Fairfax.

Peter nodded. "I was, but I didn't see any point in mentioning the fact—you having enough on without me adding complications."

"Nice of you," Knollis replied ironically. "Do you care to say where you were visiting, and why you went there?"

"As a matter of fact, I went to see Mrs. Murray."

"On business?"

Fairfax scratched his head, leaving his black hair looking like a bird's-nest. "Frankly, I dunno whether I should tell you. Other people's business and all that." He looked down at his wife, and she met his silent inquiry with a blank expression.

"You'll have gathered that Murray isn't a nice person," Fairfax remarked.

Knollis was non-committal, merely saying: "No?"

"Brenda bought the house with her own money, and gave him both house and deeds—you'll gather they were in his name. Quite by accident it came to my knowledge that the dirty dog had mortgaged the place without telling her, to raise spending money for himself."

"Well?"

"I thought she ought to know!"

Peter Fairfax took a turn across the room and back. He stood looking at Knollis with a quizzical expression on his dark features. "Sometimes you wonder whether to mind your own business or not, but Murray gave her such a rotten deal that I decided she ought to know his latest."

"You saw her, of course?"

Fairfax shook his head. "No, some other fellow was entering the place as I went down the Avenue."

"Murray, perhaps?"

Knollis regarded Fairfax mildly, and Fairfax seemed to read a warning in the pose of innocence. "Er—no, I'd seen him leave for town."

"There was the matter of your advice regarding his hedge," said Knollis. "Would it be fair to assume that you rigged his visit to Benson so that you could be sure of seeing his wife alone?"

"*Cupressus* won't grow in this soil," said Fairfax.

"I'm questioning your intentions, not your gardening knowledge," said Knollis quietly. "Would it be fair to assume that you persuaded him to see Benson last night?"

Fairfax gave a sheepish grin. "Looks very transparent, doesn't it. Yes, it would be fair to assume that, Inspector. Couldn't think of any other means of gettin' him out of the way."

"You hung around, and waited until he was clear?"

"Correct. Then went straight to the house."

"This second person was entering the house, or entering the garden by the gate?"

"Oh, through the gate!" Fairfax said immediately.

"He'd walked down in front of you at that rate?"

Fairfax flashed a keen glance at him. "No. He must have come up the Avenue."

"From the direction of the waste land?"

"Ye-es," Fairfax replied with hesitation. "Either that or he in turn had been hiding in the shadows and waiting for Murray to get clear."

"He didn't come from any of the houses below?"

"Oh no!"

"Good!" said Knollis, smiling and nodding his satisfaction. "It was a dark night, and you couldn't really say whether he came from one of the other houses in the Avenue or not, therefore you either recognised him or suspected who he might be? You did recognise him?"

"Er—no!"

"But you have your suspicions?"

"Well, yes."

"You didn't see him enter the house?"

"No, I didn't see him enter the house, Inspector."

Knollis smiled placidly. "I'm going to suggest you've got your facts mixed—either by accident or design. I'm going to suggest that this mystery man went through the gate before Murray left the house!"

Fairfax started, and coughed. "Er—why should you suggest that, Inspector?"

"There are footprints," said Knollis. "Somebody spent a fair time crouching under the dining-room window. There could have been no other motive than to hear what was being said by those inside. Therefore it was either this man eavesdropping on

Murray and his wife, or you doing the same with Mrs. Murray and this second man!"

"I see," said Fairfax. "I don't listen at keyholes, Inspector."

"Therefore you didn't see Murray leave for town. *You* saw him leave the house and walk up the Avenue, but no more! You were already in the Avenue when Murray left the house, and the stranger was already parked under the window! Doesn't that make a truer picture?"

Fairfax was silent. He seated himself on the arm of his wife's chair, and laid a hand on her shoulder. She was sitting with her hands pressed tightly together, and her eyes fixed on his face.

"Well, Mr. Fairfax?" asked Knollis.

Fairfax gave a careless shrug. "Fact is, that I expected Murray to be clear of the place earlier than he was. I got fed up with waiting on the main road—it was a ruddy cold business!—and moved down the Avenue. The other bloke was slipping through the gateway as I approached the house, doin' it sort of furtively like they do on the films, so I went across the Avenue, and a few yards lower than Murray's place, and waited. Murray came out, and the other fellow didn't—not for some time, anyway."

"By which door did he leave?"

"Not by the front door, certainly!"

"So that he either left by the back door, or didn't enter the house at all?"

Fairfax nodded. "That's what I meant."

"Did you go on the premises?"

"No, sir."

"Who do you think the man was?"

Fairfax shuffled on the chair arm. "I don't like these guessing games. They ain't fair on the other fellow. I might have been wrong."

"It's my job to decide that, Mr. Fairfax."

"Oh well! It looked—and I do say that!—like Roy Palmer, the brother of the fellow Brenda was once engaged to. Oh heck! I don't like it!" grumbled Fairfax.

Knollis gave a too-obvious sigh of satisfaction. Fairfax quickly looked up at him. "You knew all the time?"

"The name of the house," said Knollis. "I understand you suggested it to Mrs. Murray?"

"Avalon? Yes, I suppose I did in a way," replied Fairfax. "Murray was demobbed before me, and they'd just got into the house when I came back. I naturally called to see 'em, Murray having been under me on Lampo, and Mrs. Murray wanted a name for the place. Murray wasn't in, and Brenda said she wanted a name that would suggest Lampedusa to her, without actually using that name, so Avalon was obvious."

Knollis smiled wryly. "Was it? I don't understand, Mr. Fairfax."

"No, I suppose you don't," Fairfax answered. "I don't think Murray got it, either. Point is that Avalon is the place where King Arthur and his knights are supposed to be sleeping until England needs them again and all that."

"I'm still in the dark," said Knollis. "The reasoning appears to be somewhat tortuous and strained. Where the deuce is the connection with Lampedusa Island?"

"The Island of Sleep!"

Knollis sighed. "Do it in words of not more than two syllables. I'm dense this afternoon!"

Fairfax grinned. "That was what the bods on the island called it. Outside duty hours there was nothing to do but bathe, write letters, and sleep. There wasn't much to write home about, and you couldn't live in the water, so you just curled up on the old haybag and slept the hours away. Very restful, too!"

"Who suggested the purchase of the aerial photos of the island, Mr. Fairfax?"

"Brenda—Mrs. Murray. She wanted to know exactly where he was drowned, and where he was buried, and where he used to live and work. Murray wasn't at all helpful, and made out he couldn't help, so I set about the job and eventually found I could get photos from the Imperial War Museum, and a chart from a firm in the Minories. I got two sets of the photos, and gave one to her. As you know, she had the photo map framed."

"You obtained a copy of the chart?"

"Yes," Fairfax said readily. "Care to see it?"

"Very much," replied Knollis.

Fairfax found the chart and unrolled it across the dining-room table.

"*Plans in the Mediterranean, No. 193*. The top one is Linosa Island, as you see. Due north of Lampo, and clearly visible when there wasn't a sea-mist on. It's a defunct volcano, I think. Bottom map is Lampo, with a plan of the harbour as inset. Here's the lighthouse, on the north-east corner, Cape Grecale. It was well and truly pranged until it was a heap of stone and rubble. The two radio tenders were about fifty yards west of it, about here. The boys were living here, on the edge of Creta Bay. It was a sort of big dug-out, carved out of the edge of the cliff, and then roofed with steel girders and concrete. There was a little courtyard in front of it, and a built wall to stop anybody stepping into two hundred feet of sweet Fanny Adams and the drink. I used to go and sit with Murray and Palmer, drinking the old tea and watching the moon coming up over the water—wizard sight it was, too. And the island fishermen used to row beneath the cliff, with a light on each boat to attract the fish, and they'd sing Italian love-songs and call up to us—the islanders, I mean, and not the fish."

"Palmer was drowned—where?"

"Here. Point Ailaimo, on the north coast. The surface of the cliff face was like crêpe soles on shoes, sort of closely corrugated, and with bags of hand and toe holds so you could easily climb down to the water. Just here, where Palmer got it, was a widish shelf. He'd stripped his shorts and shoes off, and that's all we ever knew about his end. Three of the fishermen found him. One of them scaled the cliff and made for the radio site to report, and the other two rowed him back round the eastern end of the island to the town harbour. There were telephone landlines across the island, of course; the corporal notified us, and we went to meet them coming in."

Knollis looked up from the chart. "I want to ask you a serious question, Mr. Fairfax? Was there any suspicion of foul play?"

Fairfax lowered his gaze, fixing it rigidly on the chart. "Couldn't be done, sir. Not unless there's some means of murdering by remote control. There was the Wingco, the Adjutant, the M.O., and me. We went over the thing thoroughly!"

"Poison possible?"

"The vet. opened him up that same night, Inspector. Cause of death was definitely due to drowning!"

Knollis ran his tongue over his lip. "Murray married—what was her maiden name?"

"Brenda Morley."

"He married Miss Morley six weeks after Palmer's death?"

"Correct," nodded Fairfax.

"Why the hurry, I wonder?" Knollis asked of the apple-green distempered walls.

Nancy Fairfax moved an inch nearer to her husband.

"How friendly were Palmer and Murray while on the island?"

Fairfax pressed a hand to his forehead. "It's a long time ago now, Inspector. Impressions tend to fade, y'know. I mean, those bods were only under me for fourteen weeks all told, from transit camp at Chott Maria to Lampo, and from there back to Hamman Lif to be dispersed. Bit of a strain on the old mental gearbox, really."

Nancy Fairfax touched her husband's arm, and muttered something to him about letters.

"Well, *I* don't mind, darling, if you don't. If they'll help the Inspector I'm all for it," said Fairfax.

He turned to Knollis. "My wife says I mentioned them in my letters home, and she's prepared to read the bits that matter if it'll help?"

"I'd be grateful," said Knollis.

Nancy Fairfax left them and went upstairs. Knollis passed the intervening minutes in a closer examination of the chart.

"The sea appears to vary between four and nine fathoms off Point Ailaimo, Mr. Fairfax."

"Something like that," said Fairfax. "Still, it's on the chart, so that's that. Incontrovertible evidence."

"And from three and a half to five at Creta Bay."

"Mm!" said Fairfax, without any show of interest.

"What's the height of the cliffs at those two points?" asked Knollis.

"Probably a hundred and fifty at Ailaimo, and a couple of hundred at Creta—but the shelf was wider at Creta, being forty or fifty feet."

"And in each case a straight drop into the water? No sloping beach?"

Fairfax shook his head. "The only sloping beaches to be found were round the town harbour. Me, I'm a landlubber, but you'll see that what I call the town harbour was really three bays set something like a clover leaf. Here you are: Guitgia Bay, Salina Bay, and Palma Bay. We bathed a lot from Salina. It was nice and shallow for the boys who were just trying to learn to swim, and handy to the main camp just north-east of the town."

Nancy Fairfax came in with a handful of letters.

"We nearly burned all our correspondence the other week," she explained. "We thought we'd never read them again, but felt a bit sentimental about them—they meant a lot to us while Peter was overseas. However, so far as the relations between Paul and Dennis are concerned, I can only find one reference, in a letter dated the seventeenth of July, nineteen-forty-three."

"Please read it to us, Mrs. Fairfax," said Knollis.

"Can't make it out at all with these Murray and Palmer blokes. I mean, darling, Murray must have gone to something higher than elementary school, but he isn't quite top drawer, nor yet middle drawer—that sounds lousily snobbish of me, doesn't it, but I can't help it. It's the feeling I've got about the fellow. Palmer is educated, all right. Jolly good scout, with things to talk about sensibly, and some sort of code to run his life by—pardon me finishing on a preposition. Yet they are good pals despite having nothing in common but coming from the old home-town. Even little things like that matter out here. The island is a ruddy dump composed of rock, silvery snakes, odd fig-trees, and the vineyards. Some bod was telling me Lampo grapes are famous. They taste all right to me . . ."

"Thanks," said Knollis as Nancy Fairfax's voice trailed away on reaching the affectionate final paragraphs of the letter. "What was Palmer by profession?"

"Maths wallah at Coston's—that's the endowed school that rivals the local Queen Lizzie's Grammar School."

"And Murray was, and is, a bank-clerk?"

"Well, cashier at the local branch of Lords."

"And the surviving Palmer—Roy?"

"Departmental Big White Chief in a hosiery factory here in town. Darlington's, it is. They make 'Saucy Sue' stockings. You know the adverts. Pretty girl with bags of good leg showing, and—"

"Peter!"

"Sorry, darling. My imagination was running away with me!"

Knollis suppressed a smile. "Where does Palmer live?"

"Trent Street, with the old couple."

"And you still think it was Palmer who went through the gateway?"

"I think so, sir, but I'd hate to swear to it, and, for heaven's sake, don't say I said so."

"We try to be discreet," said Knollis. He reached for his hat, and the long-silent Scroggey folded his notebook and slid it into his greatcoat pocket.

As they reached the front door Knollis asked: "Do you think Murray would learn much of Palmer's private affairs when they were together on the island?"

"Possible," said Fairfax frankly. "When blokes get thrown together like that, and there's nothing else to do, they're inclined to say more than they normally would. Yes, I dare say Palmer opened up pretty well."

"And Murray would know about the money before he came to England on leave, let alone before he married Miss Brenda Morley?"

Fairfax nodded slowly. "There's never been any doubt about that in my mind. Murray's a first-class rat. Either Palmer told him about the money, or Brenda did when he came on leave. You can bet your sweet life he knew before he married her!"

He looked round at his wife. "There's a thing, Nance! You did the officer's-wife's duty and called on her after I let you know about Dennis's death, and gave you her address I found among his papers. Did she mention the money to you?"

Nancy Fairfax did not answer straight away. She stood with her finger posed on her lip. "No-o," she replied eventually, "but you knew about his money when you were on the island, you know!"

Fairfax's black brows raised themselves. "Did I?" he asked vaguely. "You're sure?"

"It's in one of the letters."

"Let's see," said Fairfax.

She returned to the dining-room, and came back with another of his letters. "Here we are. You must excuse Peter's weird literary style, Inspector! *Palmer's a decent cove, educated at Coston's, and now passing his time knocking sense into the little beasts at the old alma mater. He's no need to do it, being well endowed, his grandpa having given his wherewithal to him in accordance with some neat scheme intended to defeat the Chancellor of the What-is-it which I can't spell. Good hunting and Whack-Ho!"*

"Interesting—and whack-ho!" smiled Knollis.

"Queer," said Fairfax. "It's a surprise to me that I wrote the thing. I'd clean forgotten. I wonder where I got that item from? Palmer himself? We'll have to put the full amperage on the old memory machine!" He saw them down the path to the car, and closed the door very firmly as if hoping it would never open outside his house again. "Good-bye, gentlemen!" he said, and waved them off.

"This looks like being a good case, sir," said Scroggey as he drove up the Avenue to the main road.

"Depends what you mean by good," replied Knollis from the rear seat. "We've three men to consider. If Murray's alibi falls down—and I don't say it isn't an honest one—then he automatically becomes a suspect after all we've heard about him. Then this Palmer isn't shining bright with innocence. What was he doing round the house? The item from Fairfax about the money does nothing to put him in the clear. Revenge—or vengeance—is a strong emotional motive."

"He's waited long enough by the sound of things," commented Scroggey. "Wonder what triggered him off, sir—always assuming he did the job?"

"We don't know," said Knollis. "Something must have happened to add force to a smouldering hate. Force is the wrong word, but you know what I mean. The point sticking in my mind is the nature of her death, and its similarity to the way Dennis Palmer died. It surely means that someone intended her to die as he did, and to realise it as she was drowning!"

"Roy Palmer," murmured Scroggey.

"I wondered about that," said Knollis, "but we can't afford to assume anything."

Barnard was waiting for them at police headquarters. Knollis gave him a resume of the afternoon's work, and Barnard nodded thoughtfully.

"Benson's stitched up one point," he said. "Murray rang him early in the afternoon and asked to see him that night. Shortly after tea he rang again to say he couldn't make it, and apologised for any inconvenience he might have caused."

"That's something," said Knollis. "Anything else?"

"I've a man out at Murray's, working on the prints. You don't think they are Fairfax's, then?"

"Not unless he deliberately went out in heavier boots or shoes than he usually wears, and I think you'll agree that no one but a casual eavesdropper would have been so careless as to leave prints in the flower-bed. Again, I've noticed that men who were in the Services tend to wear footwear similar in type to those issued to them. Most men discovered foot comfort for the first time when they joined up. Service footwear may have been heavy, but it was well-designed."

"You're suggesting that the listener may have been a ranker? Someone wearing heavy boots?"

"No, not quite," said Knollis. "If it was an ex-Service man then I'll settle for a non-commissioned officer. They were usually issued with shoes, but not so light as the ones the officers wore."

Barnard sucked the end of his thumb and looked quizzical. "Did you know Roy Palmer was a sergeant in the tanks when he was demobbed?"

"Didn't know a thing about him," said Knollis. "If that is the case, then I think I'll take Scroggey and go to see him."

Barnard ticked off various items on his fingers. "Dennis Palmer was drowned in the sea. Mrs. Murray was drowned in a lily pool. Mrs. Murray had the money which belonged to Palmer...."

"Fairfax says he learned that Murray had pawned the house," Knollis reminded him. "Why did Murray need the money? Why couldn't he live on his salary?"

"Dunno," shrugged Barnard. "I know the fellow, but not officially. Up to now he's just been a decent little fellow working in a local bank and minding his own business."

Knollis looked across the office with narrowed eyes. "He wasn't happy with his wife. He seems to have married her for her money. She bought him the house, and it was in his name...."

"Well?" asked Barnard curiously.

"*Cherchez la femme*, Barnard. There's another woman in it somewhere!"

"There always is," sighed Barnard, "but we haven't found her yet in this case."

"What I mean is this," said Knollis. "You'd have known if he was a gambler, or a heavy drinker, or a general lad-about-town. Now, wouldn't you?"

"I know most of 'em," admitted Barnard. "That's my job, of course, to know people and what they do and don't do. Those things are noticed and automatically filed in one's mind against the day when they might prove useful. Oh yes, you're correct there, and I see what you are getting at. So we have to look for a woman!"

"What did he do with himself o' nights?" Knollis said, continuing his theme. "If he and his wife were so much at odds, then I can't see him spending his nights and evenings reading by the fireside—not his own fireside, anyway. Try the people in

Brandon Avenue. They'll know whether he stayed home or not. They always do. If he didn't—"

"The rest is obvious," agreed Barnard.

"Another point," said Knollis. "It's an important one, too. If he went out most evenings, where did he tell his wife he was going? All interesting and important points."

"I'm wondering," said Barnard. "You won't be offended?"

"I don't take offence," said Knollis, "what's in your mind?"

"I was wondering if you'd let Scroggey collect the casts and do the rounds of Fairfax, Murray, and Palmer? You look too intense, too much like a detective, and I do think your appearance tends to make people close up!"

"I know about it," said Knollis. "I've had to study methods of overcoming it. Yes, your plan is agreeable, except with regard to Palmer. I'd rather like him to get the first shaking from you and I, so why not let Scroggey invite him here to see us—y'know, information about Mrs. Murray as he remembers her when she was courting his brother?"

Barnard nodded to Scroggey. "Go to it, Sam!"

"And now I want a dictionary and a gazetteer," said Knollis. "I'm interested in the name of Salina Bay, Lampedusa. I think it should have something to do with salt."

Chapter VI
THE SUSPICIONS OF NANCY FAIRFAX

NANCY FAIRFAX watched the police car drive away, and then took a firm grip on her husband's arm and led him back to the fireside, pushed him into a chair, and stood over him. She pushed her brown hair back from her face, and shook her head sadly.

"You may be clever with electricity, but when it comes to everyday matters you're as feckless as a child! Can't you see your silliness is going to get you into trouble with the police before you've done?"

Peter waggled his bristly black moustache at her, and grinned happily. "Why on earth? I told them the truth, didn't I?"

"But not the whole truth, Peter. That was obvious, even to me, and these men are trained to know when a witness is holding back. What on earth were you up to last night?"

Peter shrugged. "Just what I said, darling. I'd made up my mind to tell Bren something I thought she ought to know."

"And what was it?" Nancy demanded firmly.

"A woman, if you must know the truth."

"Which woman?"

"Peroxided wench by the name of Dickinson. She lives in Dale Road."

"The girl he was courting before he married Bren!"

"Exactly," said Peter.

"How long has it been going on?"

Peter wriggled down into the chair, and sought his pipe, which he stuck into his mouth and sucked. "Actually, it never stopped!"

Nancy sank into the chair at the opposite side of the hearth with disgust written across her pleasant oval features. "The lout!"

"My point," Peter said dryly.

"And Brenda was so utterly, so utterly decent!"

"Again my point. That's why I thought a hint in due season might give her a clue that would lead to her getting shut of him—divorce, of course."

Nancy blinked. "She might not have welcomed the chance, Pete. To some women half a man is better than no man at all."

"She could have married again. She wasn't old, and she was still attractive—apart from the creases she'd worn in her forehead, and dark rings under her eyes. With a decent bloke she'd have bucked up and been a joy to the eye once more. Roy Palmer would have jumped at the chance."

Nancy's head came up quickly. "Roy?"

"Why not?"

"I don't know. It was a surprise you saying that."

"Why else do you think a personable fellow like he is hasn't got harnessed before now?"

Nancy shrugged her slim shoulders. "Never occurred to me, to be truthful. How did you come to learn that he was interested?"

"Oh, just through getting into his company occasionally and keeping my ears open."

Nancy leaned forward, her hands tightly clasped. "Look, Peter, what did happen last night?"

"More or less what I told the bobbies. I hung around on the main road, and Murray didn't roll up according to schedule, so I went down the Avenue on the opposite side to the house, and stood in the shadows. Roy—I'm certain it was he—was coming up. He opened the gate very cautiously, as if to make sure it didn't squeak, and vanished down the side of the house. I went across the Avenue, stood under the lamp for a few minutes, looked to right and to left, and then slipped through the gate."

He took out his pouch and began to fill the pipe.

"Go on!" Nancy said impatiently.

"Er—oh, yes! Well, Roy had gone down the right side of the house, so I went down the left. I was there quite a time, and then Paul came out and went up the Avenue. I heard voices, and then the back door closed. This is where I lied to the coppers, because I couldn't bring myself to admit that I'd listened at the window like a common cad—but I did! Brenda and Roy were in the diner. I caught snatches of the conversation. He was asking for money for his dear old lady. She's suffering from an incurable complaint, and he wanted money for a private operation. They started a row about whose money it was. They were shouting like nobody's business. She said it was hers, and he said Dennis had only left it to her as a trust, a sort of stewardship. I dunno what happened next, but it sounded like heavy furniture being moved. I felt uncomfortable about bein' there at all, so went back to the Avenue. . . ."

"And then?"

"Oh, shot back to town. I did a sort of lukewarm pub-crawl in the hope of dropping across Murray. There were one or two questions I wanted to shoot across him."

"Such as?" Nancy asked persistently.

Peter smiled whimsically. "I'll tell you when I've got the answers."

"And that's the truth, Peter?"

"More or less, yes."

"I still think you're holding something back!"

"Maybe. My memory's most unreliable!"

"Look, Peter," Nancy said, "you realise it can look bad for you from the police point of view—hanging round the house just before she must have been—well—murdered!"

"Nothing to worry about, old lady," Peter replied easily. "I think Murray must have done the job, but it looks as bad for Roy as it does for me, and I don't want to tell them more than I need because of incriminating him."

"You haven't done him much good up to now, you know!" said Nancy.

Peter raised an eyebrow. "I haven't? Why?"

"Well, you did let the policeman pump you to the extent that you admitted it looked like Roy who was hanging round the house."

"Ye-es, I suppose I did," he replied slowly. "Clever devils, these coppers, darling. Trained to it, of course! I'd have bitten my tongue off sooner than have done Roy any harm."

Nancy sighed. "You're clever in your own way, Peter, but horribly ingenuous! Anybody can get anything out of you if they go about it the right way."

"Funny, that!" said Peter. "I always thought I was fairly bright. Queer when one's own wife has to break the news that one is as dim as a farthing dip!"

She was across the hearth in an instant, her arms round his neck. "Darling! I didn't mean that! What I mean is, you're too honest. You really are, you know! That's why I fell in love with you. But honesty doesn't always do in this complicated world. I don't say we have to lie, but there are times when we have to sidestep, and temporise."

Peter laid his pipe aside and took her face between his hands. "Darling, suppose Bren had made a will in favour of Roy, or his father and mother?"

She twisted her head away, avoiding his eyes. "Oh, *don't*, Peter!"

"I heard her tell him that," said Peter.

Nancy nestled closer to him, and stared at the wall over his shoulder.

"See how my brain was working?" Peter asked. "I was wondering whether to tell the coppers that I stayed under the window and heard Roy leave the house, and then followed him and saw him get on a bus. I didn't, of course, because I couldn't make up my mind. I stalled 'em, leaving the thing open so that if I did decide I could let them pump it out of me later, and it wouldn't look so obvious that way."

She planted her hands on his chest and forced herself backward so that she could look into his face again. "Did I say ingenuous? It needs qualifying. Ingenious and ingenuous! You've unsuspected depths, Peter."

"There's a snag," he said softly.

"What is it? Can I help?"

"If I tell them that story, it leaves me the last person on the premises."

"Oh! They might think—!"

"They might think," he said grimly.

"Look, Peter," Nancy said after a moment. "You'd no motive!"

Peter brightened. "No, I jolly well haven't, have I? Why should I want to kill Brenda? Wouldn't make sense, would it?"

He hugged her tightly, and kissed her under the right ear. "You're perfectly correct, my sweet. I must be ingenuous! I never see the obvious facts, do I?"

"I love you, Pete!"

"Car stopped outside, Nance. . . ."

She drew away from him, straightened her hair, and repaired the damage to her make-up as the door-bell rang.

"I'll go, Pete."

A tall, broad man with sandy hair stood on the step. "Mrs. Fairfax? I'm Sergeant Scroggey, local C.I.D. Wonder if your husband could spare me a minute, please?"

She invited him in, and took him through to the dining-room. He was carrying a pigskin bag.

Peter nodded a welcome. "Take a pew, Sergeant!"

"Thanks, but I won't be staying more than a minute," returned Scroggey. "You know about the prints found under Murray's window? We've taken casts, and wonder if you'd mind us comparing them with your own boots and shoes? We can't go to work on the other fellow until we've eliminated you—which you'll agree is an elementary deduction. Inspector Knollis asks me to convey his apologies, compliments, and thanks."

"All wrapped up and tied with a pretty pink ribbon," murmured Peter.

Nancy hurried away, and returned with an armful of black and brown shoes, which she tumbled into a heap on the hearthrug. "Every pair in the house but those my husband is wearing, Sergeant Scroggey."

Scroggey took the casts from his bag, handling them delicately in his great hands. Five minutes later he put them back, and smiled. "We won't be hanging you, sir! Foot too small, and shoes too refined in style to fit my casts. It's a tallish guy who wears medium-width shoes."

"Not boots?" Peter asked innocently.

"Doubt it," Scroggey replied. "Boots wouldn't have allowed our man to bend his ankles so much as the prints indicate, and the impressions wouldn't have been so deep."

"Hope you find him," Peter said politely.

"We will," Scroggey assured him.

Peter escorted him to the door. "Must be an awfully interesting profession, Sergeant."

"Fascinating, sir," said Scroggey. "You never know for sure, right to the last minute, whether you're talking to the murderer or not."

"I'd wear a bullet-proof waistcoat if it was me," smiled Peter. "I wouldn't feel a bit safe, you know!"

"I always feel safer than the other fellow does!" Scroggey replied.

"Nice to feel so smug—I mean snug," said Peter.

He closed the door, and stood in the hall, watching the distorted shape of Scroggey through the coloured-glass panels as he went down the path to the car. When the car was clear of the Avenue, he lifted the telephone directory from its hook. He became aware of Nancy standing beside him. "Howard, isn't it, who lives next door to Roy Palmer?"

She did not answer, but stood looking at him with a queer expression on her oval features. Peter found the number and asked the lady who answered the call if she would oblige by fetching Mr. Palmer to the telephone—Mr. Roy Palmer.

He leaned against the wall, waiting, while Nancy seated herself on the stairs, her hands clasped nervously.

"Oh, hello! Palmer there?" Peter said suddenly.

"No names from this end, although you probably recognise the voice. Listen hard. If you've a pair of shoes with medium-width toes, get rid of them. There's a copper with the innocent air of a plaster saint wandering around with a set of plaster casts, looking for shoes to fit them. The footprints were found under Murray's window. Okay? Cheerio, old man!"

He replaced the receiver and grinned at Nancy. "I'd much rather they hanged Murray."

Nancy rubbed her cheek wearily. "What is all this about, Peter? What are you trying to do? Don't you think it's all—well—unnecessary?"

"Put it this way," said Peter, still leaning negligently against the wall, and his hands now thrust into his pockets. "Murray is a little bloke and his shoes are bound to be narrower than Palmer's. Now for a story to make the police think things out for themselves. Suppose Murray was to see Roy go to the house, and eavesdropped, and came to the conclusion there was something between 'em. He might then have bumped off Brenda."

"Peter! You wouldn't tell them that!" Nancy protested.

"I wouldn't actually tell them, darling, but I might say something to give them the idea—the idea that Paul Murray is responsible for the whole thing; responsible for killing Brenda, responsible for faking the job to make it look as if Roy did the job, so that Roy would be hanged, and Paul rid of them both at one fell swoop. If I suggest such a plot, I turn the attention of these detectives from Roy to Paul. Simple, really, isn't it?"

Nancy got up from the stair and walked to the lounge doorway, from where she looked through the far window into the side garden. She stood with her back pressed hard to the doorframe, her face lined and strained.

"It's all wrong, Peter. I thought I knew you, but you've shaken me to the roots in these last few hours. What you're doing isn't the work of a man of honour! You used to have a code. . . ."

"It's my code that's driving me," sighed Peter, without moving from the wall. "There are laws more important than police laws—or so I see it!"

Nancy nodded towards the telephone. "Do you think you should have done that? Don't you think you should tell the police the truth exactly as you know it, and leave the rest to them—the decision and the responsibility?"

"And leave Roy to be hanged when he didn't do the job?"

"Didn't he do it, Pete?" Nancy asked quickly. "Can you prove he didn't do it?"

"Funny question, that," Peter replied.

"If he did it, then he deserves to hang," said Nancy. "Murder is murder, whether a man thinks he's justified or not. The country wouldn't be safe if we all thought we could ignore the law and wipe off our own scores! I mean, nobody has the right to end another person's life—for any reason whatsoever!"

"First time we've ever differed on a major matter," said Peter thoughtfully. "That makes it awkward, my sweet. Anyway, I've gone so far now that I'll be in trouble with the coppers if they catch me out, so I just have to go on, covering myself, and covering Roy. Even if Roy did kill her, I can't see him hanged for it, when Paul Murray's doing nothing useful for humanity. Somehow, I think hanging would do Paul a lot of good! Sorry, Nance, but Paul's going to take what's coming to him. The police mind runs in well-established tracks. Mine's elastic, or shall we say mobile, and I think I can fool them."

Nancy turned her head towards him for an instant, and immediately looked into the lounge again. "It's going to be uncomfortable, Peter. If your plot succeeds we spend the rest of our lives knowing that we caused an innocent man to be hanged—and I'm no Lady Macbeth!"

"You'll stay with me?" Peter asked anxiously.

Nancy nodded, slowly and deliberately. "I'll stay with you, and stick by you, whatever you do, Peter, but please don't expect me to congratulate you!"

He moved easily across the hall and kissed her cheek. "I'm glad I married you!"

"So am I," she said with a sad smile; "it stops the neighbours from talking."

She suddenly pushed past him and ran up the stairs. "I—I've some shopping to do in town before the shops close, Peter."

She'd been gone from the house about five minutes when the door-bell rang. Peter opened the door to find Roy Palmer. He pulled him inside and closed the door.

"Dam' fool, coming here, aren't you?" he said shortly.

Roy Palmer, lean-faced and haggard, threw his hat on the hall-chest. "What the hell do you know, Fairfax?"

"The sergeant fellow has been here, checking up on my foot-wear. I thought you might be interested."

"Why should I be interested?" Palmer demanded.

"Dunno," Peter said idly. "Depends."

"What do you know, Fairfax?"

"I went to see Brenda. You got there first, but I came away first. See what I mean? The police don't know yet, but if they did they might get ideas."

"You're not thinking—" Palmer protested.

"I'm thinking nothing," said Peter, "except that Murray was a swine to Brenda, and deserves everything that can come to him!"

Palmer took a step forward. "If you think that I—"

Peter waved him into silence. "I told you I wasn't thinking anything. All I know is that you were under the window and mug enough to leave two nice foot-prints for the police—and you know how they love such playthings! Sergeant Scroggey's as pleased as a little boy with a new bucket and spade."

"You say he's checked all your shoes against them?"

Peter smiled. "I had to say that, because Nancy was listening to our conversation. Actually, there's another pair out in the shed, my gardening ones."

"How does this concern me, Fairfax?"

Peter hesitated. "Well, I'm apparently a naive sort of bloke, and Barnard and the Yard man chewed at me until they wangled an admission that I'd seen you in the Avenue, so I shouldn't be surprised if Scroggey isn't at your house, looking for you. Which shoes did you wear?"

"These," said Palmer. "The ones I'm wearing now. But look here, Fairfax—!"

"Shurrup," said Peter; "I'm thinking! My garden boots are fairly big. I got 'em that way so's I could wear two pairs of socks on cold days. They are clean, too. Now if you were to go home in my boots, and leave the shoes here! . . ."

"Well?"

Peter lowered an eyelid in a heavy wink. "You never know! They might be found on Murray's premises—hidden. You'll admit that my evidence is true, and that you did go to the house, and the coppers will think Murray was hiding under the window and listening. You'll say that Brenda told you she was making a new will in your favour."

Roy Palmer caught his arm. He was taller than Peter, and looked down on him with an advantage of several inches.

"Hold everything!" he said. "I may not have your subtle brain, Fairfax, but if you know that, it means that you were listening when I was with Brenda!"

"Of course," Peter admitted readily, "but I wasn't mug enough to leave traces! I leaned across that narrow flower-border, with my arms on the sill. My technical training has taught me to think out all the obvious mistakes first, and avoid 'em."

"She was alive and well when I left the house," said Palmer, giving Peter a hard stare.

Peter shook himself free, and patted Palmer's arm. "Of course she was, old man. Of course she was! She let you out, didn't she?"

"You don't believe me!"

"Don't let's go into all that again," Peter said in a weary tone. "For the sake of reaching agreement I'll believe that you killed her, and you believe I did. The point is, that we're both on the list of suspects, and we're both agreed that Paul Murray ought to swing for the job."

He glanced at Palmer. "Aren't we?" he asked quickly.

"Of course we are! The rat ought to have been hanged years ago!"

"Then take your shoes off while I fetch the others."

On his return from the garden hut, he dropped the boots at Palmer's feet. He picked up the shoes, opened the door of the grandfather clock, and dropped them inside. "I'll attend to them later. Fit all right? They look comfortable. Er—didn't Brenda say the new will was signed?"

"No, she didn't!" Palmer replied abruptly. "The lawyers were drawing up the thing."

"So that if Murray was listening at the window it's quite logical to assume that he'd take steps to prevent the money being signed away from him?"

"Ye-es, I suppose so."

Peter gave a long slow smile. "Even if he didn't do this job, even if you or I or some third person did Brenda in, we're agreed that Murray has a hanging due to him?"

Palmer stared into the smiling face with its smiling mouth and serious eyes. "Now seems a good time to get a few other things settled, Fairfax. What really did happen to Dennis? You know what I think, but I know nothing. You were on the island with him. You know the local conditions, the circumstances, and everything."

He backed to the chest and sat down, his hands clenched between his knees.

Peter balanced himself on the edge of the telephone table and folded his arms. "I can't prove it, Palmer, but I've always been satisfied in my own mind that Paul Murray murdered your brother. I felt it at the time, and I've known it inside me ever since, but you can't go to these police fellows with feelings and hunches. They're sub-human efforts who work to slide-rules, and with mikes. Such things don't, and can't, take into account the mysteries of metaphysics—abnormal psychological phenomena, if you like it better that way. That's why science isn't progressing, y'know. You can't take minds and souls to pieces on a laboratory bench. There are more things in heaven and all that, as Hamlet said. Yes, he murdered your brother, Palmer, and I'll stake my own life on it!"

Palmer thumped a huge fist down on his knee. "That's all I wanted to hear from you! Murray shall hang as high as Haman if I can do anything to convict him!"

"They don't string 'em up these days," Peter said lightly. "They drop 'em through a trap. Most uncomfortable method of passing out, to my mind. Undignified, too! I should hate it. Embarrassing to all concerned, or so I should imagine. However, it's good enough for Murray!"

"Too good," said Palmer, rising from the chest. "So Murray's to hang! By the way, I didn't do Brenda in, you know! I happen to have loved her."

"We've agreed on that, Palmer," Peter said patiently. He went to the door and opened it. "You didn't do it, but I should get home as fast as you can, and nobody will look more surprised than you do when you find friend Scroggey waiting for you. Go out of your way to tell them everything you can. Be frank! We need contrast, and I'm letting them drag information from me—I'm so dim that I don't realise what I saw, nor what I'm telling them."

Palmer paused on the doorstep. "Fairfax, it doesn't really matter now, but how did Murray work it? My brother, I mean?"

"I'll never tell anybody that," replied Peter, "but you can take it from me that he planned and executed the perfect murder. I doubt if it could have been done anywhere else but on Lampedusa. He's a clever little man, so watch him! Nature gave him extra brains to make up for his appearance."

"You won't tell me?"

Peter shook his head. "No, I won't tell you. You're the impulsive type, and you'd go straight to Murray and tax him with the truth. That would spoil everything. One thing I will promise you.

If our plan should go wrong, then I'll blab the Lampedusa story to the police, and once they've got him suspected of Dennis's death they'll do their damnedest to prove he murdered Brenda. Circumstantial evidence will do the rest."

"Is there any?" asked Palmer.

"There can be," replied Peter. "You see, Palmer, you don't know the whole story, and I do."

CHAPTER VII
THE OBSERVATIONS OF SCROGGEY

SCROGGEY KNEW BETTER than to knock at a front door in a street like Trent Street. It was surprising how many people simultaneously opened their doors for a breath of fresh air. He went down the ginnel at the side of the house, and tapped lightly at the back door. It was opened by a shaky old man—near-bald, and collarless. Scroggey asked for Mr. Roy Palmer.

"My son. He's out just now. Went out about a quarter of an hour ago, and I can't say where he's gone, but he shouldn't be long. Any message I can give him?"

Scroggey screwed up his lips. "No-o, not really. I wonder if I could wait for him?"

The old man muttered an apology. "Got Mother seriously ill upstairs, and somebody has to be with her all the time. A bit awkward, sir."

"I'll have a look at the garden for a minute or two," offered Scroggey. "If he hasn't returned by then, I'll call some other time. Just an old acquaintance looking him up—you know how it is when you've been in the army with anyone and find yourself in their home-town!"

The old man nodded without enthusiasm. "I don't doubt he'll be pleased to see you, sir."

"Then I'll look round the garden," said Scroggey. "Got anything planted yet?"

"My boy put the broad beans in last week. There's nothing else yet, although he says the first early peas are going in this week-end. He's done a trench and filled it with compost."

"I'll be doing mine when I get back home," said Scroggey. "Still, I'm keeping you from your wife. The name is Horrocks, if I don't see you before I go!"

He ambled down the garden as casually as possible, full well knowing what he was looking for. The winter digging had been done, and the winter frosts had broken the soil into a friable condition. The broad beans? Where were they? The average man nearly always left a few footprints on his garden, however enthusiastic he may be with a hoe. And here they were at the end of the bean rows. Half a dozen nicely impressed prints of a pair of shoes with medium toes! He couldn't very well set to work to take casts now, but it was nice to know where to find them when wanted.

He went back to the car, backed up the street, and did what he'd seen dozens of commercial travellers do; he took out a notebook and began to write in it—but it wasn't orders he was entering.

In due course he glanced in the driving-mirror and saw Roy Palmer turning into the street. He waited until he drew level, and then poked his head through the side window. "Excuse me, sir! Can you tell me where a Mr. Roy Palmer lives?"

"Well, I happen to be Palmer."

"Now, there's a thing!" said Scroggey with an air of intense surprise. "I'm Sergeant Scroggey, East Courtney police. The Chief wondered if you could give us any information that would help to fill in the background of Mrs. Murray's life. Truth is," he said in a confidential tone, "we're stuck, and eager for any help we can get—although we're not going to admit it publicly. Mrs. Murray was once engaged to your brother, wasn't she?"

"She was," said Palmer, aware that Scroggey was looking at his boots. "Yes, they were engaged to be married."

Scroggey looked up and down the street. "We can't talk here, really, can we? I wonder—?"

"Er—" said Palmer.

"Hop inside with me," said Scroggey. "It's warmer."

Palmer went round the car and joined him. "I'd take you home, but my mother's seriously ill."

"Sorry to hear it," Scroggey sympathised. "Perhaps it will be better if we run back to my office, and I'll have someone bring you home again. Worst of streets like this, isn't it? Everybody's nosy, and if anybody who knows me sees us together they'll have you hanged before Tuesday morning."

He felt Palmer draw away from him. He started the car and drove to police headquarters, meanwhile enlarging on the difficulties of a murder investigation. He left Palmer in a waiting-room for a few minutes, and went to Barnard's private office, where he and Knollis were in session.

"Got Palmer down the passage, sir," he announced. "I tried Fairfax's shoes, and he's all right. Palmer isn't. He wasn't at the house, so I took a walk round the garden. Nice prints very similar to the casts, but he's wearing a somewhat heavy pair of broad-toed boots just now!"

"That's interesting!" commented Knollis.

"A bit awkward in 'em, too, as if not used to them," added Scroggey. "He nearly overbalanced when he got out of the car."

"Still more interesting. Bring him in, Scroggey. What's the excuse?"

"Mrs. Murray's background, sir."

Roy Palmer bent his head as he came through the doorway, and then stood looking round the office. He was tall, and thin, and tired-looking, and obviously surprised to see Knollis and Barnard. He looked round at Scroggey. "I thought you and I were going to have a quiet chat," he said dryly.

"The Inspector thought you may object to taking a subordinate into your confidence," Scroggey said in a deferential voice.

"Oh, well!" said Palmer, and advanced into the room.

Barnard found him a chair and offered him a cigarette, which he refused.

"The sergeant said he wanted to know something about Mrs. Murray's past life," said Palmer. "I'll tell you what I can—anything that will help."

"Well, first," said Knollis, tapping his pen on the table, "we'd like to know something of her association with your late brother."

"They were engaged," Palmer said crisply. He didn't like this lean and slit-eyed man in the grey suit who was apparently to undertake the questioning.

"We know that," said Knollis. "Please pardon my use of the unfortunate word *association*. I didn't realise the implication until I spoke. Yes, they were engaged, Mr. Palmer. I believe your brother was accidentally drowned on Lampedusa Island. Is that correct?"

"That's so," replied Palmer. There was a lot more behind the bland mask of this Yard man than one would expect. He'd have to use his wits if Fairfax's plan was to succeed. These policemen weren't quite the dumb-clucks Fairfax thought them to be.

"Your brother had money. It's the money we're interested in. Could you tell us something of its history?"

Palmer breathed easily. They were laying out the thing just as he wanted it to be!

"I can, sir! My grandfather was in the printing business in a big way, and made a fair pile. He objected to paying death duties or any other duty to the Chancellor of the Exchequer if it could be avoided. He made up his mind to get rid of his money while he was still alive. It was simply arranged. He gave my brother a cheque for eight thousand pounds, and told him it was for division around the family after he was dead. After he was dead—please note that! That was the year war broke out. He was killed while in London on business—that was the following year. A bomb. Dennis was then trustee for the eight thousand. The old man wouldn't have done it any other way, hating lawyers and everything to do with them—a handshake had been his way of making a bond. Dennis got a bit worried when he joined up. He knew I should soon be following him into the Services, and wondered what would happen to the money if he got killed. He was going to do the whole job legally, but it was also going to be a bit long-winded—you know what lawyers are!—and what he was trying to do was stall until the job could be done properly, and at that time nobody thought the war would last very long. So he had an idea, and handed the whole sum over to Brenda."

"I follow you," Knollis said keenly.

Palmer cast a sharp glance at the two detectives. The story seemed to be going down all right, and doing its work. "Right! Well, poor old Den went west on that island, and Brenda was in possession of the money. Not a cent of it got back into our family!"

"You asked for a share, if not the whole amount?" Palmer stiffened in his chair.

"Asked her? I've demanded it, bullied her, argued with her, threatened her with a lawsuit, and generally tried to make her see sense by being sarcastic, but she wouldn't come clean with a penny. She said it belonged to her—Dennis had given it to her without conditions."

"May we take it for granted that you went round last night to have yet another try?" Knollis asked casually.

Palmer froze. Here it came, if he wasn't careful! "Last night, sir?"

"You were seen going to the house, Mr. Palmer," said Knollis. "I don't suppose you intended your visit to be secret, surely?"

The simple statement disarmed Palmer, and he fell into the trap laid for him. "No, only from her husband!"

"So you did go to the house! You admit it!"

"Er—yes!"

Palmer smiled inwardly. He could make that error pay interest from now on. Fairfax was a cunning so-and-so!

"You knew her husband was out, Mr. Palmer?"

"Yes."

"You either saw him leave the house, or saw him in town?"

"I saw him leave the house."

"You waited until he did leave it!"

"Er—yes," said Palmer, looking down at his hands. The fellow's eyes were pretty searching.

Knollis interlaced his fingers and rested his fore-arms on the table. "At what time did Mr. Murray leave the house, Mr. Palmer? This is important."

Palmer grimaced, and shrugged his shoulders. "I'm not sure to a few minutes, but I'll say five or ten to eight."

"And you waited until he was clear."

"I've said that, sir."

"You went to see Mrs. Murray then, of course. Tell me, Mr. Palmer, which door did you go to?"

"The back one."

"How did she receive you?"

Palmer found himself pulling at his collar with one finger. The job wasn't so easy as Fairfax had indicated! "Why, not too happily," he said. "It looked to me as if she'd been having a row with her husband. She was very pale, and there were two spots of high colour on her cheeks. She was very off-handed, too!"

"You asked her for money?"

"I did!" Palmer nodded. "My mother's ill with an incurable complaint. Her life can be extended if she can have an immediate operation, and that means a nursing-home. I asked Brenda—Mrs. Murray—for a minimum of two hundred and fifty pounds. I was a bit too hasty, and reminded her that it was our money anyway. We had a row over that, and then things quietened down, and she gave me a cheque for three hundred pounds."

"A cheque!" Barnard exclaimed, glancing at Knollis.

Palmer took out his wallet and handed the cheque over the table. "We've had it now, of course. They won't pay out on it, will they?"

"I don't profess to understand the intricacies of banking," said Knollis. "Tell me, did Mrs. Murray have occasion to go to the safe?"

Palmer again avoided the eyes. "I didn't know they had one," he said. "I can't remember seeing it."

"A wall-safe, behind the sideboard," said Knollis. "Now, there's a point puzzling me, Mr. Palmer. If you had a row over the money, why should Mrs. Murray give you fifty pounds more than you asked?"

"Sheer good nature, I imagine. I didn't ask for it."

"Sheer good nature—after you'd virtually accused her once more of robbing your family?" asked Knollis. "Look, your parents are both of an advanced age. Are they drawing pensions?"

"Oh, yes."

"You are really keeping them out of your salary?"

Palmer nodded. "That's why I can't afford to move to a more salubrious district. I just can't get out. I'm stuck!"

"Mrs. Murray knew this, of course?"

"Considering the amount of time she used to spend at the house when my brother was alive, she should have had a darned good idea how things were!"

"Up to last night she'd refused to give you or your brother's father and mother a single shilling?"

"That's so," said Palmer in a puzzled voice. "Where does all this lead?"

"I'm wondering about Mrs. Murray's sudden change of heart," said Knollis. "I'm reluctant to suggest this, but you didn't sell her anything, did you?"

Palmer blinked. "Sell her anything? Such as?"

"Information," said Knollis. "Information about her husband."

Palmer's eyes opened wide. He shuffled, and felt for the edges of his seat, as if unsure of its security. "Why—why do you suggest that, sir?"

"Because someone else went to the house with the same idea in mind," said Knollis, sphinx-like behind the wide table-desk. "Someone else went on the same errand, only to come away when he saw you there. Is it possible you both knew facts that you thought should be in her possession? Is that why she gave you the two-fifty, and added the fifty pounds to it, Mr. Palmer?"

"Yes," Palmer said in a low voice that was almost a whisper. "I didn't sell it to her in the usual sense of the word. She wanted to know what her husband was doing with the money he was continually begging from her, and I told her. The only condition was that she shouldn't stop the cheque."

"Yes? And you told her . . . ?"

Palmer sniffed. "I told her the truth about his carryings-on with the girl in Dale Road."

It was Knollis's turn to be surprised, but he concealed it behind a bland mask. He shuffled the papers lying before him. "See, that will be Miss—Miss—"

"Gloria Dickinson, since you appear to know all about her," said Palmer.

"Ah, yes! Miss Dickinson!"

Barnard made a queer noise into his throat, which he turned into a cough and an apology.

"How long has this association been going on?" asked Knollis. "I feel I can use the word in this instance."

"She was engaged to Murray up to him coming on leave after Dennis's death. Didn't you know that?"

"Merely checking," smiled Knollis amiably. Barnard muttered something inaudible.

Knollis turned his pen the right way up and doodled on the blotting-pad. "So the story runs something like this, Mr. Palmer. Your brother and Murray were on the island together. Your brother was engaged to Miss Morley, as she was then. Murray was engaged to Miss Dickinson. Your brother died, Murray came on leave, jilted Miss Dickinson, and married Miss Morley. That correct?"

"Correct, except that he didn't ditch Dickinson," Palmer said fiercely. "We didn't realise it at the time, but his association with her never ceased. He simply put her into the flat in Dale Road, and kept her on our money!"

"You know more about this business than we do," Knollis said. "Was there any legal loophole whereby the money might get back to your family in the event of Mrs. Murray's death? I mean, other than by being willed?"

"Not so far as I know," Palmer replied. "Dennis regularised the affair by making out a deed of gift. Of course, the money was coming back to us. She was drawing up another will—in our favour. She was ironic about it, and said Paul knew, and asked why, once it was signed, I didn't race Paul to it, and murder her before he persuaded her to destroy it!"

"And did you?" murmured Knollis.

Palmer half-rose from his chair, and sank back again, to glower across the table. It was no good trying to get tough with these people. They had the whip-hand. "The new will wasn't even signed," he said. "It was being drawn up by her lawyers."

"You say Murray knew about this new will?" interjected Barnard.

"Brenda said so, and I've no other information on it than that."

"She actually said the will wasn't signed!"

Palmer hesitated. "No, being honest, she didn't. It was an impression I got from what she said—or the way she said it. What she actually said was that there was a new will in our favour, but I'm certain it wasn't even ready for signing—otherwise, why should Murray be so interested?"

"Confusing, isn't it?" asked Knollis. "Who are her lawyers?"

"Morgan, in Bridlesmith Gate."

"And she said she'd told her husband?"

"She said that."

"And you say she looked as if she'd been having a tearful row with her husband?"

"Yes, and I'm certain of it."

Knollis suddenly came forward across the table, to peer closely into Palmer's face. "Exactly how long did you crouch under the dining-room window, Mr. Palmer?"

"Me!" exclaimed Palmer. "I did no such thing!"

"Footprints were found under the window," said Knollis. "Whoever made them was there some considerable time."

"Probably belonged to the man who saw me go to the house," Palmer suggested brightly.

"The prints are of shoes with medium toes," said Knollis. "Our informant wears pointed ones."

Palmer looked down at his boots. "These aren't exactly pointed, I admit," he said.

"Too wide for the casts we took," said Knollis. "I noticed them as you walked in the room. Army type, aren't they? Surprising how many men stick to what they got used to in the Services."

"They're comfortable," said Palmer, now at his ease.

"You always wear that style of footwear?"

"Oh, yes!"

Knollis faced him with a dry smile. "You seem to have a good friend somewhere, Mr. Palmer. Someone else is planting your broad beans this year!"

Palmer flushed, recovered his self-control, and with an excellent imitation of nonchalance said: "That's as it may be, but these are what I wear."

Knollis signalled to Scroggey, who came from the back of the room and laid the casts on the table.

Palmer eyed them. "You'll find no shoes like those in my house!"

"You should be a detective," said Knollis. "How did you know they are casts of prints made by shoes, and not boots?"

"Er—well, it was a sort of impression!"

"Of shoes," smiled Knollis.

Palmer did not reply, so Knollis rose and dismissed him, thanking him somewhat sarcastically for the information he had so readily placed at his disposal.

"That was quite a do," said Barnard. "It all swings on the new will now, doesn't it?"

"If we're following the monetary motive, yes."

"What other motive is there?"

Knollis seemed to wake from a reverie. "Hm? Oh, yes! Of course! I was dreaming."

"The Dickinson bird will be able to tell us whether Murray was there or not last night."

Knollis nodded absently. "Yes, she'll now be in a position to say where he was last night. Even supposing Murray is guilty, and supposing his girl wasn't in the thing from the start, you can bet your boots she'll have been fitted up with a sound yarn by now. Murray may play the old game, deliberately keeping us in the dark about her, letting us find out about her by accident—as we have done! Then, of course, we pump the story out of her against her will, and she'll finally admit that he was with her. That lets him down morally, but clears him of suspicion of murder. It's an old trick that sometimes works!"

"We'll go to work on her?" Barnard asked somewhat anxiously.

"In the morning."

"Sunday!"

"Good day for such an interview," smiled Knollis. "People like her think we don't work on Sundays, and we'll catch her off her guard."

Scroggey wandered back into the office, looking thoughtful.

"What's worrying you?" said Barnard.

"I was thinking, sir," replied Scroggey. "There's some monkey business going on, and I'm sure Fairfax is at the bottom of it. This boot-and-shoe problem, for instance. It strikes me that the pair Palmer is wearing might be the type a fellow like Fairfax would use for gardening. I'm sure they ain't in normal everyday use. There's a black-leady sheen about the shine, and that's how my gardening boots come up when I clean 'em—which is once a year whether they want it or not! I lay anything they've been dubbined in their early days, and it's showing through."

"Where did that idea come from?" asked Knollis, showing intense interest.

Scroggey stroked his freckled face. "I went to see Fairfax first, sir, and was shown every pair in the house—Mrs. Fairfax's own words. I went on to Trent Street to see Palmer, and he'd been gone from the house only a short time—quarter of an hour, his father said, which was only a few minutes longer than I'd been coming from Fairfax's. I had the car, and Palmer hasn't one, which means he has to use the bus.

"There isn't a telephone at Palmer's, but I'd a notion I'd seen wires running in next door, so I've checked with the exchange, and they gave me the name of Howard. I've rung them, and asked if they remembered me 'phoning Mr. Palmer some time ago. The lady remembered fetching him to the blower for me. Now Palmer was gone about forty minutes all told. . . ."

"But it took you fifteen minutes to get from the Fairfax side of town to Trent Street!" Knollis protested.

Scroggey grinned. "I haven't your endurance, sir. I'm a big man. You've had no tea, but I called in home and had a quick cupper and shoved a couple of sandwiches in my pocket."

"We'll accept that explanation of the time-lag," smiled Knollis. "Now, what are you getting at?"

"I think it might be interesting to have a look round Fairfax's outhouses sometime when they aren't at home, sir."

"Well? What's preventing you doing so?"

Scroggey nodded happily. "Thanks, sir! That's all I wanted to know."

CHAPTER VIII
THE REFUSAL OF MISS DICKINSON

THE CHURCH BELLS were ringing for morning service as Gloria Dickinson swung her undoubtedly shapely legs out of bed and wandered through to the kitchenette to switch on the electric kettle. Not that bells meant anything to her. She wasn't likely to be getting married herself, and although she had been to one or two weddings as a spectator, and once to a funeral, she couldn't otherwise remember going to church since she was christened, and as that was twenty-five years behind it meant nothing to her.

She yawned deeply, and didn't bother to cover her somewhat generous mouth with her hand. Such niceties of conduct were superfluous, although Ugly, otherwise Paul, was always pulling her up about this, and that, and the other, telling her that such things were definitely not done in polite circles. As she didn't move in polite circles she wasn't very much worried, although she pretended to be impressed by his superior social knowledge, and performed some of the rites sooner than upset him. One doesn't throw one's bread ticket in the street!

It wouldn't do to upset Paul. He was all that a girl could ask, if you ignored his pitted skin and frog-like face. He loved her, he was attentive, and he had money. He would have more now his wife had been conveniently removed.

Brenda had been a nuisance ever since she came on the scene—or had she? Life wouldn't have been so comfy if she'd married Paul without the money, and she wasn't a domestic slave like Brenda had been. She'd encouraged him to marry the girl and her thousands, so it was hardly her place to grumble. Queer how one's ideas can change in the space of half an hour, ideas it has taken years to sort out and frame into a way of living! He'd been honest enough that day when he came home from the Mediterranean on leave—she had to give him that. Marry, and they'd be happy, but would have little money. It was either marriage and no money, or money and no marriage. She'd done the quickest think of her life that night, and had the sense to throw the responsibility on him so that if it went wrong he couldn't blame her. She threw her arms round his neck, declared that she loved him dearly, but, darling, she just had no brains for this kind of thing, and she would leave him to decide what was to be done. He married Brenda Morley and her money, and put her—Gloria—in this sweet little flat! Since when life had been mainly good. Mainly. There were snags.

She fetched a half grapefruit from the refrigerator, and put it on the tray, and cut three wafer-thin slices of bread and butter to go with it. Real butter, not margarine; and farm butter, not the shop stuff. Paul was simply marvellous at finding things one wasn't supposed to have. There were distinct advantages in not being married. She held him because he loved her, and not because he was tied down by a contract and had to put up with her whether he was fed up or not. Again, a husband was always under one's feet, and that could never be said about Paul. It gave her an awful lot of time to do the things she wanted to do, and she didn't have to do things she didn't want to do just to please him. And yet there were times when she would willingly be without the money and be in possession of a marriage certificate. She was lonely.

The tray complete but for the teapot, she waited patiently for the kettle, meanwhile regarding herself critically in the full-length mirror on the wall of the bathroom, the door of which stood open. Not bad! There was no point in denying it. She wasn't at all bad-looking. Her face was long, but well-shaped and there was a kind of oriental slant to her eyes that attracted Paul from the very first; he said it made her look mysterious. Her hair had once been light brown, was now golden, and was soon to be ash, but that was to surprise Paul when this affair of his murdered wife was over. Her teeth were all her own, and good ones—they should be, considering how many dentist's bills Paul had paid! As for her figure, very self-evident in the cobwebby pyjamas, she had no regrets. When one could keep a slender shortish body and long slim legs without having to exercise or diet, then one should be grateful for the fact! Yes, she could get by!

She took one of the many packets of cigarettes that lay around the flat, and stuck a cigarette in the corner of her mouth, lighting it from a gold-plated lighter that was on the tray. The kettle was singing now. She pulled up a cork-seated stool and made herself comfortable for the remaining minutes before she could brew the tea.

She blew the smoke down her nostrils, and returned to the question that had been bobbing in and out of her mind since reading yesterday morning's papers. Why hadn't Paul been round? Had he gone sentimental over Brenda, or was he hemmed in by police and reporters? She daren't get in touch with him at his home. That would never do. She'd read a spate of detective novels and mystery thrillers in the years since Paul married, and she knew they always looked for a woman in the case. It was only a matter of time before they learned of her existence, and then they'd be round to question her—and before they did that she had to know whether Paul wanted her to deny all knowledge of him, or whether he wanted her to admit the truth about them both, and then, again, whether he wanted her to say he was or was not with her at the flat on Friday night. It was quite a problem, and one she didn't feel capable of solving without help.

If she said he had been round, then—according to the books she'd read—it would increase the suspicion against him, since they'd say he'd murdered Brenda for her sake and she was providing a false alibi to cover him. If she said he hadn't been round, they'd say he must have been somewhere, and where was he? It was awkward, and all the more so since once his two enemies, Mr. Palmer and Mr. Fairfax, opened their mouths, the police would be bound to suspect Paul of the murder.

The kettle erupted. She hurriedly switched off and poured the water into the silver teapot. She carried the tray to her pink boudoir, where her pet budgerigar was busily chattering to himself in the pale February sun.

"We're in a mess, old boy," she said. "Either our master is a murderer, or he isn't—and I'm not sure. And here's the snag. If he is, and gets away with it, we have to wonder what he might do if he casts his eyes in another direction and decides he no longer wants us. We can't live without money, and we don't want to be murdered for being in the way, so we have to use our noddles and think up something pretty quick, because either way we're likely to lose him." She stared down into the deserted street.

"There's something else. If he didn't murder her? If it was one of the others . . ."

The budgerigar said: "So what?" in a piping voice.

"So what?" she asked, cocking a shaven eyebrow at him. "So this! If somebody else did her in, it means they did her in because of you-know-what, and he might have our little Ugly next on the list. Looks as if we're in danger of losing him one way or another." She looked at the caged bird, her eyes wide, and said: "Oh!"

"Pretty Billy!" said the budgerigar.

"He never said a word that would give him away," she muttered, staring blankly at the gilded cage with its blue accessories, "but he really did do the other Palmer in! That's why he won't drink much—afraid of letting something slip. Funny I haven't really thought about it before. It's sort of slid through my mind once or twice, but I've never really thought about it until now. He's been a murderer all the time . . . !"

She licked her lips.

"He won't murder me, because I'd be no use to him dead, and all he need do is walk out on me when he gets fed up. I mustn't let him get fed up, and before the risk arrives, Billy Boy, we've to get all the money we can out of him. I'll play fair by him as long as he plays fair by me. After that it's every man for himself, and women and children first!"

Looking down, she saw a car drawing into the kerb, right against the door of the stairs which led between the two shops to the flat.

She hurried to the bathroom for her wrap, then back to the boudoir to make up her face. The doorbell was ringing before she'd reached the lipstick. She called *"Coming!"* in a loud voice, and carried on with great deliberation. It could only be the police. Blind 'em with cosmetic science and a little discreet exposure! Keep 'em occupied with everything but what she might know about Friday. Then act silly and brainless. That was the way to fool clever men. Heck, didn't she know from experience!

She lit another cigarette, carefully arranged her wrap so that it suggested more than it revealed, and went to the outer door. She unlocked it, and opened it a mere inch, peeping round it nervously. "Who—who is it?" she murmured feebly.

"The police. Can you spare us a few moments, please?"

She gave an uncertain laugh. "Well, really, I mean, I'm only just having my breakfast."

"We won't keep you from your breakfast more than two minutes," said the red-faced man with a pleasant smile.

She looked the two men over. The red-faced one looked all right. The other—the thin one—stood solidly and rigidly, like an undertaker come to measure a corpse, and wearing the professional air of mourning.

She opened the door very slowly. "We-ell, I suppose it will be all right," she said. "There *are* two of you. I mean, a girl has to be careful! You—you have a card or something to show you're *really* policemen?"

"I'm Inspector Barnard, Courtney C.I.D.," said the red-faced man. "This is Inspector Knollis of Scotland Yard."

"Scotland Yard!"

"Scotland Yard," said Knollis.

"That's different!" she said eagerly. "This is exciting. Come straight in. Would you like a cup of tea—it's fresh!"

"Thanks, yes," smiled Barnard. "I had breakfast at seven, and am getting a bit thirsty."

Gloria smiled archly as she led them to the boudoir. "Seven? There isn't such a time! I don't believe it!"

"Take it from me, Miss Dickinson, there are even earlier hours than seven—my God, yes!"

She made a lot of fuss in parking them in the chintz-covered chairs in the window. She fetched cups and saucers, and poured their tea with her little finger stuck out at right angles in the manner favoured by Paul, who knew all about etiquette.

"You live here alone?" Knollis asked frigidly, meanwhile looking round the room as if expecting to see the feet of another body sticking out from under the furniture.

Gloria nodded happily. "That's the wrong line, Inspector. On the pictures they always say something about it being a nice little place I've got here!"

"I'm not in pictures," said Knollis. He sipped his tea, and it seemed to thaw him to some extent. "It is a nice little place though. You live here alone—oh, I've asked you that, haven't I?"

"You didn't get an answer, Inspector," said Gloria. "Yes, I live alone, apart from Billy Boy there. He's my sole companion."

"You know Mr. Paul Murray?"

"Paul? He is one of my friends, yes!"

"One of them?" Knollis asked pointedly, meanwhile glancing round the showy luxury.

"He's my friend," said Gloria.

"That's better," said Knollis. "I don't think we need beat about the bush, Miss Dickinson. Mr. Murray is responsible for the upkeep of this flat?"

"Er—"

She took another look at him, and changed her mind.

"Yes."

Knollis nodded. "If we're frank with each other, we can save time. You were once engaged to him?"

"Yes."

"That would be about seven years ago?"

"Yes, when we got engaged."

"You would be quite young then?"

"I was seventeen when I was engaged. It was broken off when he came home on leave in nineteen-forty-three."

"Why?" Knollis asked shortly.

"He fell in love with another woman, and married her," Gloria replied with a shrug.

"Then why is he keeping you going here?"

"He thought he owed me something. I promised not to sue him for breach of promise and damage his career."

"That sounds suspiciously like blackmail!"

"No! Oh, no, it wasn't that!" she protested. "Paul suggested it himself because he said I'd been so decent over the whole thing. I mean, I didn't want to hurt a man I still loved!"

"You go out to work?"

"Well, no."

"So he's looking after you pretty well," said Knollis. "I take it he calls from time to time to see if you are comfortable and happy?"

"Occasionally, Inspector. He doesn't forget me."

"I can well believe that," Knollis said dryly. "Did he call on Friday evening?"

Her heart took a leap. So here it was! She put her fingers to her forehead. "Friday? Friday?"

"Friday evening, Miss Dickinson."

The way to take came to her with the swiftness and blinding brilliance of revelation. She dropped her hands to her lap, looked him straight in the eyes, and said boldly: "I can't tell you, Inspector!"

"You mean you won't, Miss Dickinson?"

She shook her head vigorously. "Not until I've seen him! It's not my place to say another thing about him. I can't interfere in his private affairs. He'll surely tell you himself if you ask him!"

Knollis sat back and looked at her with a twisted smile. He looked at Barnard, and then back at her. "I see," he said.

Gloria mentally rifled the pages of the detective novels she had read. "You can't make me say anything about him, you know!"

"We know," said Knollis. "That's the trouble!"

Barnard leaned forward with a coaxing smile, all friendliness and honeyed sweetness. "Miss Dickinson, a woman has been murdered."

"I'm sorry," she said. "Honestly I am, but I didn't do it!"

"Mr. Murray was away from his home at the time," said Barnard, "and while there's nothing whatsoever to connect him with the murder, well, he just can't prove where he was at the time. That's awkward for him, isn't it? And you do see the point, don't you?"

"You want me to say he was here?" said Gloria.

Barnard laughed in what he intended to be a hearty fashion. "Good gracious, no! We only want you to tell us whether he was or he wasn't. If he was here, then it's obvious he's a real gentleman, and risking suspicion of murder rather than bring your good name into the affair—"

Knollis coughed behind his hand.

Barnard glared at him, and turned to Gloria with a smile. "Not that it would be made public, of course! Oh, no, you've got us wrong, Miss Dickinson! If he was actually here, it's a point in his favour!"

Gloria nodded her blonde head, and gave him smile for smile. "I'm sure it is, but if that's the way he feels about it, then I'm more certain than ever that it's up to him to tell you whether he came or not."

Knollis groaned.

She turned her smile on Knollis. "And that's another thing. I know Paul's no murderer, but even if he was, and he wanted me to go into the witness box and swear he *was* here—I'd do it!"

"Whether he was or not?" said Knollis.

"Whether he was or not!"

"That's perjury!" said Barnard in a shocked voice.

Gloria nodded. "I know! I read books!"

"It—it isn't honest," said Barnard, fumbling for some way of bringing her down.

"I know that, too," she replied. "You both went round it very nicely when you came in, and thank you for doing it, but facts are facts, and Paul really is my man. He's always been married more to me than to the one who's been murdered—and I'd actually hang for him if necessary!"

"We're not asking you to do anything so dramatic as that," protested Barnard. "We're asking you whether you can say where he was between eight and nine on Friday evening!"

She shook her head firmly. "Not until he gives the word!"

Barnard pushed his cup and saucer on the tray and got up. "We're wasting time, Knollis."

Knollis ignored him. "See, the entrance to the flat is between a butcher's shop and a newsagent's, isn't it? All we need do is go round the customers and we'll soon find out whether he came or not."

"The shops were both closed by seven," Gloria said smugly, "and Paul never comes while they're open. He is discreet, you know!"

She showed them from the flat, apologising step by step for her inability to help them, but they really must see her point of view!

Before they were down the stairs she was in her bedroom, changing into brown slacks and a golden-yellow sweater. Over them she pulled a camel-hair travelling coat, pushed her feet into brown walking-shoes, and hurried down to the street clutching a handful of coppers.

The telephone kiosk was ten yards away. She rammed the pennies into the slot and dialled Paul's number. Nothing happened. She got her money out, and tried again. She tried four times in all, and then swore as the door thudded back when she flung it open and hurried to the flat.

The policemen weren't as dim as she thought they were. They didn't mean her getting in touch with Paul, and that was serious! It showed they really did suspect him, and all she could do was spend the day trying not to bite her lacquered nails. And Ugly would be itching to get in touch with her, and just daren't try it, knowing they were watching him. She'd stick by him through thick and thin, just to spite the policemen. She'd stick by him to the last penny. Well, to the last fifty pounds!

CHAPTER IX
THE REMORSE OF MURRAY

MR. CHARLES BENSON was not surprised when Knollis and Barnard visited him at noon that Sunday. He had been expecting someone from police headquarters since the Saturday evening paper informed him of Mr. Paul Murray's visit to a well-known nurseryman.

Barnard he knew, knowing him as a friendly fellow who would always share a drink in the club they both frequented, and refuse to be drawn on the subject of his work. Privately, Benson didn't blame him. It was always wise to leave one's work behind for an hour now and then.

It was the other officer, Knollis, who interested him now. He had read of him. Who hadn't, if it came to that? Knollis had fallen for more than his due share of murder cases, the kind that catch the public eye, and various periodicals had published at least six different accounts of what the man was like, and how he set about the investigation of these murder cases. One of them should approximate to the truth.

It was obvious from the first that he was not approachable. There was an air of reserve about him that distinctly said: Keep Off! He was of medium height, a slit-eyed man with high cheekbones who walked with a straight back and almost military precision. Benson wondered if he was soulless, and then if he was putting on an act, and finally gave up the riddle and invited them both indoors.

"I was expecting you, of course," he said. "The bit in the papers about the local nurseryman made me think you might be dropping in. Mr. Murray did make an appointment, of course."

"Did he keep it?" asked Barnard.

"No, he cancelled it, Inspector. You see, I got the 'phone call during the early afternoon. He said he intended planting a *cupressus* hedge along his boundary fencing, but his friend Fairfax had told him it wouldn't grow in the local soil, and had suggested asking my advice. He was to be here about eight o'clock.

Then, after tea, he rang again to say he couldn't make it, and would ring me some other time to make a new appointment."

"You went out that evening?"

"Yes, Mr. Knollis," said Benson. "I usually turn out about half-past seven. I'm a bachelor, living alone, and the house gets a bit dreary. I like company, you know!"

"Look, Mr. Benson," Knollis said; "would you say it was the same person who rang you both times?"

The plump nurseryman hesitated, and blinked at Knollis wonderingly. "I never thought about it? I'd no reason to think it was anybody different."

"That's all right then," smiled Knollis. "We aren't trying to put any ideas into your head. That kind of thing doesn't do. You know Mr. Fairfax?"

"Oh, yes! Very pleasant fellow who'd go out of his way to help anybody if he could. Bit weird in some ways, but then, who isn't!"

"How weird?" Knollis asked.

"Well, he looks a bit queer for one thing. I don't know anybody so dark for one thing, and then those heavy eyes of his always seem to be looking at something miles away. You can see he's thinking about two or three other things even when he's talking quite intelligently to you. Still, he's a fellow I like to get talking to in the club."

"Thanks for your help," Knollis said abruptly. "We can leave you in peace again."

Outside, Barnard scratched the back of his neck and looked quizzically at Knollis. "Well, where do we look next? Shall we have another go at Murray?"

"Yes," Knollis replied. "I think we should ask for a more detailed account of his conversation with Fairfax."

Murray was sulking when they arrived at the house. His flat face was sunk on his chest, and his hands thrust deep into his pockets, the picture of dejection.

"I'm getting sick of all this," he complained. "There's a policeman hanging round the house all the time, and a plain-clothes fellow always at the top of the Avenue."

"My dear fellow," explained Barnard, not too truthfully, "he's there for your protection—both of them are. Until we know why your wife was killed, we simply have to keep a watch on you in case an attempt should be made against you. But we haven't come to chat about that. We'd like an account of your meeting with Mr. Fairfax on Friday. Lunch-time, wasn't it?"

Murray raised his head. "Fairfax has told you that?"

"With a little persuasion," said Knollis. "How did you meet?"

"We ran into each other and got talking about this and that and the other. He knows this place, and I mentioned our idea of planting a hedge along the back to cut out the wind. He said a good thorn hedge was as good as anything, and I said I was thinking of *cupressus* because it massed together better than thorn and didn't make a garden look so much like a hedged field. He said *cupressus* wouldn't grow in limy soil, and suggested seeing Benson. He added that he knew Benson would be in that night, and it wouldn't be a bad idea to 'phone him and make an appointment. I thanked him, and said I'd do so immediately after lunch when I got back to the bank."

"Which you did?"

"Yes."

"At what time?"

"It would be about quarter to two."

"Now look," said Knollis. "At what time did you leave the bank that night?"

"Half-past five."

"Did you 'phone Benson again?"

Murray stared at him. "There surely wouldn't have been any point in that?"

"Not if you still intended to see him."

"Well, I did intend seeing him, and I went to see him. I've told you so."

"And he wasn't in?" said Knollis.

"He wasn't in," Murray said irritably. "I called at the Crown for a drink, and then decided to walk home when I saw the tail light of the bus vanishing up the street. February nights aren't exactly the right ones for hanging about waiting for buses."

Knollis sighed. "That's a straight enough story! Now suppose your wife had willingly given that three hundred pounds away, Mr. Murray? Would you be willing for the recipient to keep it?"

Murray shrugged, and looked at Knollis as if he considered the question a stupid one. "Would I have any alternative? What is gone, is gone."

"And if she gave him a cheque for the same amount, considering it was for a worthy cause, would you be prepared to honour her wish?"

"Depends whom she gave it to," said Murray. He glanced quickly at Knollis. "You know who has it?"

"We know who has the cheque," said Knollis. "We're giving away nothing you won't learn later. She gave Mr. Roy Palmer a cheque for the amount. His mother is suffering from cancer, and the money was to pay for an immediate operation and whatever else might be needed for her comfort."

"In that case . . ." said Murray. He looked at Barnard and Knollis in turn, questioningly. "The cheque was for the same sum as that missing from the safe!"

"That has occurred to us," said Knollis. "Where did your wife keep the cheque-book?"

"In the sideboard drawer."

"So she wouldn't have to open the safe on that account, would she?"

"Of course not."

"I don't suppose you know the numbers of the notes?"

Murray shook his head. "No idea. She drew the money herself. She liked to have money in the house."

"You're absolutely sure you came straight home from the Crown, and walked it?" Knollis asked, watching Murray narrowly.

"I've told you the truth," said Murray. "Why do you doubt my word?"

"We aren't doubting it," said Knollis. "We're trying to prove your story in your own interests."

"What else could I have done?" Murray challenged him.

"Shall we be frank?" asked Knollis. "Benson wasn't in when you got to his house, and we've consequently no proof that you ever went there—I'm giving you the worst possible view of your own story, remember! I should add that you are under no suspicion regarding your wife's death, but we must clear you completely before we go to work on the person we do suspect. That clear?"

Murray nodded. "Yes. Please go on. This is interesting, and may help me."

"Benson wasn't in," Knollis continued, "so we've no proof that you ever went to the house. On paper it could look as if you told that story, but actually never went farther than the main road, from where you went down the field to the boundary fence, and there lured your wife into the darkness. . . ."

"My God!" exclaimed Murray. He stared at Knollis and Barnard for a full minute, and then asked: "But look here! Why didn't Benson wait for me? He knew I was going. I'd made an appointment!"

Knollis decided to tell him the truth, hoping by doing so to shake him into revealing more than he intended.

"Someone rang in your name to say you couldn't keep the appointment," he said quietly.

Murray started. "Someone—rang—in my name? But only Fairfax knew I was going. Brenda didn't know until I got home in the evening!"

"Quite so, Mr. Murray!"

"Then it must have been Fairfax!"

"We think so," said Knollis.

"Fairfax—to murder Brenda," murmured Murray. "It doesn't make sense!"

"Wait a minute!" said Knollis. "There's no suggestion that Fairfax did murder your wife, nor that he came here to do so."

"Then why should he slink round while I was in town? It still doesn't make sense!"

"He wanted to see your wife alone," said Knollis.

Murray allowed that to sink in, his pock-marked little face screwed into a grotesque mask. "He could have caught her alone without cancelling my meeting with Benson!"

Barnard blinked and looked across the room at Knollis. "He's right, you know!"

"Of course he's right," Knollis replied calmly.

"Why did he want to see her?" asked Murray. "Queer idea, cancelling the appointment, surely?"

"He'd certain information to put into her hands."

"Oh!"

Knollis waited patiently, while Murray's twitching face revealed the searching in his mind for the one fact Fairfax might have wanted to pass on.

"Was the score so heavy?" Knollis asked gently.

Murray put his hands over his eyes and did not make an answer.

"We've paid a call on a young lady this morning," said Knollis. "A young lady who lives in a flat, wears transparent pyjamas, and keeps a budgerigar. She makes an excellent cup of tea."

Murray's face rose above his hands. He rose and walked to the far side of the room, from where he stared back at them with wide eyes. "You've seen Gloria," he said flatly. "If ever she's found murdered you can come straight round here and arrest me, gentlemen. She's been asking for it since 'forty-three."

"Perhaps you'd care to tell us," said Knollis.

Murray backed to the fireplace, stood on the square, oak curb, and rested his back against the mantel.

"She's been the cause of all the trouble," he said. "You'll probably find who it was who told Fairfax—oh, I know what she told him! The gold-digging little devil—and she used to be angelic! She told him she was my mistress. Well, it's true, and I couldn't get rid of her. I'm not getting sentimental or even penitent, but your sins do find you out. When I married Brenda I—well, I married her for her money. Yes, that's better out of my system! I married her for her money, and kept Gloria at the flat.

"As time went by I learned I'd made a mistake. Brenda was good, and I began to love her. Gloria had become a habit, and

I couldn't keep away from her. Then she began to change, and all she wanted of me was money, money, and more money. I was in a fix. Brenda bought the house for me when we married, and gave me a thousand for myself. Gloria got the thousand, although heaven knows what she's done with it. Then she found my source of supply running out, and hinted it would be just too bad if Brenda got to know about her. I borrowed five hundred on the house, and Gloria got that as well. . . ."

He stared miserably at the carpet. Knollis and Barnard waited, loth to break the continuity of the confession.

"Brenda found the papers, and we had a first-class row about it on Friday before I went out. She said she hated me, and I told her I didn't hate her, but loved her. I tried to find a way of bringing about a reconciliation, but she told me to get out. She wanted to think. I've loved her for three years, and tried to make her love me, but there was Gloria in the background all the time, and I knew I was in a trap. May she finish up in—"

"Quite!" said Knollis.

Murray looked up. "I told her last week that the holiday was over. I told her I'd still pay the rent of the flat, although heaven knows how I was going to do it, but she'd have to economise and try to realise that I was running two places. It was then she threw out another threat. It's a wonder I didn't kill her that night. I smacked her face and threw her across the room, and then got out before I did something desperate. She's seen the last of me. Oh, I know she'll finish me in Courtney. I'll get out and make a fresh start where I'm not known, but if she follows me I'll swing for her!"

"Mr. Murray," said Knollis earnestly. "On your honour, did you or did you not go to the flat last Friday evening?"

Murray beat his fist on his leg. "Inspector, I swear I didn't see her on Friday evening!"

"Did you go to the flat?"

"Aren't those two the same question?" asked Murray.

"No," said Knollis. "They aren't!"

Murray grimaced. "Well, if you're so meticulous, I'll say I neither went to the flat nor saw her on Friday evening. Is that satisfactory?"

"Was she expecting you?"

"No, I never went to see her on Mondays or Fridays."

"And you did go into town to see Benson, and then walked home?"

"Walked home slowly," said Murray. "I was trying to think up a way out of this mess I was in. I'll swear it in court."

"Tell me," said Knollis, "what was Miss Dickinson's attitude towards your wife?"

"One of contempt when we first married, and then she began to hate her as the money ran out, wishing she was dead so that I could marry her. She'd some hopes! What a wonderful honeymoon she'd planned! Milan, and Venice, and Florence, and Rome! A bigger and better house when we came home, and a car, and lord knows what else. She might have let Brenda die first! Money had grown on trees for years, and she thought it would keep growing, like fruit, year after year."

"Why didn't you see her on Fridays, Mr. Murray?"

Murray shrugged. "An arbitrary choice. I couldn't see her every night, because I had to keep up appearances here. She wanted some freedom, too, so we casually picked those two days."

"I think a few pennies are dropping," said Knollis.

"I can't hear them," replied Murray.

"Changing the metaphor," said Knollis, "you're in the ring, and it's the man outside who sees most of the game. What did she do on Mondays and Fridays?"

"Pictures, or the theatre. She obviously had to take herself on such outings. I daren't be seen in town with her."

"A woman could have done it," Knollis mumbled to himself.

"If it was Gloria—" exclaimed Murray.

"You'll do nothing of the kind," warned Knollis. "Why did your wife have such a sum of money in the house, Mr. Murray?"

"I don't know," Murray replied slowly. "I think it may have been because, like Gloria, she'd never been used to it, and it made her feel good to know she could go to the safe and get a handful of notes just when she wanted them."

"She banked with your branch of Lords?"

"Oh, yes, of course."

"If she drew the whole three hundred at once we can assume a possibility of obtaining the numbers?"

"Yes, I think so."

"Will you care to investigate the matter for us?"

"I certainly will," said Murray. "They don't want me down at the bank just at present, but I think they are going to have me! Where did the money go, Inspector?"

"I've a shrewd idea," said Knollis, "but I can't prove it. A lot depends on whether they went before or after her death. I think I can find out. Yes, I'm sure of it!"

"I'll be very interested," Murray said sarcastically.

"We'll go and do it now," nodded Knollis.

When they reached the Avenue Barnard complained: "Don't you ever eat, Knollis? My tummy's flapping on my backbone."

"Oh, well, we'll go to lunch," Knollis said reluctantly. "I never think about food when I've a job like this on hand."

"What was Fairfax playing at?" asked Barnard as he drove back to town. "It's certain he was responsible for the second call to Benson, cancelling the appointment."

"I see it like this at present," Knollis replied cautiously. "People like him usually go about a job in the most complicated manner. His intention was to acquaint Mrs. Murray with Gloria Dickinson's existence. He'd wangled Murray into promising to see Benson, and it was a shrewd move on his part, obviously thought up quickly when he ran into Murray. Mrs. Murray, like any other wife, wasn't going to accept the accusation readily. She *knew* where he was! He'd gone to see Benson. So Fairfax could tell her to ring Benson and prove it! If Benson was out, there could be no reply."

"But if Benson was in!" protested Barnard.

"Fairfax was waiting in the Avenue. Surely that tells you he was waiting for Murray to get clear. Then he could dodge in and pitch his story before Murray got to Benson—and Fairfax had to allow for Benson being at home, and Murray catching him there! So if Mrs. Murray rang Benson *before* her husband got there all that Benson could tell her was that he wasn't expecting him—and in either case Fairfax produced the same effect!"

"Clever!" muttered Barnard.

"Conjecture," Knollis shrugged, "and unsupported by fact as yet, but I do think it is a possibility. Fairfax is a clever fellow, and I'm beginning to wonder. Yes, I'm seriously beginning to wonder!"

CHAPTER X
THE THEORIES OF JENNINGS

TWENTY-SEVEN YEARS of police work had provided Knollis with a deep fund of experience on which to draw, and he had not accepted Paul Murray's story so easily and completely as Murray might have wished or expected. He was inclined to agree with Barnard that Murray was not responsible for his wife's death; beyond that point he suspected him of lies and evasions in the interests of some obscure personal reason.

"You see," he explained to Barnard at police headquarters that Sunday afternoon, "he tells of being a considerate and chivalrous husband, and that clashes with Mrs. Fairfax's story of the woman's body being bruised, and the explanation given to her by Mrs. Murray. Murray's covering-up seems to indicate a connection with the Dickinson girl—and if that seems so obvious as to be elementary I'll apologise for mentioning it!"

"I still don't get it," said Barnard.

Knollis clicked his tongue with impatience at Barnard's not-unexpected failure to see into the depths of his mind.

"Suppose Dickinson refuses to say he was with her?" Knollis suggested. "That leaves him without an alibi—and that he does really believe he's suspected is indicated by his manner. His refusal to admit that he was at the flat may still be part of his plan. We'll see as we progress!"

Barnard chewed on the stem of his pipe. "You know, Knollis, we can't do much at all until we've broken Palmer down, until we know exactly what he overheard as he crouched under the window, and we can't do that until we find the shoes and prove they belong to him, and that he was wearing them on Friday evening."

Knollis considered him through veiled eyes, and nodded slowly. "Fairfax has them, of course. He's a peculiar mixture of the clever and the naive. He tends to confuse the functions of strategy and tactics, and that's where he helps us even when attempting to hinder us. Scroggey calls on Fairfax to check the casts, and it would be obvious to Fairfax after what he'd already told us that Scroggey would then go on to see Palmer. Scroggey has established the fact that Palmer was fetched out by a telephone message. Where to? Where else but to Fairfax's house, so that he would be out when Scroggey called. And when Scroggey does contact him he's wearing shoes—boots—which apparently do not belong to him. We've two good lads on our hands! Both Murray and Fairfax may be innocent, but are trying to conceal some fact or shield some person."

"I wonder how much Fairfax knows about our work, about police procedure?" Barnard pondered. "Does he understand search warrants?"

"I should imagine so," Knollis answered. "Most people who read crime novels know something of them, and I regard Fairfax as above normal where intelligence is concerned. What have you in mind?"

"There are two things Fairfax could do with the shoes once he was in possession of them," Barnard went on reflectively.

Knollis raised his eyebrows in a silent question.

"Destroy them is one," said Barnard.

"Boots and shoes aren't easy to destroy," said Knollis. "You've seen that when investigating fires."

"And the other," said Barnard as if not interested in Knollis's comments, "is to hide them. Now policemen dig gardens, investigate drains, search houses thoroughly, and go to quite a lot of trouble when really looking for anything they badly want to find—don't we?"

"Fairfax wouldn't want them destroyed," said Knollis. "They would be extremely useful to him if suspicion attached itself to him and he had to clear himself. That may be why he wanted to get them away from Palmer."

"They won't be safe in the house!"

"Then have Fairfax watched!"

Barnard shook his head. "No, have his wife watched! Fairfax is too crafty to run into danger."

"Might be as well to have Palmer watched as well," suggested Knollis. "I don't know what stock of shoes he carries, but those he was wearing last evening are going to be too heavy and noticeable for a man in his position."

He broke off and scowled. "The shoes are important, Barnard, but I'm interested in the island affair, and have the feeling that whatever happened on it is the foundation of the whole case. In fact," he said, getting up and walking to the window to look down into the courtyard below, "I'm thinking of clearing up that end of it while you attend to the local details."

"I'm not happy about that," said Barnard. "Still, you're in charge of the case."

"It's this way," said Knollis over his shoulder; "both Murray and Palmer are suspect, with Fairfax trying to gum up the works with the object of covering one of them—Palmer most likely, since he owes Murray no affection. At the moment we're working on the assumption that Palmer was after the money, but if it's proved that the will in his favour wasn't signed, and if it's proved that he knew it wasn't signed, then even though all the evidential facts suggest his culpability we've no motive to attribute to him—unless we fall back on the revenge one. Hints have been thrown out to suggest that Murray murdered Palmer's brother. It seems an unreasonable accusation on the face of it, and if Palmer was murdered he was murdered by a trick. Murders are committed both by commission and omission, as we both know full well. It could be that Roy Palmer murdered Mrs.

Murray for the revenge motive, waiting all these years until the time was just ripe."

"How could Dennis Palmer have been murdered?" Barnard asked, and his tone intimated that he was throwing Knollis a direct challenge.

"Salina Bay," said Knollis. "The name intrigues me. I know no Italian, but as some of our own language derives from the Latin, as does the Italian of course . . ."

"There may be something in the accusation," said Barnard doubtfully. Brightening, he added: "Even if it's proved beyond all reasonable doubt that Dennis Palmer's death was an accident, it will reduce the possibilities in this case, and on that score alone it may be worthwhile going into. How do you intend to set about it?"

"I want photographs of Murray, Fairfax, and Dennis Palmer—Jennings should be able to supply those from the files of his paper; most people land in the local rag at some time or other. Then I want a signal sent to Royal Air Force Records, asking for the names and home addresses of the men who served on Fairfax's island crew with Murray and Palmer. Now Roy Palmer believes that Murray killed his brother—which is becoming a hackneyed phrase round here. He wasn't on the island, so where did he get the notion from? Fairfax? Fairfax believes in Murray's guilt, and therefore there was some peculiar feature that aroused Fairfax's suspicions right from the start of the affair. What is it? Where can we get a clue?"

"Dunno," said Barnard.

"I want a set of those Lampedusa photographs from the Imperial War Museum as quickly as they can supply, and a copy of the Admiralty chart—a firm in the Minories supplies them."

"Going direct—or through the Yard?"

"The Yard," said Knollis. "The Old Man's authority can speed up matters. We can get the teleprinter busy tonight, and there's no reason why we shouldn't have all we need by late tomorrow night, or early Tuesday morning. And then we'll go to see the member of the old crew who lives the nearest to Courtney."

Barnard stretched himself. "There's little else we can do today, is there?" he asked hopefully.

Knollis turned from the window with a smile. "Where can we find the editor chap, Jennings?"

"Brandon Club, most likely," sighed Barnard. "Do we want him?"

"He lives in the Avenue. He may have seen something without realising what he saw. We can't neglect—"

"Going to say any avenue?" asked Barnard with a grin.

Knollis nodded.

"It's an excuse for a swallow, anyway," said Barnard, "and my throat is like a brick kiln."

They spent ten minutes in the teleprinter room, and went by car to the Brandon Club. Jennings was leaning against the bar in his favourite position, talking to Holmes. He turned briskly towards them as they entered the bar, nodding his bird-like head. For once, his breast-pocket was empty of pens and pencils.

"The cops!" he greeted them. "What'll you have?" With drinks before them, Knollis and Barnard settled down to steer the conversation round to the Murray affair.

"Can't we sit down?" pleaded Barnard. "My feet ache—been on 'em since six this morning."

"One advantage of my job," smiled Jennings as he led the way to a table in an alcove. "On weeklies, at any rate, we don't have to work Sundays. My reporters do, but the editor has the day to himself. How's the case progressing? Anything for me yet?"

"Only questions," said Barnard. "Knollis is wondering."

Jennings looked across at Knollis, his head askew. "Wondering what, Inspector?"

"We know you live in the Avenue."

"Straight across the way from here," said Jennings.

"What time did you come in this club on Friday?"

Jennings pursed his lips. "Oh, getting on for nine. Holmes and I were on our first glasses, and waiting for the news, when Murray charged in."

"You came across from home?"

"No, I'd been scrounging round town, as is my wont. That's business, of course, and coming here always signifies the end of my day, and an hour's relaxation before having supper and going to bed."

"Hunting news?" asked Knollis.

Jennings nodded. "We've three posh pubs in town which are patronised by the elite and the self-styled and would-be elite, and it's surprising what you can pick up from them at times. I spend half an hour in each on Friday and Saturday evenings. Quite a few people are press-shy, you know, and won't send in stuff, so I amble round picking up odd items. It goes in a chatty column we call Around St. Margaret's—which is the parish church."

"Interesting," Knollis murmured in an unconvincing voice. "I was really wondering if you saw anyone hanging around the Avenue as you came here?"

"Can't remember seeing a soul," replied Jennings. "No-o, I'm certain there was no one about. Cold night, you know! Not even a courting couple to be seen."

"This question is off the record," said Knollis. "Did you see Murray in town?"

"No. Definitely no! I did not!"

"You know Mr. Palmer?"

"Roy Palmer? Yes."

"See him?"

"He was in the Crown and Woolpack when I called."

"Time?"

"Dead on seven o'clock."

"You saw him leave?"

Jennings hesitated before answering. "Ye-es, and it couldn't have been many minutes after I went in."

"He spoke to you?"

"We nodded across the room to each other."

"How did he look?"

"We-ell," Jennings said hesitantly, "as I say, I didn't see him close to, but he looked a trifle flushed to me, as if he'd put one or two down pretty quickly. That may be unfair of me."

"Tell me, Mr. Jennings," Knollis said keenly; "you knew that his brother died during the war?"

Jennings squinted over his tankard. Knollis smiled inwardly. The fellow knew something.

"I knew that," Jennings said shortly.

"Still off the record," said Knollis. "You people often hear things you can't use in your papers. Have you heard any ugly rumours regarding Palmer's death?"

Jennings lowered his tankard to the table and gave a short and unhumorous laugh. "Rumours! It's a wonder Roy Palmer hasn't found himself in court before now on charges of slander, defamation of character, and lord knows what! I've twice heard him, when well and truly lit up, saying that his brother's death was no more an accident than if somebody had deliberately shot him."

"Like that, eh?" murmured Knollis. "When in his cups, has he ever hinted at a certain person being responsible?"

Jennings plaited his hands and smiled blandly at Knollis. "That's where he used to settle down and mumble that those who knew something really knew something! Beyond that cryptic remark he wouldn't go!"

"Not even under the persuasion of your questioning, your expert questioning?" asked Knollis.

"You don't think—" began Jennings.

"I do," interrupted Knollis. "Hang it, man, it's your job to persuade people to talk, and I can't believe you'd trip over a titbit like that—even if you could not use it!"

"Oh, well," sighed Jennings.

"Since he talked when lit up," said Knollis, "we can assume that quite a few people in town know what he thinks about his brother's death, even if they have no clue to the identity of the accused person?"

"Quite a good few," Jennings agreed.

"And you pumped him," Knollis said bluntly.

"He asked for it," Jennings said in self-defence. "Always hinting at a perfect murder. You know about my hobby, so what do you expect me to do but dig into it? I was bound to be interested. You know far better than I do that the whole thing is a paradox. If a murder is discovered, and somebody—anybody—is suspected, then it isn't a perfect murder. On paper, there's never been such a thing committed."

"You believe that?" said Knollis.

Jennings rattled his finger-nails along the edge of the table before answering. He looked up with a quizzical, deprecatory expression on his bird-like features. "You know more about crime than I do, Inspector. Yours is first-hand experience. I've read a deuce of a lot of cases in the hunt for the ones that can be written up to provide popular appeal—which means a titillating mixture of the sensational and the salacious! Some of the cases have been near perfect, but there's always that one flaw that spoils 'em from an academic point of view—which you'll agree is the only one I, as a writer, can take."

"There are unsolved jobs on the files, you know," Knollis reminded him.

"Unsolved doesn't mean perfect," persisted Jennings. "The terms are not synonymous. In the unsolved cases there's always been a person suspected, whether proof was forthcoming or not."

"Not always," said Knollis.

"Well," said Jennings, "shall we say there are first-degree murders and second-degree murders—both to be designated perfect? If a culprit is suspected, and the job can't be proved against him, or if he isn't suspected, but some innocent person is and suffers for the crime, then we have a second-degree perfect murder."

"And your first-degree ones?" Knollis murmured politely.

"The really perfect murder mustn't even look like murder. It must assume the appearance of suicide, misadventure, or natural death."

"And you thought the Palmer death might prove to be a first-degree perfect murder, according to your classification?"

"There's the paradox," Jennings smiled faintly. "Once it was discovered, it wouldn't be one. Nevertheless, it did seem to me that Roy Palmer had a feeling about the affair—that and no more. It wasn't evidence, nor even logical suspicion, and I'm prepared to say it was founded on nothing more substantial than prejudice against Murray."

"So he told you it was Murray!" Knollis said with an air of quiet satisfaction.

Jennings shrugged. He was reluctant in manner, as if he was aware he'd admitted too much, and yet realised that he must ride the horse now he was mounted. "Ye-es," he said. "I don't think he's right, mind you. He has a theory, and has made the facts fit and justify it in his own mind, but it concerns only the predisposing causes, and doesn't deal with the way in which his brother was murdered."

"There's all the difference in the world between ratiocination and rationalisation," said Knollis. "I'd like your own version of the matter."

Jennings wasn't comfortable. "It's a bit too much like teaching one's grandmother to suck eggs," he apologised. "Palmer worked it out round the money. Dennis had money belonging to the family. He had a premonition that he wouldn't come back. He handed the money to the girl, and he didn't come back. Murray was with him. Murray married the girl, and got the money. Therefore Murray must have known about the money, must have wanted it, and must have murdered the man."

"He told you all that at once?" Knollis asked.

"He told me none of it actually," Jennings confessed. "I've merely fitted together his ramblings and tried to interpret them—probably wrongly. I'm not a detective. I was interested in the possibilities of the affair solely because my hobby is criminology. I knew where to find him most Friday evenings, and so made it my business to keep dropping across him as if by accident. He usually got lit up, or partly so, without any encouragement from me—which wasn't my way. I simply let him talk to a sympathetic listener."

"He never suggested the manner of the death?"

Jennings gave a wry grin. "Candidly, Inspector, I don't think he has a clue. It was just an idea which built up in his mind to obsession point. Me, I'm neutral, and have no ideas or opinions.

A writer's job is to watch, and write. He shouldn't judge nor condemn. He isn't capable of it, anyway."

"Who is?" murmured Knollis. "Wasn't it Dr. Johnson who said even the Almighty didn't propose to judge man until the Last Day?"

"Another point, while we're at it," said Jennings. "When the fellows started coming back from the war I went around looking for stories for a series—queer adventures, curious incidents, unknown acts of bravery, and so on, and went to see Peter Fairfax amongst others. Palmer's name cropped up, he being a Courtney man, and from what Fairfax told me I'm prepared to say, after twenty-five years of journalistic experience, that Dennis Palmer's death was as pure an accident as any I've reported."

"We know the details," Knollis warned him, fearing he might go on and on like the proverbial brook.

"Then you'll agree with me?"

"No English coroner could have reached any other conclusion," Knollis said ambiguously. "You say Palmer didn't stay more than a few minutes in the hotel on Friday? Did he usually stay in until closing time?"

"Can't say," Jennings replied. "I usually went in about seven, and was never later than eight leaving, having my other calls to make."

"The Crown and Woolpack, you said?"

Jennings nodded.

"Fairfax patronises that hotel, doesn't he?"

"I've seen him at various times. I wouldn't call him a regular patron."

"Ever seen him with Roy Palmer?"

"We've all three been together on a few occasions. Always seemed to me that Fairfax was sorry for Palmer, and while not exactly encouraging him he didn't put the wet blanket on him by telling him not to talk rot."

"Fairfax was there last Friday?"

"I didn't say that," said Jennings, shaking his head. "I didn't see him."

"You're still sure you saw no one hanging around the Avenue on Friday evening?"

"Certain of it, Inspector. What my wife saw is another thing, and you know all about that."

"You'll know the town pretty well," said Knollis.

"Know a girl by the name of Dickinson, living in Dale Road?"

Jennings laughed. "You mean Glorious? Murray's specimen?"

"So well known?" Knollis asked with raised brows.

"Not generally, perhaps, but certainly to we fellows. Little gold-digger if ever there was one."

"You mean she's—er—promiscuous?"

"Heavens, no!" Jennings protested. "She's just got Murray on a string. No, I think she plays fair in the sense of sticking to him, but she fleeces him like nobody's business!"

"Now how would you know all this, Mr. Jennings?" Knollis asked in the gentlest of voices.

"It's my business," Jennings retorted. "I'm district correspondent for a national daily as well as editor of the *Weekly News*, and I've something of a reputation as a news ferret. Apart from which," he added wryly, "we've a competitor in the next town who's trying to knock a wedge into our circulation by using a couple of columns of Courtney news, so I have to be on top of my job all the while. My directors are understanding fellows, but they won't hesitate to replace me if I can't keep the nose of the *News* ahead of the rival. With a girl like Glorious, well, you never know. She's rated as an adventuress as far as I'm concerned, and you never know when a story's going to break with one of her type, so I've kept tabs on her. She's also a good model when I've been writing up these cases."

"Your book-writing won't keep you?" Knollis asked.

Jennings grimaced. "Your friend Dr. Johnson said literature was a good walking-stick but a pretty poor crutch. He also said nobody but a blockhead ever wrote for anything but money, which is beside the point! No, the income from my books is a useful addition to my salary, but I could only starve if dependent on it."

"What do you know about the Dickinson girl?"

Jennings hunched his shoulders, and lowered them again. "Oh, a bit of an angel, and a bit of a bitch. I'm told she leads Murray a nice dance, knowing she's got him where she wants him."

"Does she hold him by threats, or by what goes as love?" asked Knollis.

"Iron hand—velvet glove," Jennings said laconically. "That's a horrible cliché, but it'll serve. She takes as fast and hard as she can, and yet the people in Dale Road say she's awfully good to the kiddies in the neighbourhood, to beggars, old people, and animals. I do happen to know that last year she gave a hundred pounds to the children's ward at the local hospital—and that anonymously."

"Probably tithing," suggested Knollis. "You know, giving a tenth of her income to good works."

"Conscience ointment," Jennings scoffed.

"Or a genuine interest in children," Barnard pointed out quietly. "You never know, she might have wanted one or more—and she can hardly have them in her present circumstances. It's far too easy to condemn, and you said yourself, Jennings, that a writer shouldn't do it!"

"I'm human," said Jennings, as if admitting the fact while not rejoicing in it.

Over a second drink Knollis nodded thoughtfully. "So that's how Palmer reached his conclusions! A hint here, an opinion there, an apparently insignificant fact from somewhere else. He puts two and two together and makes six. Dreadfully evasive and misleading."

"Even a heavy rainfall starts as a mist in the sky far above our heads," said Jennings.

"But the conditions have to be just right before the mist can turn to rain," said Knollis. "That's just the point, Mr. Jennings. The conditions were just right for the murder of Mrs. Murray— and the murderer knew they were holding steady for him."

He paused and looked round the intense faces.

"How did he know they were right? How did he know the circumstances were auspicious? That's the question!"

Chapter XI
THE CORNERING OF FAIRFAX

Nancy Fairfax left the house shortly after nine o'clock on Monday morning, a shopping-basket over her arm, and her heart and mind filled with misgivings and doubts. Peter was undoubtedly clever, and yet she had the feeling that he was playing a risky game in trying to fool the police and make it look as if Paul Murray and not Roy Palmer was responsible for Brenda's death. This morning's errand was Peter's solution of the problem of what to do with Roy's shoes, the shoes in which he had crouched under Paul's window on the fatal night. It wasn't safe to have them in the house, he didn't want Roy to have them back, but he did want it to look as if Paul had owned them, had listened under his own window, and had tried to destroy the evidence without losing a serviceable pair of shoes.

There was a telephone kiosk halfway up the street, and as she came up to it a man blundered out to ask her the time. She pushed back the sleeve of her green jacket, and showed him the watch Peter had bought for her last birthday. He thanked her, and backed into the kiosk again. As she had never seen him before she didn't know he was Detective-Officer Duggan, nor that as she turned the corner of the street he was reporting to his headquarters.

She joined the short queue for the bus, boarded it when it arrived, and dismounted when it drew in at South Parade, the lower side of the Market Square. She saw a bulky man standing with his back to a shop-window; saw him, but did not pay any particular attention to him. He appeared to be waiting for someone who had not come on the bus, and he turned away and followed her along the Parade and into Station Street.

She went into the Twenty-four Hour Repair Service branch shop, and took a brown-paper parcel from the shopping-basket, unrolling it on the counter and explaining that she wanted them soling and heeling. She gave the name of Dickinson—Miss G.

Dickinson, Dale Road—and was presented with a receipt and the information that the shoes would be ready in a fortnight.

The bulky man had meanwhile walked back to the corner of South Parade and Station Street and unlocked the police telephone box affixed to a lamp standard.

"Gregory reporting. She's gone into the Twenty-four Hour shop. I'm going back."

He collided with her as she came from the shop, raised his hat and apologised, and glanced at her empty basket, empty but for her handbag, before stepping aside. He waited outside the shop until Barnard and Knollis joined him, and then followed them into the shop as witness-if-needed. Knollis stood back and let Barnard do the talking.

"A young woman's just brought a pair of men's shoes in for repair," said Barnard.

The assistant, a cripple, looked hard at him. "She has, but that's her business!"

"My name's Barnard. In case you don't know me, I'm Inspector Barnard of the East Courtney Police, and I'm a detective. I want to look at those shoes, please."

The assistant's manner changed. He became anxious to help. "You mean the ones brought in by Miss Dickinson?"

Barnard's head went forward on his shoulders. "Eh?"

The assistant checked his counterfoil. "Miss G. Dickinson, Dale Road."

"Well I'll be hanged!" said Barnard. "Hey, Gregory, it was Mrs. F., wasn't it?"

"It was, sir."

"Very neat," commented Knollis.

He joined Barnard at the counter, and produced the casts from his pockets.

"Perfect, Barnard! This right one, for instance; nail knocked in slanting, bent over, and knocked down into the leather. Temporary repair made by an amateur, as I'm sure our friend will agree. All the wear on the outer edges of the soles. Yes, these are the shoes!"

Barnard took over again. "We'll have to borrow these, against a receipt, of course," he told the assistant. "We must ask you to keep the matter under your hat—you can tell your manager, but nobody else."

"If the lady calls again, sir?"

"She won't," Barnard assured him. "As much chance of her calling as there is of a teetotaller walking in the front door of a pub for a pint!"

Knollis was examining the shoes closely. "Cherokee Skins. Know anybody who sells this brand?"

"If they were bought in Courtney they'll be from Henson's on North Parade—top side of the Market. They're the sole agents for all the Cherokee stuff."

"You can describe the lady who brought them?"

"I think so, sir. She was wearing a green tweed costume with a heavy green coat over it, and a green hat with a feather in it. She was good-looking, and had light-brown hair."

"Fair enough," said Barnard. "You may be asked to identify her later."

The manager of Henson's was not prepared to say whether the shoes had or had not been bought at his branch, but he certainly sold the brand.

"Is your trade casual, or do you know most of your customers?" asked Knollis.

"Quite a few of them are regular customers, coming year after year."

"You know a Mr. Fairfax?"

The manager shook his head.

"Mr. Paul Murray?"

The manager looked up eagerly. "The one whose wife has been murdered?"

"That's the one!" Barnard said quickly.

"No, I don't know him, sir."

Knollis swore under his breath, while Gregory smothered a smile.

"Mr. Roy Palmer?" asked Knollis.

"Oh yes, he's been a customer for years—except for the war years when he was overseas."

"How long have you been managing this branch?" asked Barnard. "I seem to remember seeing you about for a good many years."

"Two years before the war, Inspector. I came here from South Wales."

"Palmer was a customer then?"

"Ye-es, I think I can say so. His name was on our mailing list, anyway."

"These shoes his size?"

The manager spread his hands. "I can't go so far as to say that. I haven't such a good memory. He's fairly tall, so they're somewhere near his size."

Knollis interposed. "Can you tell us when these shoes might have been bought?"

"It's the Cherokee Swiftfoot style. They came on the market eighteen months ago."

"Still selling?"

"Very well. They're a popular shoe."

"Does the amount of wear suggest how long ago they might have been bought?"

The manager smiled. "I'm no magician, Inspector. One man can wreck a pair in three months, and another keep a pair decent for three years. I can't help you."

"Have they been repaired since they were bought? Can you tell us that?"

The manager turned them over in his hands. "They haven't been repaired, sir."

Outside in the street Barnard said: "This is a spot of luck!"

"Spot of good work on your part," Knollis corrected him. "I'm wondering, Barnard, if Murray was telling the truth yesterday, and if Mrs. Murray was lying that day at the Fairfax tea-party— about the bruises, I mean."

"Where else could she have got 'em but from her husband?"

Knollis got into the car and sank back with his arms folded. "She and her husband seem to have done a lot of covering up.

Both tried to hide their troubles from the outside world. She had to tell Mrs. Fairfax something when the bruises were noticed, and it seems to me that if she deliberately accused her husband of the damage after so much covering up, then she might have been choosing the lesser of two evils and hiding something more shameful than the fact that her husband was in the habit of beating her. I think we should have another chat with Glorious!"

Barnard looked at him from the corners of his eyes, but Knollis's features were unreadable, so he sighed and said to Gregory, who was driving: "Dale Road, Greg!"

Gloria was suspicious of them from the first, and invited them in only because they practically forced their way into the flat. "You'll get me a bad name!" she protested.

"Decided whether Murray was here last Friday?" asked Knollis.

She shook her blonde head, closing her eyes to add emphasis as she replied: "I have not, Inspector!"

"You knew his wife?"

"I should have recognised her if I'd met her in the street, but I hadn't met her socially—naturally!"

Knollis paused a moment, rubbed his chin, and then asked: "See, when did you last meet?"

"We never did meet—not in the sense you mean!"

Knollis looked askance at her, his manner suggesting he knew more than he was prepared to admit. "Sure of that, Miss Dickinson? Sure she never came to see you?"

She studied her lacquered nails, and made no reply.

"About two months ago?" added Knollis.

"So you know," she said slowly, and still without looking up.

Knollis smiled at Barnard. His hunch had proved correct. "Tell us about it, Miss Dickinson."

"I was getting short of money, and sent a note to Paul at the bank. He forgot to destroy it, and she found it when pressing his suit."

"Go on," said Knollis.

She took a cigarette from a box on the table, and turned away from them as she lit it. "She came to see me, and got nasty.

I told her a few home-truths about me being able to make him happy when she couldn't. The conversation got a bit hot, and she hit me."

Barnard flashed a suspicious glance at Knollis. He turned to Gloria Dickinson. "Hit you!"

"Hit her," Knollis said in a complacent tone.

"Yes, she hit me," said Gloria. "That's where the battle began. I lammed into her, and she didn't look so good when she left."

"The grisly details, please," said Knollis. "Where did you hit her?"

"Where it hurt—on the—er—chest. Her clothes got a bit torn into the bargain."

"And this was—when?"

"The week before Christmas. I've a hot temper, and went straight out to the 'phone and rang Paul at the bank to tell him about it, to sort of prepare him for what would be waiting for him when he got home. He came round the following night to apologise for it all, and said he'd given her another to be going on with, and she wouldn't be seen in public for quite a few days."

Barnard gave a queer laugh, and Knollis looked down his thin nose.

Gloria blew a smoke ring to the ceiling, and wrinkled her nose. "I didn't like that. Two women settling their differences in an ancient style is one thing, but it's quite another when a man starts banging a woman about. If he's capable of hitting one— you see what I mean?"

"Made you careful?" suggested Knollis.

"Made me broke over Christmas," she said sarcastically. "I've got some money, but it's tied up. I daren't ask him for any more while he was in that mood. He's a fiery little devil when he gets going!"

"Still prepared to hang for him?"

She smiled wryly. "Well, not that, but I'll go a long way towards it."

"What size shoes does he wear?"

"Paul? Six and a half. I bought him a pair of slippers for Christmas—to wear here."

"Can I see them, please?" asked Knollis.

She fetched them, and Knollis and Barnard took one glance at them and saw there was no comparison with the shoes in which they were interested. Fairfax, like so many amateurs, had forgotten a vital fact, that Murray was short and Palmer was tall, and the odds were against their shoes being of even approximate size.

Knollis hustled Barnard down the stairs to the street.

"Where next, sir?" Gregory inquired.

"Round to see Mrs. Fairfax while her husband isn't at home to put answers into her mouth. He tends to monopolise the conversation."

"This sort of turns Fairfax into a liar," said Barnard.

"Elementary," Knollis said dryly. "He isn't the only liar in this town. Mrs. Murray knew about Glorious, and Murray knew she knew about her. Fairfax knew about her—and that makes his story of going to tell Mrs. Murray about Gloria nothing but a fancy story for our amusement. It's a queer case, Barnard, and I can't see how it's going to end—but it is going to end. I assure you of that!"

He was little nearer the solution when he had once more talked with Nancy Fairfax.

"In an earlier interview," he said, "you told us that Mrs. Murray had a black eye early in January. How early in January was it?"

Nancy Fairfax poised a finger on her lip. "It must have been New Year's Eve, now I come to think. We'd managed to persuade them to come and see the New Year in with us. Yes, it must have been, because they haven't been since."

"Was it a fresh black eye, or one in its later stages?"

"It had got the greeny appearance," she replied. "Brenda explained it had been such a mess she hadn't dared to be seen out all Christmas."

Knollis ran his tongue round his cheek. So Mrs. Murray had experienced three thrashings, and not two as he'd thought. The first was on the occasion of the anniversary of Dennis Palmer's death, the second when she went to see Gloria, and the third when she got home. Faulty logic had produced another evidential fact. That was queer!

He leaned forward in his chair. "I appreciate your loyalty to your friend, Mrs. Fairfax," he said, "but how long had Mrs. Murray been aware that her husband had a mistress?"

She looked up, startled. "Oh, that!"

"That!" echoed Knollis.

"Er—well, she'd been suspicious for some time," Nancy Fairfax said hesitantly. "Paul was going out quite a few nights each week, and Brenda said there was nothing to worry about when he came home a wee bit beerish, but it caused her to think when it was gin and scent she could smell."

"When did she confide in you to this extent?"

"The night of those awful bruises, and that makes it the twelfth of August, the anniversary of Dennis's death on the island."

"You told your husband?"

"I did. Yes. I was worried, and wondered if there was anything we could do."

"Did Mrs. Murray know the other woman's name?"

Nancy Fairfax shook her head. "I don't think so. I don't think she ever knew, or she'd have told me."

"Would she, indeed?" murmured Knollis.

"My husband knew her," Nancy Fairfax said surprisingly. "The men-folk in town had apparently gossiped pretty freely about the affair—and it's we women who are supposed to do that!"

"One more question, Mrs. Fairfax," said Knollis. "Do you think she accused her husband of his infidelity?"

"I can't say," she said. "She may have done. I've wondered since if that is really why he hit her, and she told me about it being over Dennis's death to cover him to some extent. She was in an awfully muddled state that night!"

"She would be," agreed Knollis.

They left, and through the glass-panelled front door saw Nancy Fairfax busy on the telephone as they drove away.

They went to find Fairfax at his works, and were taken through the shops until Fairfax was located in a wooden-walled office set in a corner, surrounded by machinery and noise.

"Oh, hullo!" Fairfax greeted them. "Come in and have a smoke. Or perhaps you chew gum? I wish you could chew some, actually. I use it for sticking bits together when I'm experimenting, and it's an infernal bind having to chew it all myself. Hardy, my assistant, is always willing to have a go, but it pulls his top set down, and that ain't always comfortable. Nearly swallowed them once, I remember—"

"We're wasting time," Knollis said crisply.

"No wish to keep you," said Fairfax.

"The story about the shoes is what might be called phoney," said Knollis.

"The—er—shoes? Shoes?" Fairfax murmured.

"The story you hoped would be accepted. The story you suggested, but never told. After Sergeant Scroggey called to check the casts against your footwear you 'phoned Palmer through his neighbour, and asked him to come to your house—"

Fairfax raised a finger. "Error there! He came of his own accord, and against my wishes!"

"You warned him that Scroggey was on the trail of the shoes which had left imprints under Murray's window. When he arrived, you lent him a pair of your own boots which were not shown to Scroggey, and then contrived to place the shoes in a safe place. Your wife took them to town this morning and parked them with a firm of shoe repairers in the name of Dickinson. We have them in the car if you care to see them."

Fairfax brushed his bristly black moustache with the back of his hand. "Not much good, am I? Not smart enough. Thought I had a good all-round brain, and it seems it's a specialised one, and a bit dim in other departments. Oh well! What do we do now, Inspector? It's your turn to call the tune."

"Get down to brass tacks," said Knollis, "and we'll start at the beginning! You believe that Murray killed Dennis Palmer?"

"Yes. As sure as I am of the sun coming up the right way in the morning. None of the old adage for me!"

Knollis raised an eyebrow. "Old adage?"

Fairfax grinned. "The one about a sunset at night being a shepherd's delight, and a sunset in the morning being a shepherd's warning."

Knollis stifled a smile. "What created the suspicion in your mind about Murray?"

Fairfax scratched his head.

"How did he do it?" asked Knollis.

"Divine inspiration in both cases," replied Fairfax. "It came to me, and it came to him. Intuition told me."

"I've a respect for it," said Knollis. "How did Murray work it?"

Fairfax eased himself on the table and sat with legs swinging and a bland expression on his dark features. "That, as Mr. Edgar Wallace's Bosambo used to say, is my mystery, Inspector, and will remain so. You can't condemn a fellow on intuitive notions, and you can't prove he did it, but I assure you that Palmer was murdered, and that by Paul Murray. His alibi was perfect. He was a good mile away at the time, and there were twelve or thirteen bods with him, while Palmer was alone at the foot of a deep—or high—cliff. I ask you!"

"There's another point we've established," said Knollis. "Mrs. Murray was aware of Gloria Dickinson's existence. You were aware of her knowledge, and therefore your story of going round to acquaint her is a blunt lie."

"Them's harsh words where I come from," chaffed Fairfax. Then he smiled, and nodded. "You're correct, of course. I cut the cherry tree, papa; I cannot tell a lie—"

"Why did you go to the house?" interrupted Knollis.

"On the other hand," added Fairfax, "I cannot tell you the truth. That is another of my mysteries. Sorry to be unco-operative and all that, but there we are."

"Since you went round," persisted Knollis, "and apparently wanted Murray out of the way while you were there, it would seem obvious that the matter concerned him."

"Or that it didn't," said Fairfax. "There is that angle to it as well, isn't there? As a matter of fact, it didn't concern him, which is why I didn't want him present. As a further matter of fact it didn't concern Brenda, either! That intrigue you?"

"You feel intensely about Mr. Dennis Palmer's death," said Knollis. "You didn't go round with any intention of harming Mrs. Murray?"

"Good job I didn't," returned Fairfax. "It would have been too late by the time I got a chance."

"Too late? But she was alive when you were listening at the window!"

"True, Inspector, but she was dead within a few minutes of Palmer leaving the house."

"How do you know that?" Knollis demanded quickly.

Fairfax grimaced. "You may as well have the story since this is confession day. When I heard Palmer about to leave I was on the path that runs along the right side of the house—the right as you face it. To the left is the gravel drive leading to the garage. If he left by the back door it seemed obvious he'd take the normal way to the front gate, and I didn't want him to run into me. He did come that way as it happened, and I heard him walk down the street, or avenue."

"Down it!"

"Towards the waste land. I wasn't sure what he was playing at, so I stayed doggo on the drive for quite a few minutes. There was the chance that he was so absorbed in his own thoughts that he'd made a mistake and turned right instead of left—as if leaving his own house for the bus to town. Matter of habit, see! That being the case, there was the risk of him realising his mistake and turning back. So far as I know he didn't come back, and so I assumed he was taking a short cut to avoid the risk of running into Murray. There's a rough track running at right angles to the bottom of the Avenue, so I suppose he took that way back to town.

"Anyway, I stuck around and was going to the front door when a shaft of light came over the garage. I knew Brenda was on the step. She started calling the cat. The cat, or some cat, started to howl as if the Inquisition was working on it, and I heard Brenda call again. She seemed to be going away from the house. I waited a little longer and went to investigate."

"Then you found her?" asked Knollis.

"I'm telling you the thing as it happened," said Fairfax, somewhat irritably. "I found her in the pool, and there was a long branch on the edge of it. I nearly tripped over it, so slung it out of the way. I switched off my torch, and was wondering what to do when I heard someone calling her. It must have been Murray, so I vaulted the fence and squatted down in the darkness to see what was what. Murray came along, also with a torch, and found her. He stood there gibbering for some moments, and then hared it back to the house as fast as he could. I decided it was no place for me to be found, since he'd probably gone to 'phone you fellows, so I made for town as fast as I could."

"Since when you've done your best, or worst, to make things difficult for Murray. Not so much by direct statement as by inference and insinuation!"

Fairfax scratched his black head. "Ye-es, being truthful. Dennis Palmer was a member of my crew!"

"Yet you made something of a friend of Murray!"

"The ends must justify the means," smiled Fairfax. "I still want to read about him being hanged for murdering Brenda—or Dennis. I don't care which."

Knollis got up and opened the door of the office. "I hope you sleep well o' nights, Mr. Fairfax!"

"I've every anticipation of doin' just that," said Fairfax. "Oh, I know it looks as if Murray was clear of the place of death again, but a fellow who's done one trick can do another. I think he did one—but don't know how he worked it."

CHAPTER XII
THE ADMISSIONS OF PALMER

BARNARD RANG MORGAN, the solicitor, later in the day, and had a chat about Brenda Murray's will.

"The new one was in the process of being drafted," he said to Knollis as he replaced the receiver. "It was not signed. The existing will leaves everything to Murray, which clears up that! It really does boil down to Murray now, and all we have to do is break his alibi. It stands to sense it was Murray," he added, seeing the look in Knollis's eyes. "Fairfax told us that Palmer went down the street when he left the house, and Mrs. Murray was dead a few minutes later. What happened, as I see it, was that Murray did her in, and then nipped up the field to the main road, and came down the Avenue to make the discovery. It's been done before!"

"And Palmer could have gone down the street or avenue," protested Knollis, "and up the field instead of taking the track back to town."

"What had he to gain?" Barnard protested in turn. "He had the cheque, and so was it likely that he'd want her dead before he'd cashed it?"

"With the three hundred in notes in his pocket," said Knollis, "the cheque makes a nice alibi—exactly on the lines you've just laid down."

"You believe he has them?"

"I believe it even if I can't prove it."

"Murray might have whipped the money himself," said Barnard. "He might have taken it before his wife's death, or even afterwards."

"Then why report it to us?" asked Knollis. "It was his own money once his wife was dead, and he could take it or leave it or do as he liked with it. And if he spends any of it, and the numbers of the notes are supplied, we'll trace it back to him. A cashier wouldn't make such an elementary mistake. It doesn't make sense, Barnard."

Barnard sniffed his agreement. "We're still stuck with Palmer and Murray," he said. "That's quite a point of yours about Palmer's possible return, but I don't think it feasible. He'd got what he wanted."

Knollis stubbed his cigarette. "I've sent for him. He should be here any minute, and we can smack him down on his original story."

Barnard shook his head, stubbornly refusing to accept Knollis's policy of an open mind and no theorising until a sufficiency of facts justified it. "Murray has the best motive," he said. "He knew that a new will was up and coming, and the only way to stop her signing it was by doing away with her before Monday."

Knollis made no answer, and there was silence in the office until Gregory appeared in the doorway to announce the arrival of Roy Palmer.

Knollis was a courteous man by nature, but there were times when he was deliberately rude with the object of upsetting a witness. He greeted Palmer without rising, and pushed a chair towards him with his foot, meanwhile keeping his eyes fixed on his long features.

Palmer looked nervously around the room, from Barnard and Knollis on either side of the table-desk to the officer sitting remotely in a corner with a pen and notebook.

"Take a seat," said Knollis.

Palmer perched himself precariously on the edge of a hardwood chair.

"We've something to tell you," said Knollis. "You went to the Murray house on Friday evening. You didn't want to be seen, so you went down Fairholme Avenue, across the waste land, and parked yourself at a point in Brandon Avenue from where you could watch the house and approach it cautiously. You crouched under the window of the dining-room, and eavesdropped on a conversation between Murray and his wife. When Murray left for town you went to the back door, gained admission to the house, and had an interview with Mrs. Murray, during which she gave you a cheque for three hundred pounds. You then left, going down the Avenue instead of up it to the bus route.

"Sergeant Scroggey called on Mr. Fairfax to check his shoes against casts taken of the prints found under the window. Fairfax telephoned you through a neighbour after Scroggey left, warning you that he was probably on his way to see you. You immediately went to see him. You left your shoes with him, and went away in a pair of his boots. Early this morning Mrs. Fairfax tried to put them in safe hiding by leaving them in town to be repaired. She left them in the name of Miss Dickinson, of Dale Road."

"I—" began Palmer, and then closed his mouth tightly.

"Yes?" said Knollis.

"Nothing!"

"We're not concerned with the ethics or otherwise of listening under windows," said Knollis, "but we do want to know exactly what you heard! Incidentally, the shoes do match the prints, and they are a pair of Cherokee Swiftfoot style, bought from Henson's on North Parade less than eighteen months ago. The sole of the right one had sprung, and some amateur had attempted a clumsy repair. All this to convince you that we are not bluffing, and know far more than we intend admitting. That correct, Inspector Barnard?"

"Quite correct," Barnard said in his best official tone. "And there are beautiful footprints in your garden, Mr. Palmer."

Palmer grunted. "You do go to work, don't you?"

"It's our job."

"Well," Palmer admitted reluctantly, stretching his long legs across the office floor, "I did listen under the window, not so much to hear what was being said as to know when Murray was likely to leave. They were having a whale of a row. Murray was on to her about Dennis, saying he was fed up with her one-time fiancé haunting his bedroom. Brenda got wild, and accused him of coarseness. She said she hated him, and Murray was seemingly a bit upset at that, saying he didn't hate her, and he wondered if things would have been any different if they'd had children, and then taunted her with not regarding him as good enough to be the father of her children—only Dennis could have filled that role, he said. Then they got on to money matters. She said he'd spent a thousand she gave him, and now she'd discovered that he'd mortgaged the house, borrowing five hundred on it. She told him that Morgan had drafted a new will, and every cent would come back to us—we Palmers."

He paused for a minute, and stared thoughtfully at the wood-block floor.

"Funny people," he went on. "A minute later they were discussing a new hedge as if the row hadn't taken place. He must have gone into the hall, for their voices were raised as if calling over a short distance to each other. She asked if he was coming back, and he said he was. She gave him a broad hint to stay out because she wanted to think. He said he'd come back to tell her what he'd done about the hedge, and then go up to the club."

"Ah!" exclaimed Knollis. "Please go on, Mr. Palmer. This is vastly interesting!"

"Oh, and she said she'd wipe off the mortgage, but the deeds must go into her safe deposit at the bank."

"Anything else?"

"Nothing vital," Palmer shrugged. "I think Murray must have asked something about the cat, because I heard her say she'd call him in later; he was busy courting somebody or other's cat. I heard the front door bang, and then heard him going up the Avenue. I went to the back door and she let me in. I've told you the rest."

"She was emphatic about him not staying in?" asked Knollis.

"Very emphatic," replied Palmer. "She wanted to think out what they were going to do. She definitely did not want him at home before the club closed."

"And the cat was then out?"

"Yes, I'm sure of that as well, Inspector."

"Did Mr. Fairfax know your mother was ill?"

"Yes, I told him some weeks ago."

"He knew she needed this operation, and urgently?"

"Yes."

"How long had he known that?"

"I saw him in town either last Tuesday or Wednesday, and he asked after her, so I told him the whole thing."

"Did you mention the financial difficulty?"

Palmer hesitated. "I suppose it came out in the course of conversation, naturally. I think I may have said I didn't know how the devil I was going to raise the money, and was a bit worried."

"You think you said that," said Knollis. "Did you, or didn't you?"

"Probably I did."

"Did he suggest any means of raising the money?"

"He did mention the possibility of Mrs. Murray helping me."

"Then you did mention the financial aspect," said Knollis. "Did he know you were going round to see her?"

"I don't think so. No, it was later, when I'd thought it out, that I decided to try her."

"Did you see Fairfax on Friday evening?"

"For a few minutes, in the Crown and Woolpack. We had a few words on this and that, and then I left."

"When you go in a pub," said Knollis, "do you usually have just one and come out, or do you have what might be called a session?"

"Well, an hour or so."

"What time did you leave the hotel?"

"Something after seven."

"What did you do then?"

"Walked slowly to Fairholme Avenue."

"Roughly a twenty-minute walk, I believe," said Knollis. "You arrived in Brandon Avenue shortly before seven-thirty. What did you do when you left the Murray house?"

"I suppose you've traced my movements and are trying to trap me," Palmer said bitterly.

"There's no suggestion of a trap," said Knollis. "It's essential that we should know the movements of everyone who was near the house at the vital time."

"I went back up Fairholme Avenue, and caught a bus back to town. I went to see Gloria Dickinson."

Knollis stiffened. Barnard's legs shot out under the desk, and he wriggled into a straighter position.

"Yes?" Knollis murmured in the most unconcerned voice he could muster.

"I'd made up my mind to work off a score on Murray, and I think it was neat."

"I'm sure it was," Knollis said softly.

Palmer's long face features twisted into a sly smile. "I went to queer his pitch—for good!"

"Do explain," said Knollis.

"I told her Brenda had made a new will, leaving everything to me, and that Murray was broke flat and finished. She seemed interested."

"You got the satisfaction you sought?"

"At the time, yes," Palmer said reluctantly.

"And now? Has the thing gone sour on you, Mr. Palmer?"

Palmer made a gesture of hopelessness. "No point in it now, is there? You'll be hanging him before long."

"Now that is an interesting point," said Knollis. "What makes you think so?"

Palmer glanced up. "Well, he did murder her, didn't he? It's obvious he did, to stop her signing the will in my favour. I mean, he was the only one who knew she was going out to call the cat in! I read about that, of course."

"You knew she was going out to call it in," Knollis said firmly.

Palmer jerked upright. "Me?" he asked, pointing a finger at his own chest.

"You heard her tell her husband she would call it in later!"

"Yes, but—"

"But what, Mr. Palmer?"

"I'd no reason to kill her! You can't say a thing like that!"

"Reasons aren't always obvious, Mr. Palmer," said Knollis. "Did you really want all your brother's money back? Did you, Mr. Palmer?"

Palmer studied the backs of his hands for a time. "Apart from what was needed for my mother, I wouldn't have touched it with a bargepole—but surely that clears me of—of what you're suggesting!"

"I'm thinking of the vengeance motive, Mr. Palmer," said Knollis. "The minds of murderers work in queer and unnatural ways. They don't follow normal and logical lines of reasoning. You've long been of the belief that Murray killed your brother, deliberately and wilfully, and that Mrs. Brenda Murray betrayed a trust in marrying Paul Murray and hanging on to the money instead of sharing it out. Now—hypothetically—your mind could have worked like this: you murder Mrs. Murray and so avenge the betrayal, and you murder her knowing that a new will in your favour is due to be signed in a few days, and so you believe suspicion will rest on her husband, he being in a financial mess. That way, you get rid of both of them, and as you obviously regard the money as tainted you don't care a hang what happens to it afterwards—once you have sufficient to cover the operation expenses."

Palmer grunted, and shuffled uncomfortably.

"You see," Knollis continued, "you could have gone down the field—down the Avenue, I should say, and up the field behind the house, lured the cat by some means or other—"

He broke off, to stare hard at the opposite wall with its calendar depicting a nude girl at a well.

"I was saying," he went on absently, "you could have lured the cat and then waited with it until she opened the door to coax it from its wooing of the neighbour's cat. . . ."

"You're making it look black for me!" Palmer protested.

"Merely pointing out that it doesn't do to accuse people so freely," said Knollis. "The circumstantial evidence against yourself is more convincing than that against Paul Murray. You see, when you'd got the cheque you'd got all you wanted!"

"Not much point in murdering her before the cheque was cashed, surely?" exclaimed Palmer.

"Ah, but there was the three hundred pounds in notes," smiled Knollis. "The cheque makes a lovely story for you—you've rubbed it in twice since you came into this office. Paul Murray happens to know there was three hundred pounds in the safe that day, and you were the only person to enter the house!"

"Murray could have taken it to give that impression!"

"Murray didn't know you'd been to the house, Mr. Palmer. That fact is established!"

"Unless he did what you've accused me of doing! If he was waiting in the field at the back of the house he'd have seen me leave—and who was better fitted to coax his own cat to him!"

"I know the answer to that one now," said Knollis with a smile.

Barnard raised an eyebrow, but said nothing, while the man in the corner steadily continued with his shorthand notes of the interview.

"Fairfax also thinks I did it," Palmer grumbled. "Seems I'm in a tight spot."

"And he was actually outside the house at the time," said Knollis, "not sitting in this office trying to make a picture from a thousand jumbled pieces of jigsaw puzzle. And he tells of the sound of heavy furniture being moved, and the wall-safe is behind the sideboard!"

"He can confirm my talk with Brenda, anyway," said Palmer, "and can tell you what time I left, and Gloria Dickinson can tell you what time I got there and left."

"And if she denies that you were there at all?"

"She can't!"

"You don't know her," said Knollis. "She's refused to say whether Murray was or was not at her flat that night—and he's closer to her than you are!"

Palmer got up, and stood there, tall and thin, sucking the end of his thumb. "How the deuce can I convince you?" he asked.

"Candidly, you can't," said Knollis. "If you're innocent you've nothing to fear, and I'm not trying to accuse you, but showing you the foolishness of trying to condemn Murray when you know less about his movements than we do about your own."

"I've really nothing to worry about, as you say," nodded Palmer, "but it isn't a comfortable feeling when you know the police might be suspecting you of murder! Anyway, Gloria Dickinson can prove I was there—and it was a good job I didn't get there ten minutes earlier!"

Knollis looked up, sharply. "Why? Was Murray there with her after all?"

"Oh no, but she'd been out. She was just entering the flat as I turned the corner into the road. There's a lamp outside the door, you know, so I saw her very clearly."

"She'd been out, eh?"

Palmer shrugged. "Looked as if she'd just dropped off the bus. It runs off the main street and down Dale Road to turn round.

It goes down Dale Road, turns right into Harbourd Road, then right again into Howe Street, and so back into the main street to start the run back to town. The stop is a few yards before her flat, and the bus was just changing up again as if it had dropped her."

"The time?"

"Nearly nine. Why?"

Knollis shrugged in a casual manner. "Oh, only checking your story. How did she receive you? Did she know you?"

"I introduced myself. She was a bit flustered, and seemed preoccupied, so I had quite a job at first making her pay attention."

"How did she take your news?"

"With one blonde eyebrow lifted thoughtfully, and both eyes looking me over as a possible prospect to replace Murray."

Knollis got up and clapped Palmer between the shoulder-blades. "You've nothing to worry about, Mr. Palmer. Just tell us the truth, and any details as they may occur to you, and everything will be all right. I'll have Gregory run you home now."

"Home be blowed!" said Palmer. "I'm going for a swallow after this grilling."

"Well, be careful how you spend that three hundred pounds you never had," said Knollis, "because we'll have the numbers in a few hours!"

He smiled as the door closed behind Palmer, and turned to Barnard. "What buses run past Gloria's flat, Barnard?"

"Twenty-threes."

"Interesting," Knollis said sarcastically. "That tells me a lot! But where do they run to?"

"Right to the western boundary of the town, and through the town centre."

"Past Brandon Avenue?"

"Oh yes!"

"Send us victorious, happy and Glorious!" said Knollis.

Chapter XIII
THE PECULIARITY OF CRETA BAY

JENNINGS ARRIVED at police headquarters a mere few minutes after Barnard and Knollis the next morning. Being well known in the building, he was not challenged as he passed the inquiries office, and walked quickly along the corridors to the C.I.D. office and pushed open the door without knocking. Knollis and Barnard were bending over the large table in the middle of the floor, studying what appeared to be a large map.

Barnard looked round, and his fresh-complexioned features showed his annoyance. "How did you get here?" he demanded.

"Walked," Jennings said lightly. "Any objections?"

"We like people to ask, and then to knock," Barnard replied. "It isn't the public library or the post office."

Jennings ignored the snub. He walked to Barnard's side, nodded affably to Knollis, and looked round the table. "An Admiralty chart, eh? And photographs. *Plans in the Mediterranean*, eh? Linosa and Lampedusa. So that's the line you're taking, is it?"

Knollis straightened up and placed his hands on his hips as he stared hard at Jennings. "And if one word gets out of this office, Mr. Jennings, somebody will be going down another line!"

Jennings shrugged this second snub away. "After nearly thirty years of journalism I think I know the ethics of the business, Inspector. I know I can't publish this stuff, and I wouldn't attempt it. What I'm really after is inside gen on procedure for when I eventually write the case up in one of my volumes—and that may be years ahead. So far as present needs are concerned I'm always ruled by you people, aren't I?"

"You'd better be," said Barnard shortly.

"That's all right, so long as we know where we stand," said Knollis. "Know anything about this island?"

"Only what I've heard from Palmer and Fairfax at various times. Seems to be a rocky place, with a deep ravine called the Aria Rosso running across from a point just outside the town to the north-west coast. It's terraced, and practically everything that grows on the island grows there—apart from odd fig-trees, and a handful of vineyards at the eastern end of the island. Before the war there was a sardine-canning factory in one of the bays on the east coast, but Fairfax said it went out of production when the war moved into that area."

Knollis perched himself on the corner of the table. "Has Fairfax ever mentioned any peculiarity of tides—such as there are in the Med.?"

Jennings shook his head. He looked round the table. As well as the plan and the photographs, there was a list of names with addresses attached. He smoothly jockeyed into a position from where he could read them.

"You—er—think there's something in Palmer's suspicions regarding his brother's death?" he asked in a casual tone.

"We can't say," Barnard said with complete frankness. "We are looking into the matter now."

"It does seem that Murray is the favourite," said Jennings thoughtfully.

"Does it?" asked Knollis. "What makes you think so?"

"I've interviewed 'em all for the *Argus*, and to me the thing is obvious. Oh, I know it's one thing suspecting a man, and another proving it, but if Murray doesn't hang for this job . . ."

"What did they tell you?" asked Knollis.

Jennings took his time in answering, bringing out his cigarette-case and offering it round. Not until three cigarettes were lit and the air charged with blue smoke did he say: "No more than they told you, of course. Fairfax and Palmer both think, or say they think, Murray killed her, and candidly he hasn't a leg to stand on. Point is, as I see it, that Mrs. Murray's murder was just the final stage in a plan. Murray murdered Dennis Palmer so he could get the girl and the money, then he married the girl and the money, and then he murdered her to get rid of her and have the money all to himself. Palmer told me that a new will was to be signed in his favour. I've checked with Morgan. Being a lawyer he naturally wouldn't admit anything to me, but on the other hand he wouldn't deny it, and by now I've learned how to evaluate a negative answer."

He sucked a tooth for a moment, and then said: "Thing I can't understand is why he didn't get himself rigged with a decent alibi. Glorious Dickinson could have provided one like nobody's business. No reason why she shouldn't, either! She stands to get plenty out of it."

"Concise summing-up of the case against Murray," said Knollis.

"Trouble is, she wouldn't give him a break," added Barnard. "Couldn't, because she was out on a trail of her own the same night."

Knollis kicked his ankle. Barnard, in a reproachful voice, asked: "What the—!"

Jennings smiled, his bird-like head askew as he glanced down at Barnard's leg. "You're not letting slip anything I don't know. I've seen her. She came as clean as a whistle—for a consideration. You see, gentlemen, she thinks the money is going to Palmer, so she's lost a certain amount of interest in Murray, and didn't mind giving me the facts in return for a little folding money to keep things going."

"Go on," said Knollis, dangerously calm. "Where did she go?"

"To see Mrs. Murray."

"What?"

Jennings nodded nonchalantly, enjoying his triumph. "Point is that people will often talk to the press when they won't to the police. Oh yes, she went to see Brenda Murray!"

Knollis retained his appearance of calm. "Let's have the rest," he suggested. Then he held up a hand.

He flicked over the switch of the inter-office telephone. "Sergeant Scroggey there? Hello, Sergeant. I want you to fetch Miss Dickinson in for questioning, and I'm not too faddy about how you get her. Keep her on ice till I want her."

He switched off and turned back to Jennings. "Now, what did she tell you?"

Jennings lit a new cigarette from the old stub, and blew the smoke down his nose. "She was suffering from an old complaint—shortage of money. She couldn't seem to be able to get any more out of Murray, so she went along to see his wife. Method was to tell her that she—Gloria—had no reputation to lose, that she was short of the necessary, and if Mrs. Murray couldn't supply she'd see to it that the story of Murray's association with her was well and truly spread round town, bringing humiliation to Mrs. M. Nice girl! I can't think why he didn't murder her out of the way. He might have made a go of it with his wife then. Still, when you're in a trap . . . !"

"Nice girl," echoed Barnard.

"She got there at some indeterminate time before nine," went on Jennings, thoroughly enjoying his present role. "She got no reply at the front door, so went round to the back. The door was open, and that outside light switched on. She started to investigate, and went indoors. She was actually in the house when Murray came home! She hid in the pantry when she heard his key in the lock. She saw him go looking for his wife, and then chase through the house and up the street, so she also went—across to my side of the Avenue, and to the first handy bus."

"How long have you known all this?" Knollis asked.

"Since very late last night. I covered 'em all between eight and half-past ten—Murray for the second time. Why else do you think I'm round this morning?"

"To see what else you could pick up," said Knollis.

Jennings fidgeted with the row of pencils sticking from his breast pocket. He nodded at the plan of the island. "Having given you that, what about giving me your line of this Dennis Palmer business? Fair do's!"

"We don't know anything," Knollis admitted. "All we know is what you yourself know. Palmer was bathing here, at Point Ailaimo. Two men were on duty in radio tenders here, just west of Cape Grecale. Murray was bathing with about a dozen other men in Cape—no, Creta Bay. It doesn't make sense, does it? All concerned believe Murray murdered him by a trick, and the discovery of that presumed trick is the problem of the moment."

"Doesn't look easy!" Jennings agreed as he stared at the plan.

"We can only surmise that he went for private swimming practice because he was sensitive of his incompetence. What I want to know is why he didn't go to the beaches round the town harbour—the only points on the island where there are long and sloping beaches. There must have been other men also learning to swim. Did Murray recommend Point Ailaimo? If so, why? And why did Palmer fall for it? He should have known that a bathing-place at the foot of a hundred-and-fifty-foot cliff was hardly a suitable spot for a man to learn to swim—especially when he had no companions! The thing doesn't make sense!"

Jennings pointed to the list of names and addresses. "What are those?"

"Members of the crew with which Palmer served—Fairfax's crew."

"I see," Jennings said slowly, nodding his perky head. "You think one or other of them may have the key to the problem?"

"We're hoping."

"Where does the nearest live?" asked Jennings.

"Anfield, wherever that is," replied Knollis.

"Sixteen miles north of Courtney."

"And you're not having the address," said Knollis. "If I find you've dug out the man and interviewed him before we do, there'll be a stink in this town!"

"I wouldn't do it," murmured Jennings in an unconvincing tone. He put on his hat, buttoned up his coat, and ambled to the door. "Interesting case, this! I'm indebted to you for allowing me to see it from the inside. Makes a deuce of a difference, you know!"

"So long as you don't blow anything before the time is ripe. . . ."

"I won't, Barnard!" Jennings assured him. He gave a jaunty salute, and left them.

"I suppose we can rely on him?" Knollis asked doubtfully.

"He's safe enough. Ardent amateur type—and a bit afraid of us, which is as it should be. He'll wait until he does his next book, and then go to town on the affair, quoting how Inspector Barnard said this to him and Inspector Knollis of the Yard said that to him. That'll be his special glory. Anyway, he dropped us a nice plum over Dickinson! We can't grumble if he trespasses a wee bit. The gents of the press do their best for us. Shall we have Glorious in now?"

He pressed a bell-push.

Gloria Dickinson was either reluctant or overawed, for she had to be pushed into the room by a none-too-gentle Scroggey, who then stood just inside the door to make certain she didn't attempt a sudden exit.

"Information has reached us to the effect that you visited the Murray house on Friday evening," said Knollis without any pre-amble. "Do you care to deny it?"

"Been bullying my friend, Mr. Jennings?" she snorted indignantly. "Well, I was there, and I've nothing to be afraid of, and I didn't do it!"

"Take a seat," said Knollis.

"I'll stand. I'm not staying!" she retorted.

"Why did you go there, Miss Dickinson?"

She patted her blonde waves, and sniffed. "A girl can't live on fresh air. I wanted money badly."

Knollis slid round the table and took a seat. He put his elbows on the table and balanced his chin on his clasped hands. "Now I wonder why you need so much money, considering how much you've had from Mr. Murray since he was married?"

She studied her varnished nails.

"You aren't a selfish person," said Knollis, "nor a greedy one, otherwise you wouldn't have donated a hundred pounds to the children's ward of the local hospital last year. I wonder why you did that? Are you very fond of children, Miss Dickinson? Or is there some other reason?"

She kept her eyes on her nails.

"I take it," continued Knollis, "that the donation was a mark of gratitude? Perhaps some child known to you was cured of some disease, or underwent some treatment, which saved its life. . . ."

He stretched his hand towards the telephone. Gloria Dickinson took a step forward, and then halted again.

"The secretary or the almoner could possibly clear up the matter for me," said Knollis. "I mean, it's so unusual for a person to use money in that way when it has been obtained . . ."

"Don't, Inspector! Oh, please don't!" Gloria exclaimed. "You know, don't you?"

She opened her handbag and took out a photograph, which she passed over the table to Knollis. Barnard moved round to stand looking over his shoulder with amazed eyes at a boy of about seven years of age, a boy with a peculiarly flat chin.

"This—this boy is yours!"

"Hers and Murray's," said Knollis.

Gloria Dickinson at last found the chair offered her some time before. "David Murray," she said. "He's known as David Murray Thorpe. Paul doesn't know of his existence. He was born after Paul went overseas—he was in the North Africa landings. I've never told him."

Barnard looked down at Knollis, and his hand clamped tightly on his shoulder.

"The money has gone to this lad," said Knollis. It was no question, but a fact of which he was sure, just as he had been sure of the boy's existence.

"He's with foster-parents in Westerby. They are very good to him, but they won't leave me alone. They're always after more money. They found out who his father was, and keep threatening to tell him," Gloria said in a sad voice.

Barnard grunted, and moved away from Knollis's side, to stand with his hands in his jacket pockets, staring at her with wide eyes. "You've been dunning Murray for cash with which to pay these people so that he'll never learn he has a son! That's some complication, by heck!"

"Where did the visit to Mrs. Murray come in?" Knollis asked gently.

She looked at her nails again and made no attempt to answer.

"How did you hope to get the money from Mrs. Murray?" asked Knollis. "I can guess now, but I'd prefer you to tell me."

"It's the first time I've had a photo of him in my handbag," she said. "I was taking it to show her on Friday night—if she wouldn't help me. She daren't have refused then. I was going to tell her the whole story. *She* wouldn't have wanted him to know he had a son, and being a married woman she wouldn't have wanted it known that her husband had—a son. I didn't want to be mean to either of them, but you must see that I had to have the money. I didn't care what I did or what happened so long as Paul didn't know!"

"You had the thing nicely tied up," said Knollis. "Now tell me, Miss Dickinson; who did you see in the garden on Friday night?"

She looked very surprised at the question, but no more so than Barnard, who seemed to be experiencing a series of shocks from the interview.

"I honestly don't know who it was," she said, "but when I was hiding behind the bushes there was someone else right at the end of the garden. I heard them moving about just after Paul came running back to the house."

"The remaining question is this, Miss Dickinson," said Knollis. "Can you now say whether Paul Murray was with you on Friday evening?"

"I did not see him to speak to, and he was not at the flat," she replied.

"How did you get out of the Avenue without being seen?" asked Knollis, anxious to have Jennings's evidence confirmed.

"I followed Paul to the Avenue, crossed the road, and stood in a gateway for a few minutes. There was a tree just inside it that threw a shadow. I saw Paul rush from the club with two men with him, and I knew something was badly wrong, so I went to the main road, and then caught the first bus home."

"You were followed into your flat by Mr. Roy Palmer."

She glanced cautiously at him. "Ye-es."

"What did he want?"

A puzzled look crossed her made-up face. "I don't know! He said he'd come to tell me that Brenda Murray had made a new will in his favour, and that Paul was finished. I don't know why he came!"

"What would you have done if the new will had been signed?" asked Knollis, and immediately knew he had made a mistake.

Her head came up. "Isn't it?" she asked in a tone of mingled surprise and elation.

"Er—no," said Knollis. He had gone too far to turn back.

She threw her coat back over her shoulders and took a deep breath. "Phew! Then Paul didn't kill her after all!"

"You thought he did?"

She sat looking at them for a time, her tongue wandering round her cheek. "That's wrong," she said, addressing nobody in particular. "He wouldn't have killed her if the new will had been signed, because—it—would—have—been—too—late!"

Knollis and Barnard watched her silently.

Her eyes suddenly bulged with horror. "I've—I've let him in for it. You've trapped me into saying that! I didn't intend saying it! It isn't true. Paul didn't kill her!"

"We haven't trapped you," Knollis said gently. "You merely spoke your own thoughts aloud. Oh, no, we haven't trapped you, or tried to do so, Miss Dickinson. All we wanted to know was where you were on Friday night. We know, because you've told us of your own free will. That is all there is to it."

She got up and moved closer to the table. She was obviously going to tell Knollis what she thought about him. And then she glanced down and saw the chart lying beneath her eyes. She started, bent over it for a second, and then looked straight at Knollis, incredulously.

"Lampedusa!"

"It's an island in the Mediterranean, Miss Dickinson."

"Lampedusa!" she whispered. "Then you know! *You know* now!"

She looked from Knollis to Barnard with frightened eyes. "He doesn't know that I know anything about it—he'd kill me if he even thought I knew. And now *you* know!"

Knollis and Barnard met her searching eyes with expressionless faces.

"That's why he never had more than a few beers. He was scared of talking. That's why he had a bedroom of his own at home—he was afraid of talking in his sleep!"

She ran round the table and grasped Knollis's arm. "How did he do it, Inspector? I've got to know! Don't you see I've just got to know!"

"We think it was a trick," said Knollis.

Gloria nodded. "That would be it! Paul's good at tricks. He tricked me and he tricked Brenda when he married her. He tricked her again when he—when he killed her. Nobody but Paul could have thought about that cat trick! Oh, God, what am I going to do now? I'll have nobody to help me—and there's David to keep!"

"Wait a minute, Miss Dickinson," said Knollis. "You didn't say it, but your story of what you saw in the garden surely suggests that Murray was shocked by what he'd found in the garden pool—which was obviously his wife's body. I wouldn't jump to conclusions."

"You mean . . . ?"

"People in this country are innocent until they are proved guilty," said Knollis.

He signalled to Sergeant Scroggey. "Take Miss Dickinson through and get her a cup of tea, Sergeant. Then see her home."

Knollis went alone to interview the ex-R.A.F. man at Anfield, although driven by a constable. He had some difficulty in contacting him, but eventually ran him to earth in a billiards saloon, where he was passing the morning before going on the afternoon shift at a local works.

"Your name is Roach, I believe," said Knollis. "I'm Inspector Knollis of New Scotland Yard. You were on Lampedusa Island during the war?"

Roach, a tall man with heavy features and a high-pitched voice, showed immediate interest.

"That's correct, sir."

"With two men by the names of Murray and Palmer?"

"I was, sir."

"Where can we talk privately? Care to come with me to the local police station?"

"My home's only two streets away, if that will do."

Knollis agreed, not particularly wanting the official atmosphere as a background to the interview. At Roach's house he unrolled the chart, and laid the photographs side by side on the table. "You were billeted here, I believe," he said, sticking his finger on Creta Bay.

Roach agreed with the position of the living-site.

"And working—where?"

Roach pointed out an approximate position to the west of the bombed lighthouse, and one that agreed with Fairfax's statements on the subject.

"Any idea what I'm investigating, Mr. Roach?" asked Knollis.

Roach threw a cigarette into his mouth and chewed the end reflectively. "Paul Murray's the one whose wife was murdered last week?"

"Correct," said Knollis.

Roach looked down his nose. "Murray was a little stinker even on the island, so heaven knows what he's grown like since then. We always reckoned he had something to do with Den Palmer's death—especially as he married his girl so quick. That anything to do with what you're after, sir?"

"Correct," said Knollis briskly. "We understand each other excellently, so let's get down to work. Let me be frank and say I'm working to a theory rather than to a set of facts. It's the wrong way round, but I want to prove or disprove my theory. How many men were in the crew?"

"Seven. One corporal, two leading-aircraftmen, and the other four were either A.C.1s or A.C.2s. There were two radio tenders, three men to each tender, doing eight-hour listening watches in turn, and the corp. in charge of both jobs."

"You were with Murray?"

"No, the other crew. Murray, Palmer, and a fellow called Howies were together on the Air-Sea Rescue job."

"You seven were more or less isolated at the light-house end of the island?"

"Oh, yes, sir," said Roach. "It was only a mile as the crow flies from the main camp, but there was no proper road, and the rock was darned rough, and you had to make detours which added nearly another mile, and it just wasn't worth making the trip unless you had to go sick."

"So that you were thrown together more than would normally have been the case?"

"Yes, sir. That's so."

"Plenty to do in your spare time, your off-duty hours?" Knollis next asked.

Roach shrugged, and grimaced. "Practically nothing! The mail came when some remote official on the mainland thought fit to send it—the Raff were always badly served with mail and comforts, and we'd nothing to read that we hadn't read ten times before."

"So you . . . ?"

"Talked, bathed, slept. We called it the Island of Sleep."

"With regard to the talking," said Knollis. "I've no experience of such conditions, but do men tend to get intimate in their conversations?"

"Well, yes. There's nothing else to do, and when you've talked out all the trivial matters you get down to deep things like philosophy, and sex, and your own lives and the way you're running them."

"You'd say more about your private affairs than you would normally?"

"Oh, yes," said Roach. "For one thing, if you drop anything private, you don't expect the other fellow to blow it around because he's probably told you something pretty similar."

Knollis nodded. "I must be careful. I don't want to push too many leading questions at you. That isn't fair even to my own theory. How much did you know about Dennis Palmer?"

Roach scratched his head. "I can't say. I remember nothing now, but I reckon we all talked ourselves out on the island before we got to the point where we didn't bother to talk to each other at all."

"Murray and Palmer were friendly?"

"Very thick, sir. I do remember that. They both came from Courtney, and that always makes a difference."

"The bathing?" Knollis asked as casually as he could. "Was it safe?"

"Rattling good bathing where we were," replied Roach. He bent over the map. "There was good bathing here in the town harbour, too. We used to dodge Palma Bay, and Guitgia was a bit far out when we had Salina to go at—and Salina was really good, with a long sloping beach. We only went there when we had to go back to the main camp for parades and had the rest of the day off. We stuck to Creta."

"The chart gives a depth of three and a half fathoms," said Knollis. "Surely that's fairly deep? Could you all swim?"

"No, but we used to bathe there. Palmer couldn't swim a stroke, and Murray could, but wasn't too hot. I'm fair, and the others were okay."

Knollis took a deep breath. "Look, Mr. Roach, I've been told that at this point where you bathed you dropped straight off a ledge into about twenty feet of water!"

"That's correct, sir."

"But you've said Palmer *couldn't* swim!"

Roach laughed. "He didn't have to swim in that cove, sir. He couldn't *sink*!"

"Why on earth not? It doesn't make sense!" said Knollis. He was almost trembling lest the solution he had reached by sheer thought should be swept out of his reach by some answer from this solid-minded ex-airman. "Why on earth not?" he repeated.

"It was like this, sir," said Roach. "The bathing-place was queer, like a tall barrel with a couple of staves knocked out, or a well standing up instead of going down. There was a shelf about—oh, ever so wide—ran round the landward half of it, and it had been cut out into pans about three feet square and six inches deep. You could fill one of them with seawater, go and bathe, and when you came back the water was evaporated, and you had nothing but salt. Heck, the saltiness of the water in that cove was so's you could stand straight up in the water, and just *couldn't* sink!"

"You couldn't sink," murmured Knollis.

"You couldn't dive in it, sir, let alone sink. If you did, you went in about a foot, and it was like jumping on a spring mattress. I've never seen it like that anywhere else, although it was fairly heavy in Salina Bay—"

"Salina gets its name—"

"From the salt," said Roach. "It's fairly salty all along that southern coast, but it reaches its peak in Creta Bay."

"Below Point Ailaimo?" Knollis asked with suppressed excitement. "Did you ever bathe there?"

"Not me!" exclaimed Roach. "I don't know whether such things are possible, me being no scholar, but some of the boys went once and told me it was nearly like fresh water—looked for all the world as if by some queer business all the salt was washed round to the east and south sides of the island, and piled up in that cove."

"Was Palmer worried about his inability to swim?"

"Both he and Murray were. We pulled their legs a bit too much. Murray said Palmer could do as he liked, but he'd dam' well learn to swim by hook or by crook. He'd find some quiet spot and practise until he could hold his own with the rest of us."

"Ah-h!" sighed Knollis. "Murray said that? Not Palmer?"

"Palmer was a bit quiet over his duff swimming. He was a big fellow, and I think he had the idea it made him look unmanly."

Knollis smiled at Roach. "You remember all this very well indeed. You're not helping your memory on, by any chance?"

Roach shook his head. "I was through North Africa and Italy and Greece, and there are months I can't remember a single thing about because they were all the same, but when you get dumped on what is nearly a desert island it's a different matter. There's something proper adventurous about it like the books we read when we were kids. No, every bit of those weeks on Lampo sticks out a mile."

"Fair enough," said Knollis. He traced a finger across the chart. "Murray was coming from the direction of Ailaimo, according to the evidence given at the enquiry—or inquiry. Palmer was walking in that direction, and they met. They had a short chat, and Murray returned to his billet, afterwards spending the afternoon in your Creta Bay barrel. Palmer went to Ailaimo, climbed down the cliff, and was drowned. . . ."

Roach grasped the edge of the table with both hands, and stared up into Knollis's expressionless lean features. "God! So *that's* how he did it, sir!"

"Who? Did what?" Knollis asked in a cold voice.

"Murray killed Palmer," said Roach in an apologetic voice, as if Knollis's iciness had frozen his ardour. "We knew something queer had happened, but none of us were capable of thinking it out as you've done, sir. When we got to the mainland we were shoved in a transit camp at Hamman Lif, in the Bay of Tunis. Four of us were posted away from there together, but Murray didn't want us, so he went to the orderly room and wangled a new posting. He went to a radio-location outfit that went from Bizerta to Cape Spartivento in Southern Italy. The old bush telegraph works, you know, sir, and from time to time we got news of the old crew-fellows, which is how we got to know about him marrying Palmer's girl. He didn't want to be with us. I can see why, now you've told me how it was done."

"I haven't told you anything of the kind," said Knollis. "What you have guessed must be kept to yourself. You see, Mr. Roach, it can never be proved. It was a perfect murder. It looked like an accident. It can never be proved!"

"And now he's done his wife in, sir!" said Roach.

Knollis shook his head. "I owe you something for the way you've helped me. No, Mr. Roach, Paul Murray did not murder his wife. He loved her. Someone else murdered her. There are three alternatives. It may have been someone who wanted Murray to hang for a murder he hadn't done because he hadn't hanged for one he had done. It may have been some person with an urge to commit a perfect murder. It may have been someone who wanted to wipe off an old score owed by Mrs. Murray. That is all I can tell you."

He suddenly gave an open and friendly smile, gathered the photographs together, rolled the map, said "Thanks!" in a charming voice, and was gone from the house, leaving Roach staring down at an invisible map of Lampedusa that still seemed to be spread across the table. He slowly glanced up at the clock. It was time to be getting ready for dinner if he was to go to work today. As he turned away from the table he murmured to himself: "My Gawd! There was only one really clever fellow on Lampo. All the rest were clots, officers, and men! Mr. Fairfax— my Gawd!"

CHAPTER XIV
THE EVIDENCE OF THE SEALYHAM

KNOLLIS, on his return from Anfield, picked up Barnard, and together they went to Fairfax's place of business. Knollis reported on his interview with Roach on the way.

"You know," said Barnard, "you'd a rough idea what happened there almost from the start, hadn't you?"

"It was bound to be something like it," said Knollis. "At first I jumped to the obvious explanation that tides and currents were to provide the solution, and then the name of Salina Bay gave me the new idea. Anyway, that's settled now, and we'll see what we can drill out of your friend Fairfax."

Fairfax was busy on some experiment, his bristly black hair standing on end, and a far-away expression on his dark features.

"We're winding up this case at last," explained Knollis in the naive manner he could affect at times. "Only one point remains to be cleared up so far as you are concerned—your purpose in visiting Mrs. Murray on Friday evening."

"It isn't relevant to the case," replied Fairfax, "and I'm busy!"

"There are a limited number of reasons why you should have gone," said Knollis. "You either went to inform her of her husband's association with Gloria Dickinson, to inform her of the mortgaging of the house, to kill her, or to put in a preliminary plea for Roy Palmer whom you guessed would call on her to beg money. She knew about Miss Dickinson, and you knew she knew. She knew about the mortgaging of the house. . . ."

Fairfax laid his pliers aside and leaned against his bench with folded arms. "I didn't go to kill her."

"So you did go on behalf of the Palmers."

"Well, if you insist, yes," admitted Fairfax.

Knollis nodded affably. "You're a damned nuisance, Fairfax, and have been all the way through this case. You may find yourself in trouble later. May I put it to you that you've let your code run riot? That you've an over-developed sense of justice? That ever since Dennis Palmer's death you've been on the look-out for opportunities to even the score on his behalf?"

Fairfax's mouth took on a wry twist. "Seem like that to you, Inspector Knollis? Makes it sound like a pose, the way you say it, but you're a pretty good psychologist. I hated Murray's guts from the moment I suspected he was responsible for Palmer's death, and then I got to detest Brenda for her betrayal of him."

"You cultivated the friendship of the Murrays with the sole purpose of finding an opportunity of avenging Dennis Palmer?"

"Yes, that's true enough," sighed Fairfax. "Even my wife didn't approve, but I'm still prepared to see Murray swing if I can work it. That honest enough for you?"

He looked at them with frank and bulging eyes. "You blokes evidently now believe he killed Palmer."

"We do," agreed Knollis, "and, like you, we realise we'll never be able to prove it in a court of law. I should tell you we've seen a member of your old crew, a man called Roach."

"A good bloke," nodded Fairfax. "I remember him quite well. He had ideas, too?"

"He thought the whole affair was fishy, but had no ideas, Mr. Fairfax. I had, as it happened, and by questioning him managed to learn what you refused to teach me—the peculiar nature of the cove in Creta Bay."

"That's it," said Fairfax. "I didn't want to say what I thought because the whole theory sounded so screwy. I was puzzled at the inquiry, and as we were leaving the island the next day I hadn't a chance to do any real investigating, so had to think the thing out, and I could only come to one conclusion—the one you've also reached. It flatters my ego that a trained fellow like yourself should agree with me! Isn't there some way we can get him?" he asked, cocking a questioning eye at Knollis and Barnard in turn.

"He'll never swing," said Knollis.

"But for his wife?"

"He didn't murder her, Mr. Fairfax," replied Knollis, "so put that idea out of your mind, and don't try to put it in ours! Mrs. Murray was not—repeat not—murdered by her husband!"

They left him, and went to find Roy Palmer at his place of business. Knollis went straight to his point.

"We're not interested in more than one point at present," he said, looking up into the tall man's face. "We must have a straight answer to a question. Did Mrs. Murray give you the missing three hundred pounds?"

Palmer ran his tongue over his lips. "Yes, I have the money. She gave it to me quite freely."

"Why?"

"She'd given me the cheque," Palmer said in a halting voice, "and somehow I was suspicious. She'd handed it over a bit too readily considering her previous attitude towards money. I wondered if she'd given me the cheque to get me out of the house, and intended stopping it. I challenged her on it, so she dragged the sideboard from the wall and got the notes from the safe. She said it represented every cent in the house other than her housekeeping money."

"And you hung on to the cheque!"

"Er—yes," Palmer said. "Perhaps it wasn't quite honest, but she was distraught and didn't seem to realise what was happening, so I decided to hang on to it and try to cash it before she could do anything about it. It was our money, anyway!" he said, in a sudden attempt to justify his action.

"That's a matter for your own conscience," said Knollis, "but now we know you have the money we don't have to waste time hunting it, and yet another item can be crossed off the list. By the way, when did you last eat kippers—or buy them?"

"Kippers?" murmured Palmer hazily.

"Kippers!" said Barnard.

"Kippers," said Knollis.

"Months ago," replied Palmer. "Why?"

"I'll ask the questions," said Knollis. "You stick to answering 'em, please!"

Barnard waited until they were outside, and then asked: "What the deuce is on your mind this time?"

"Kippers," Knollis replied absently. Then he looked round at Barnard as he was getting into the car. "Remember Mrs. Fairfax expressing surprise when her husband brought them home?"

"Yes, of course."

"There's the clue," said Knollis. "I don't think Fairfax did buy them. I think he found them in the field when he vaulted the fence behind Murray's house—y'know, when he heard Murray calling his wife."

"One of us is mad!" said Barnard, rubbing the back of his neck wonderingly.

"The cat! The cat!" Knollis snapped impatiently. "Don't you see what is before you, Barnard! The kippers were used to lure the cat! Whoever used them for that purpose left them there! Fairfax found them, probably slipped on them in the darkness, and being an intelligent man he realised their purpose there. He knew, as he knows now, that Murray didn't and couldn't have murdered his wife, but hating Murray as he did, he snatched at opportunity and removed what he regarded—so rightly!—as a vital clue which, if left, would help to clear Murray. Oh, and there's another thing, Barnard. The kipper trail was laid while Murray was still at home."

Barnard ran his handkerchief round his collar. "If it wasn't February I could sweat. Go on and explain, but it's going to be sheer madness to me!"

"When I first called on Murray," said Knollis, "we were standing in the garden when a white Sealyham terrier dashed round from the front of the house, sniffed excitedly at the ground round the back door, and followed some trail up the garden, and through the back fence into the field."

"Well?"

"Murray said it was a neighbour's dog, and it and his wife's cat played together as if both of the same animal family. But here's the point, Barnard! Having reached a certain spot in the field it nosed around, looked puzzled—as dogs can—and went away, not following any particular trail!"

"But that would be the spot where the cat came to its sticky end," protested Barnard. "The cat was carried away from there by Duggan, so it couldn't have left any further trail of scent for the dog to follow! Lord, don't make theories round non-existent facts!"

"It was also the spot where Fairfax found the kippers and picked them up. The dog was following an unusually *urgent* scent, with something at the end of it worth rushing for!"

Barnard shrugged. "It seems screwy to me, but if that's what you think, then let's go back and bone Fairfax about the kippers. That's the only way to prove or disprove your point."

"Yes, why not?" said Knollis. He gave an order to the driver.

"This means it was Palmer," said Barnard thoughtfully.

"And why?"

"Palmer was at the house when Fairfax arrived, and Palmer would be laying the trail when Mrs. Jennings saw Fairfax hanging about in the Avenue. That's all right, but how the heck do we prove it?"

"I've a few ideas wandering around in my head," said Knollis, and not another word would he say until they were once more shown into Fairfax's laboratory.

"Now what?" Fairfax asked testily. "I'm trying to do a tricky experiment in magnetics, and it's just one interruption after another today!"

"If you'll only come clean with the whole story we needn't bother you again," said Knollis. "As it is you're feeding it to us in serial form."

Fairfax sighed wearily. "Okay, Inspector. I think I must give up trying to fight you. You seem determined not to hang the little swine!"

"Those kippers," Knollis said directly. "Can you show us the exact spot where you found them?"

Fairfax looked down his nose. "The kippers, eh? So you're wise to that one as well, although heaven only knows how you dropped on it. Yes, I found them. They were lying beside the cat. I had my torch with me, and after Murray bolted back to the house I had a look round, having trodden on something soft and squashy which proved to be the cat. I couldn't dispose of the cat, but I did take the kippers. I mean, you look so darned silly carrying a dead cat over your arm, don't you?" he said with a winning smile.

"I hope you enjoyed eating them for breakfast," said Barnard, wrinkling his nose.

"I only ate one, and that was quite nice," grinned Fairfax. "The oiled paper was torn at one end, and pussy had tackled the head. Cats are clean eaters, and I don't eat fishes' heads, so what?"

He offered his cigarettes round, and tapped his own down on the bench. "At that time I didn't think Murray was responsible, but now I think he was putting on an act in case anybody was watching. You never know in a suburban avenue, what with courting couples and all that. He done her in all right."

"We'll listen to your theories," said Knollis, blowing a series of perfect smoke rings to the ceiling of the laboratory.

"I've been back there in daylight," said Fairfax, "and from the back fence you can see the back of the house all right, but you cannot see the side of the house down which the concrete path runs! Now Murray could have gone out, as we know he did, ostensibly to see Benson, and could have gone into the field from the main road, and got over the fence. He *knew* the cat was out, and that Brenda was going to call it in later. I've had a chat with Palmer, and he told me that. In my opinion Murray had the kippers, and *he* laid the trail, and *he* waited in the darkness, and *he* murdered Brenda. He must have been up there when I went from the house to the garden, he must have seen me, and he must have realised that being a curious type I'd wait to see what happened—hence the act he put on of discovering Bren! I bet he had a fit when he missed the kippers!"

"It makes a good story, Mr. Fairfax," Knollis said gravely; "a very convincing outline of what could have happened."

"One thing remains to be done," said Fairfax with an expansive gesture.

Knollis's manner indicated a deep respect for Fairfax's opinions. "That is, Mr. Fairfax?"

"Prove that he bought or otherwise acquired the kippers, and there you are!"

"There we are!" said Knollis. "I'm grateful for your advice, Mr. Fairfax. Very grateful indeed!"

As soon as the car pulled in at police headquarters Knollis walked quickly to the sergeants' room and looked round the door. "Scroggey! I want a blood-hound!"

Scroggey got out of his chair and stared. "A—what, sir!"

Barnard appeared at Knollis's side. "Inspector Knollis wants a bloodhound," he snapped. "Get him one as soon as possible, Scroggey!"

"Have it outside Murray's house at eleven in the morning, please," said Knollis.

"I'll go straight to Woolworth's," said Scroggey.

"What was that?" asked Barnard.

"I said I hoped the result would be well worth the trouble, sir," Scroggey replied gravely.

"I thought you did," nodded Barnard, and turned to follow Knollis back to the car.

"Trent Street," said Knollis. "I want to see Palmer again."

"Won't he still be at business, sir?" asked the driver.

"Well, then, drive to his office!"

Barnard looked askance at Knollis. This was the first time he had seen his companion warmed up, and free of his usual restricting iciness. He evidently had the thing tied up now, but to ask him for an explanation would be like asking him to undress in the street. He lay back in his seat and sighed.

For a full hour they went over and over Palmer's statements, checking and re-checking them. From there they went to Dale Road to see Gloria Dickinson. There was no answer to Barnard's knocking, so Knollis pushed past him and tried the door. It was unlocked, so he put his head into the room and called her name. There was still no reply.

"Wonder if everything's all right?" he said. "Better have a look round, just in case."

They entered the flat, closing the door behind them. Knollis knocked at the bedroom and bathroom doors, and peered into each room in turn. Then Barnard called to him in a low voice. "Knollis! Look here!"

Knollis joined him in the middle of the sitting-room. He was staring down at a small table on which lay a thick wad of writing-paper and a business card.

"Jennings's professional card," said Knollis. "So he's on the trail again!"

"See what she's writing!" said Barnard. "Jennings is apparently getting the story of her association with Murray for the *Argus*! And look at the nerve of it—sheer brassiness! See how it starts! *Now that Paul Murray has paid the penalty for the murder of his beautiful young wife the full story of his life with her can be told* . . .

"That's pure Jennings," commented Knollis. He flicked the sheets. "About two thousand words up to now, and she's even hinting that he murdered Palmer as well. This is going to be a hot story!"

"What do we do?"

"Let her finish it," said Knollis, and then smiled. "We may be able to 'borrow' it when it is finished. It should be vastly interesting. We'd better get out and pretend we haven't been here."

They went down the stairs to the street, and then Barnard tugged Knollis's arm. "That her in the call-box?"

"Looks a deal like her," said Knollis. "In which case she's seen us. Better wait and say we couldn't make her hear. It'll look bad if we drive away."

The door of the kiosk slammed, and Gloria Dickinson hurried towards them, a more sober and less glamorous creature than she had been three days before.

"I wondered if it was you when I saw the car pull up, but I'd just got my friend, and couldn't come straight away. I was going to the cinema with her tonight, but I've a fearful headache, so won't be going," she said quickly. "Is there anything you want?"

"Not if you've a headache," smiled Knollis. "We wanted to check your statements, but tomorrow will do."

At eleven the next morning they met Scroggey and his bloodhound at Avalon. He was standing on the edge of the pavement, swinging a pair of kippers.

"Three days and a half," said Barnard. "It's a long shot."

"I know," replied Knollis, "but we daren't leave the experiment untried. There's been no rain, and the scent, if it existed at all, should be there yet. You say the dog was following the cat's trail. I say it was chasing the kippers. If the hound acts as the Sealyham did, then I'm right and you're wrong, and vice versa—and that won't worry me one bit, because I'll at least have disproved what might otherwise mislead us!"

The scent was given to the bloodhound at the front gate, with Murray looking on curiously from his door-step. The hound nosed round the pavement and the path leading to the house, but didn't appear to find any scent of interest. Scroggey then led it round to the back door, where it showed signs of life, dragging him up the garden to the pool, round its eastern end, and to the fence, where it tried to force its way between the chestnut palings.

"Do we lift him over or take down the fence?" asked Scroggey.

"The easier way would be to loosen two of the palings and let him go through under his own steam," suggested Knollis, and beckoned Barnard to help him.

The hound squeezed through the gap, and made for a point a few yards away. Here it circled, and then stood with a puzzled expression on its miserable face.

"Proper depressed it looks!" said Scroggey.

"Now give it this," said Knollis. "It's a piece of rag I whipped from Fairfax's laboratory yesterday, one on which he was wiping his hands when we went in."

The dog took the new scent, quested for a time, and made up the field to the main road. Here it gave up, the trail obviously being lost in the thousands of others which must have existed.

"You win!" said Barnard. "The trail was laid from the back door of the house!"

"We now wind up the case," said Knollis with a happy smile.

"How?" Barnard asked bluntly and hopefully.

Knollis demurred. "I'd rather not tell you until I've proved my theory. You might laugh at me again."

Barnard shrugged his shoulders. The man was impossible! He watched Scroggey lead the hound back down Brandon Avenue to the van, and then coughed to attract Knollis's attention from the reverie in which he was indulging.

"There's one thing I'm unhappy about, Knollis," he said in a loud voice.

"Hm? Unhappy about? Such as?"

"The coincidence of all those people being at the house on Friday evening."

"Their presence was almost inevitable," said Knollis, brushing the difficulty away with a flat hand. "Gloria was there because she knew Murray wasn't going to visit her, and because she knew he didn't stay home o' nights with his wife. Fairfax arranged for Murray to be out so that he could make his visit. Palmer was taking a chance of Murray being out—and waited until he went out. The thing is clear enough to me."

"If she hadn't been murdered it would have been some night for her!" commented Barnard. "Three visitors going round for money! One to persuade it out of her, one demanding it from her, and the other actually blackmailing her!"

CHAPTER XV
THE EVIDENCE OF REFLECTION

KNOLLIS WAS IN a deeply thoughtful mood as he left Brandon Avenue. He dropped off at his hotel, nodded vaguely to the mystified Barnard, and went to his room. He worked with his notebook until lunch, and afterwards settled down to sift the evidence, comparing statements, counter-statements, and amended statements in the endeavour to find the vital fact, or a linking of facts that would lead him to Brenda Murray's killer.

The murder was premeditated. There was no doubt about that. It was committed by someone who knew of the domestic strife between the Murrays. It was committed by someone who knew the domestic arrangements of the house, by someone who knew of Mrs. Murray's nightly practice of calling in her cat—whether she was successful or not, by someone who knew she was generally alone each evening after half-past seven or eight o'clock. It was committed by someone who could be seen in the Avenue without any undue interest being taken in his presence. The forked branch had been prepared beforehand, and left in a convenient spot. The kippers—the bizarre and vulgar factors in the case—were no spur-of-the-moment notion; they too had been included in the detailed plan. The trail had not been laid before that evening. It could not have been laid before that evening. And it seemed reasonable to assume that it had not been laid before Paul Murray went out. . . .

Knollis raised his head from his notes, to stare at a garish oleograph on the wall, of a nude Psyche bathing at a well without soap, towel, or clothes to put on when her toilet was completed. Cats are wanderers! You can't simply lay a kipper trail from a back door to a given point in a field and guarantee that a cat will obligingly appear on time, follow it, and give itself into your hands as per Bradshaw! Therefore the kipper trail had been waiting outside the door when the cat was first let out, so that the cat was caught, and *then* confined, until it was needed for its part in the drama.

That factor changed the whole face of the case.

At what time was the cat let out? He consulted his notes and then turned to the Common Notes in the back of his diary. The sun set at nine minutes past five on the twelfth of February. Murray got home from business at half-past five. Jennings had once seen Murray turf the cat across the front lawn. . . .

The picture was developing now, emerging from the elusive mists of sub-consciousness. The cat was probably let out when Murray came home, and called in when he went out each evening. If Murray could be persuaded to confess his dislike of the animal . . . !

As his gaze wandered round the bare hotel room it came to rest on his dispatch case, thrown idly on the bed. His eyebrows rose for a second, and then the lids closed down until his eyes were no more than narrow slits concealing his inner thoughts.

"So that was it!" he said aloud. "Good lord!"

He reached for his hat and coat, wrapped a scarf warmly round his neck, pulled on his gloves, took the dispatch case from the bed, and went down to the lobby.

"Where do I get a bus for Brandon Avenue?" he asked the porter.

"Across the way, sir. Twenty yards up."

Knollis almost ran from the hotel, and when he got to Murray's door his heart was beating excitedly, although his face, as usual, was set and expressionless.

Murray was a pathetic sight as he opened the door. His pock-marked and flat little face was drawn. There were new wrinkles in his forehead. His head seemed to have settled on his shoulders like that of a tortoise withdrawing from its enemies. His hands were fidgety, and his mouth twitched as he nodded to Knollis and asked him indoors.

"This is between you and me," said Knollis as he followed Murray into the dining-room. "We're going to clear the decks. I want the answers to two questions."

"Go ahead," said Murray. "You're the straightest man I've met for a long time, and I trust you."

"Are you aware that nearly everybody in this town believes you killed your wife?"

Murray turned away to stare through the window at his garden. "My God, aren't I!" he exclaimed. "The reporters believe it, too. They haven't left me alone for more than an hour since my wife died. I can't even get out for a drink now!"

"You'll soon be able to go out for as many as you want," said Knollis. "My second question is: do you genuinely want your wife's murderer to be caught and hanged, or are you prepared to let the whole thing go?"

"I'm not vindictive," said Murray over his shoulder, "but finding her murderer is the only way I'll be cleared, and I have that to consider. Verdicts of Non Proven are unsatisfactory."

"Now let's get down to the questions you aren't going to like," said Knollis. "The answers to them, if you'll come clean, can solve the mystery. Did you love or hate your wife's cat?"

Murray turned and propped himself against the window. His flat chin tightened. For a moment his eyes sought to avoid Knollis's, and then he nodded to himself as if he had reached a decision. "I hated the blasted thing!"

"Did you ever knock it about when your wife wasn't present?"

"Not actually knock it about in the sense you mean," said Murray. "I was never deliberately cruel to it, but I did occasionally lob it a fourpenny one just to be going on with."

"Your wife either knew, or suspected, your dislike of her cat?"

"She knew—definitely," Murray replied grimly.

"Had she a regular time for letting it out?"

"Mostly just before we sat down to tea."

"Why did you hate it, Mr. Murray?"

"Why?" asked Murray. He searched the ceiling for the answer, and seemed to be hesitating, reluctant to expose his mind and heart.

"If you want to be able to walk through the town with your head up—" Knollis said cryptically.

"She thought more about the damned animal than she did about me," Murray said suddenly. "I suppose you can say I was jealous of it!"

Knollis sighed. "Tell me, Mr. Murray; did she call in the cat before you went out—as a general rule, I mean?"

Murray shook his head. "That was ruled by hygienic reasons, Inspector. If it was a bad night Fluffy was put in the coal-house. If the weather was decent she'd allow it up to two hours, and would generally go to the back door to call it in as I was going out by the front door."

"Now carry your mind back to last Friday," said Knollis. "Can you remember the time she let out the cat?"

Murray nodded. "Almost as soon as I got in. Tea was ready and waiting. I was in a foul temper over my wife's perpetual mourning of Dennis Palmer, and she saw it, and if the truth is told she sent the cat straight out, more for its own safety than for its nightly run. Is that frank enough for you?" he asked with a cynical smile.

"We're doing very nicely," Knollis said with a friendly nod. "I'm getting what I want."

"You've a line on the man at last?"

"As this is a private chat between you and I, the answer is 'yes,'" replied Knollis. "I'm going to take you into my confidence and tell you what happened, because I think you may be able to help me still further when you know the truth. It was dark by a quarter-past five on Friday. You got home at half-past. The cat was let out as soon as you got home. Now somebody came to the house with a pair of kippers, and laid a trail of scent from your back door to the field beyond your fence. The cat followed the trail when it was let out. Somebody out there in the darkness waited for it, caught it, and took it away. After you'd gone, Palmer called, and after he'd gone your wife went to call in the cat. That person in the field was now back from wherever he'd been, and tortured the cat so that its cries brought your wife running to its aid. You know the rest. Now what I want you to do when I've gone is to sit down and think back to Friday evening, trying to remember who you saw before getting off your bus and coming in home for tea. When you've got it, come straight to the office and tell me—and don't say a word to anyone else. Not to anyone!"

Murray blinked.

"I know who was responsible," said Knollis, "but I don't want to prime your imagination. You've to find out for yourself, and whatever you remember will constitute my proof against the culprit. Oh, and can I borrow the gloves you were wearing on Friday, please?"

Murray gave him a queer glance, but went to the entrance hall and returned with a pair of brown kid gloves which Knollis put in his pocket. "I can prove your innocence with these. If you didn't handle the kippers . . . ! See the idea?"

Murray stood nervously, his mouth twitching. "I'm not afraid, Inspector, but I'm weary, completely tired out. I haven't slept since Brenda went."

Knollis took his arm and led him to the framed photographic map of Lampedusa. "I'm relying on you to help me, if only to wipe this off," he said. "You see, Mr. Murray, this is Point Ailaimo, where Dennis Palmer was drowned. This is Creta Bay, where you were bathing at the time, in a cove described as being like a barrel with two or three staves knocked out. The water has an exceptionally high salt-content and it is virtually impossible for a bather to sink in it, while at Point Ailaimo . . . !" He felt Murray sinking on his arm, and let him gently into a chair. "The least you can do is to help me, Mr. Murray."

Murray put his elbows on his knees, and covered his face with his hands. Tears began to slip between his fingers. Knollis patted him on the shoulder. "We always pay, you know, Murray! It's one of the laws of the universe, the law of compensation. You've paid somewhat heavily, I believe. You've never known a moment's happiness since you left the island, have you? I know the truth about what happened to Dennis Palmer. So does Peter Fairfax. Neither of us can prove it, so we're going to forget it. You're young, and you've a chance to make a fresh start when this case is cleared up."

"The money's going back to the Palmers," said Murray from behind his hands. "I'll sell up, and get out and see what I can do with what's left of my life."

Knollis let himself out of the house and went back to town, to the mortuary. He asked the attendant to fetch the cat's body from the refrigerator. He examined it thoroughly, and then asked the attendant: "You prepare bodies for autopsies?"

"Why, yes, sir."

"What is the name and telephone number of the police surgeon?"

"Dr. Ponsonby, sir. Courtney four-nine-five."

"While I ring him, I want you to start shaving the animal. Leave the neck ruff and all four legs, please."

The doctor agreed to come to the mortuary at Knollis's request, and then Knollis rang Murray.

"Knollis here. I want the feeding-times—yes, when your wife fed the cat. Milk and bread at breakfast, scraps at lunch, milk only at night? That correct? Thanks."

He sat watching the attendant until the doctor arrived, a short and dark man with thick-lensed glasses.

"I'd like you to open up the cat, if you will," said Knollis.

The doctor grimaced. "Oh well, it shouldn't be too high if it's been in the fridge."

"First," said Knollis, "I'd like you to look at its neck and legs and tell me if you think it was ever tied up. You see, I think it was confined for an hour or more, and a tied cat would struggle and probably damage itself."

The doctor eventually pointed to a graze on the cat's neck. "What about that?"

"Could it have been caused by the strangulation?"

"I wouldn't say it was caused by anything else," said the doctor. "It was handled very harshly, you know!"

"I'll cross that off then," said Knollis. "I've no use for guess-work, even my own. Now open him up, please."

"What are we looking for, Inspector?"

"Stomach contents. It was killed about half-past eight. It had scraps for lunch, and nothing but milk afterwards."

"It's a lie," the doctor said shortly afterwards. "Digestion had barely started, and there's a good meal of white fish in its tummy."

Knollis went back to the telephone, ringing Murray once more.

"Knollis here," he said. "I know the word lunch is often misused, but you do lunch in town when at business, don't you? Does that really constitute your dinner, the heaviest meal of your day? Or do you have dinner in the evening? Your meal in town is really your dinner! So your wife lunched at home, and alone? Mostly! She did on Friday? Can you tell me what she had? Vienna steaks. One more question, please. Was there any fish in the house? No, nothing to do with kippers. I'm refer-ring to white fish. Your only fish meal last week was on Tuesday, when you had plaice for tea. The bits—how long would it take Fluffy to clear them? He'd have them for dinner next day, and they'd only last one meal. Thanks."

He turned away from the telephone with a contented expres-sion on his lean features. "Hear that, Dr. Ponsonby? Its last fish meal was Wednesday noon."

"It last ate fish on Friday evening," said the doctor. "It's ele-mentary!"

"It's nice to hear that," said Knollis. "One other point, please. You performed the autopsy on Mrs. Murray. Can you remember anything about the contents of her stomach?"

"No fish," the doctor said shortly.

"Good!" said Knollis.

Now satisfied on quite a number of points, Knollis returned to the hotel and added them to his written score. The experi-ment with the bloodhound proved that Fairfax had taken away the kippers—if any proof was needed—and Murray's further ev-idence, plus the examination of the cat's stomach, had taken the case several steps nearer the eventual solution.

Two items needed consideration now. Where had the cat been confined, and where had the forked branch come from? Suppose, and only suppose, that either Fairfax or Palmer were responsible for the murder. Both lived at the opposite side of town, and it would be impracticable to take the cat home and then bring it back again. Against that was the improbability of anyone parking in the field behind the house for what might have been a three-hour wait; it was February, and the temperature had hovered round the forty mark for well over a fortnight. . . .

He glanced at his notes. The cat had been fed, and well fed, judging by the contents of its stomach. Knollis searched his mind for knowledge of cat behaviour. His own two sons had kept pet cats at various times—along with pigeons, toads, newts, lizards, and the other weird creatures which had attractions for school-boys. There were times, such as when the family was going out, when the cats had perforce been confined in the wash-house.

How did a confined cat behave? It generally mewed piteously to be let out, and that for hours. A confined cat is an uneasy animal. So if Fluffy had been confined by a stranger, and in a strange place, it would almost certainly have attracted the attention of neighbours, so that idea was out! Where then?

Knollis narrowed his eyes, and visualised the Brandon Avenue area. There were twenty houses in the Avenue, and below them an expanse of waste land on which were piles of bricks, heaps of sand, *and* a derelict workmen's hut! And Roy Palmer had gone *down* the Avenue when leaving Avalon. He had admitted that himself, and had been seen by Peter Fairfax.

And that belied Knollis's confident assertion to Murray that he knew the person responsible for his wife's death!

He clicked his tongue. All this work for nothing! All the patient investigation of witnesses and suspects, all the running about, and all the brain work for this—the humiliating admission that his theories were invalid!

Oh well, it was a bad general who couldn't admit his mistakes and then change his plans. He would have to start again.

Not eager to return to Brandon Avenue by bus, he rang police headquarters for a car. When he went down to meet it, he found Barnard sitting in the rear seat with a smug smile on his face. "Thought you might need some help," he said.

"I didn't," snapped Knollis. "I'm not in the mood for company. The case has gone flop on me. Until ten minutes ago I had my man on Teddy Jessop's trapdoor with the rope round his neck, and now I haven't a notion who was responsible for Mrs. Murray's death! It's damned annoying."

"Sorry about that," said Barnard. "I thought you were going too fast, but didn't like to say anything to you. You know, Knollis, you're not an easy man to talk to!"

"There are times when I don't even like myself," said Knollis. "Anyway, I'm going to talk to you now, so please listen and don't interrupt. Oh, and we're going to Fairholme Avenue," he said to the driver.

"Fairholme, sir? Not Brandon?"

"Fairholme," said Knollis, getting into the car. "Got a torch, Barnard?"

Barnard patted his pocket. "There's another in the glove box. Now what's eating you?"

Knollis told him of his visit to Murray and to the mortuary, and then asked if Barnard had any news.

"Gloria seems to be getting on with her literary work. I had a man make several runs past the flat on the top deck of a bus, and he could see straight into the place. Nothing else to report," Barnard said shortly.

Darkness had fallen, and when the car reached the top of Fairholme Avenue Knollis told the driver to switch off his lights and drive straight down the Avenue and pull up on the waste land. There he stepped from the car, took the spare torch, and led the way along the narrow footpath to the bottom of Brandon Avenue.

"There's a hut somewhere below here," he said.

"More to the left, I think," replied Barnard.

They came to the hut. The winter winds of several years had pushed it over at an angle, but it was still possible to open the door and fasten it back to a staple knocked into the outer wall. Knollis swept the beam of the torch round the inside of the hut. "What do you see, my friend?" he asked quietly.

"A sack, a baked-beans tin, and a cracked plate with a decorated rim."

"Now go in."

Barnard obliged, and was followed by Knollis, who then switched off the torch.

"What's that?" asked Barnard. "That glow in the corner."

"Remains of raw fish in the bean tin. That explains why the contents of the cat's stomach were so little digested."

"What's this all about?" asked Barnard in the darkness.

"I thought I'd explained on the way," said Knollis, switching on the torch again. "The cat was confined here until Chummy needed it."

"Looks as if we were both wrong," grumbled Barnard. "I still don't know who you'd got lined up for the job, but I was on the wrong track with Murray. It was Palmer who came down the Avenue when he left Murray's house—and he had the nerve to admit it! Shows how over-confident these fellows can get! Still, it's the usual mark of the killer, and always their undoing. His undoing, her undoing, their undoing."

"I have no pen, he has no pen, she has no pen, so where are all the pens?" said Knollis. "I'm feeling much happier now, Barnard. We'll take a walk up the backs of the houses in the Avenue and look for lopped trees. I can't see our man bringing his materials from town if they were available locally."

It was when they reached the top of the Avenue that Knollis came to a dead halt, and Barnard gave a dry chuckle.

"This will shake Sherlock Jennings! Usual suburban gardener who chucks all his garden waste over the fence!"

At their feet lay a heap of sawn and hacked-off branches of sycamore.

"It would be a simple matter to collect one of these, trim it, and take it to the hut," said Barnard.

"To descend to the vernacular," replied Knollis, "it would be money for old rope. Very nicely planned, and very neatly executed. All the work could be done after darkness fell, and all that was then needed was either a really good alibi, or no alibi at all!"

"Why no alibi at all?" queried Barnard.

"You wouldn't need one if you thought you weren't going to be suspected. The trouble was that the Murray house had so many visitors within such a short time. That's the factor that has upset the whole thing, from the killer's point of view as well as ours."

"I think Fairfax suspected Palmer all the time, don't you?" asked Barnard.

"Probably so, but regarding him as justified, he did his best to shield him. You only need an alibi if you've a logical motive that you know will be considered by the investigators," he added in what appeared to Barnard to be an irrelevant manner. Then he said: "You've still got Gloria's place watched?"

"She's being watched," said Barnard.

They sauntered to the main road, just in time to see Jennings get off a bus and walk down to the Brandon Club carrying a dispatch case.

"Looked a bit full to me," said Knollis. "Streetlight gives queer effects, but you never know! Suppose you ring your office and see if he's been to Gloria's? Meanwhile, I'll slip down Fairholme and collect the car and driver."

Barnard was waiting outside the kiosk when he returned. "He called half an hour ago. They think he's got it from her."

Knollis reached into the car and brought out his dispatch case. "We'll have a drink at the club and see if I can make a mistake and walk out with Jennings's case instead of my own."

Barnard whistled. "Risky, isn't it?"

"Will he be able to prove intent?" Knollis asked with a naive smile.

Barnard prodded him in the back. "Come on. I'll try anything once. She must have put loads of stuff in her story—knowing it can't be used by Jennings until Murray or somebody has swung for it."

The nine o'clock news was on when they got in the club. Jennings and Holmes were propped against the bar like two china dogs, neither of them looking particularly intelligent, but both apparently listening.

"On me," said Knollis, as Jennings signalled an invitation.

"Not a member," Jennings said shortly, and waved a hand to the barman.

Knollis looked down casually. Jennings's case was on the floor, resting against the bar counter, and his gloves were on top of it. He placed his own beside it, but nearer to Jennings than himself, and then busied himself with the tankard pushed across the counter by the barman. He waited patiently until Jennings had apparently heard enough of the news, and then grinned at him. "We're going to arrest you for assisting in a murder, Mr. Jennings. How long ago did you cut your sycamore trees?"

Jennings blinked. "You don't tell me—!"

"We do," said Barnard. "The branch was very obviously taken from that very untidy heap of garden waste just over your fence."

Jennings looked past them to Holmes. "Now there's a thing, Holmes! The murder done with one of my trees! That's really something for the book!"

He looked back at Barnard. "When did you find out?"

"A few minutes ago. We were following a trail up the backs of the houses and fell over the heap in the darkness. Just one of those odd spots of luck, you know!"

"Got the hound on the job again, eh?" murmured Jennings.

"Taking me too literally," said Barnard, "and it doesn't give you the right idea. No, one of the characters in this tragedy said he came that way, so we were looking for clues—any old clues we can lay hands on. The job isn't going too well, is it, Knollis?"

"Not by any manner of means," Knollis answered in a despondent tone. "Well, I think we should get back now, Barnard."

"We only called in to tell you about the branch," said Barnard. "Thought you might like to be the first to know."

He swung round so that his body came in between Knollis and Jennings for a few brief seconds, and then, as they both said good night to Jennings he seemed to get in the way considerably, and so covered Knollis to the door.

They hurried down the concrete path to the car, and clambered in.

"Headquarters—like blazes!" said Knollis.

Chapter XVI
THE DEPARTURE OF PAUL MURRAY

KNOLLIS LOOKED IN the inquiry office on his way into the building. "Sergeant! It's a sin to tell a lie, but if Mr. Jennings 'phones or calls, we've been in and gone out again. We're looking for him, having taken his dispatch case by mistake."

The sergeant, an old-timer, gave a heavy wink.

"We can't get it typed out tonight," complained Barnard as they trod the long corridor to his office. "It'll be awkward if Jennings manages to corner us."

"There are dictaphones in the building," said Knollis. "Two men reading it can wipe off five thousand words an hour each, and it can be transcribed by morning."

"That is an idea," said Barnard.

The manuscript proved to be six thousand words long, and was fully recorded within the hour. It was repacked exactly as found, and the case sent to the front office ready for when Jennings should call for it, which would probably be morning, on his way to the office of his paper.

Gloria Dickinson's story proved to be a shocking one—shocking by the number of lies it contained. She told a story of being seduced by a man she really loved, and being left by her heartless love for another woman he married for her money, giving her—Gloria—no more than a pittance on which to bring up the child. For the child's sake she had not taken him to court; rather would she struggle on in poverty than take the child's name into the shameful atmosphere of a court to be talked about by people with nasty minds.

"Not bad going!" commented Knollis. "The poverty bit tickles me. So far as we know she's had every cent of fifteen hundred pounds out of him. Poor girl! What about passing the hat round the warehouse, Barnard?"

"Thing that amuses me," said Barnard, "is that while she wouldn't face a court, she don't mind slashing out the story to an audience of something like a million readers. Ah, well, if the *Argus* ever uses the story, it will be lapped up like cream."

Knollis walked across the office for his hat, intending to call the day ended.

"Wonder why she never told Murray about the kid?" mused Barnard.

"He's been a bit of a rat in some ways," replied Knollis, "and he may have descended to murder on the island, but there are peculiar inconsistencies in human beings, and I think he'd have insisted on marrying her if he'd known about the boy."

"Why the deuce didn't she tell him then?" continued Barnard. "Isn't that what she wanted—marriage?"

"If she wanted the boy to have money, and the education that money can bring, then the answer is 'no.' Seems to me she was prepared to forgo a great deal to see her boy well and truly launched."

"There is that to it," agreed Barnard. "She's a weird type. I sometimes wish I could see inside people's heads. It would help in this game."

"I wish I could see inside my own," said Knollis with a short laugh. "I've my old feeling that the solution to the whole thing is there. I've experienced it before. It seems to me that the subconscious mind collects the facts, and slowly pieces them together until the complete picture is formed, but no hint is given of it until the job is finished." He walked across to the door.

"Barnard," he said, "you needn't look at me as if I'm mad. I've given you a very private opinion."

Barnard picked up the thick wad of evidence from the table and riffled the pages with his thumb. "All this, and perhaps more, is in your head, eh? I've thought about the affair until my head aches, and can't get a clue to the solution."

"That's the whole point," said Knollis. "You have to relax and let the mind go to work in its own way. You plant a daffodil bulb, knowing full well it will grow, and produce leaf, and flower, and seed—but it won't if you take it up every day to see how it's progressing. That's why I'm going to bed now, and I won't be seeing you before ten in the morning—"

He was suddenly pushed back as Gregory burst into the office.

"Oh! Sorry, sir! Call from Murray's neighbour. His wife reports hearing something like a shot from the house some time ago, and they've failed to get any reply to their knocking. Sergeant Scroggey's gone straight on."

"You don't get your sleep," said Barnard.

Scroggey and a detective-officer were still trying to gain an entrance by normal means when Knollis and Barnard arrived. "No joy, sir!" he reported.

"Push in one of the glass panels in the door," Knollis ordered.

Scroggey drew back his arm and sent a large gloved hand through a small pane above the lock. He threaded his arm through. "No key, sir."

"Break the door in!"

Scroggey turned the knob with his right hand and threw his left shoulder against the door. Barnard joined him, and they gradually forced the lock-box from the door-frame.

Knollis pushed them aside and walked into the house. A thin strip of light showed under the dining room door. Knollis cautiously entered the room.

"He's done it, Barnard!"

Murray was sitting at the table, his head and shoulders slumped over it. A revolver lay under his face. Beside his left hand was a letter. The top of his head was blown away.

Knollis touched nothing, but went round the table and read the letter. Barnard joined him.

"So the Thorpe's ran out of money, eh?" said Barnard. "It was time he was told he had an eight-year-old son, and if the money for his keep was not forthcoming Mr. Thorpe's lawyers would consider taking the matter to court. That's clear enough, but why's he shot himself?"

"He had no money," Knollis said softly. "I'll bet he hasn't a cent to his name until his wife's will is proved. The poor devil couldn't do a thing about it!"

Barnard wriggled the letter from the table, revealing a photograph of Murray's son which had lain beneath it. "Sent the evidence as well, eh? Lord, the kid really does look like him!"

Knollis nodded to two keys lying on the sideboard. "He didn't mean being disturbed. . . ."

Dr. Ponsonby, the police surgeon, entered the room. "This end the case?" he asked, after a quick glance at Murray.

"No," said Knollis. "Murray didn't murder his wife."

He broke off and bent over the revolver. "Italian, probably a war souvenir. Hey! Shine your torch on the butt, Barnard. Bit more to the left. There, that's right!"

He straightened himself and stared at Barnard and the doctor. "It isn't suicide!"

"Not suicide!" exclaimed Barnard. "But everything points to it, man!"

"There's blood and hair on the butt of the revolver, Barnard," Knollis said slowly. He walked round Murray, grimacing at the mess of what had once been a head. "Neatly conceived, easily executed—exactly as was Mrs. Murray's murder. Murray was hit over the head with the revolver. When unconscious, he was tipped back and the barrel of the revolver pushed into his mouth. That effectively removed all signs of the coshing!"

He took the letter from Barnard's hand. "A semi-illiterate letter—but written on a good-class bond writing-paper. I don't believe it. Where's the envelope?"

"Posted in East Courtney," said Barnard. "It looks as if Chummy has slipped at last."

"He slipped earlier—if only my blessed mind would work properly," said Knollis. He looked round the room. "Everyone remember that, for the time being, he committed suicide—with particular reference to our nosy friend, Jennings. Where's this town where Murray's child is living?"

"Westerby? About nine miles south from here."

Knollis turned to Scroggey. "Fetch the Thorpe man in for questioning, Sergeant."

Scroggey turned briskly and left the house.

"Once we've traced the writer of this letter we've got the whole thing settled," said Barnard.

Knollis shook his head, earnestly and solemnly. "No, that isn't so, Barnard. Now leave everything. We've to fetch Gloria out of bed. I know how the whole affair was worked—and the peculiar thing is that it could never have happened at all if Fairfax hadn't taken a crew containing Murray and Dennis Palmer to Lampedusa."

He was looking round the room as he was speaking, and suddenly made a bee-line for the hearth, from which he picked a screwed-up piece of pink paper.

"Barnard! Palmer's cheque! The one given him by Mrs. Murray on the night she died. See, haven't we another sergeant with us?"

"Richardson's outside."

"Get him to invite Palmer to the station—and better tell him to take another fellow with him in case Palmer tries to refuse. We can't take chances now. And while Richardson and Scroggey are collecting their people, we'll see Glorious!"

Gloria Dickinson took a dim view of being fetched from her bed in the early hours of the morning. She didn't look quite so glamorous as in daylight, and even the carelessly folded wrap and the diaphanous pyjamas did little to gain any respect for her from Knollis. She was no more than a gamin of little intelligence, smart but not clever.

"Is this the only time you could think of to come and see me?" she protested angrily as she let them in. "Think a girl never wants to sleep?"

"I know the answer to that," Knollis said crisply, "but I'm too much of a gentleman to say it. You've had a letter from Thorpe at Westerby. I want to see it!"

She hesitated, and then went to the bureau, over-awed by Knollis's firm and official tone of voice.

Knollis and Barnard compared it with the letter found by Murray's head. Knollis nodded to Barnard, and walked to the bureau and pulled a sheet of note-paper from the top pigeon-hole. He turned and held it to the light.

"Identical! Miss Dickinson, you wrote a letter to Mr. Murray yesterday."

She pointed a finger at her breast. "Me?"

"You," said Knollis.

"I did nothing of the kind!" she protested.

"Enclosing a photograph of your boy!"

Gloria shook her netted blonde head. "Not me!"

"You showed us a photograph of the boy, Miss Dickinson. I'd like to see it again."

She blinked, and put a long forefinger to her lips. "Now, where on earth did I put it?"

She went to her bedroom, and came back with her handbag, ferreting through the miscellany it contained. "I must have put it back in the bureau!"

Knollis and Barnard waited patiently while she went through her play-acting.

"I don't know what I've done with it!" she said at last.

"You have only that one?" Knollis asked casually.

"Oh, yes, it wasn't safe to have more—not with Paul in and out of the flat."

"Let her have it!" Barnard said in a low voice.

"I think you should know the truth," Knollis said solemnly. "Paul Murray is dead. He committed suicide tonight."

Neither Knollis nor Barnard moved as she blinked at them, put her hand to her heart, and slowly sagged to the floor.

"So she didn't know," said Knollis. "That settles one more point. There should be some brandy about somewhere, Barnard. I'll get her on the settee."

"Bit blasé, aren't you?" muttered Barnard as he went to the kitchenette.

"No time for emotionalism at this stage of the proceedings," replied Knollis as he manhandled Gloria Dickinson across the room.

A quarter of an hour elapsed before she was anything like herself again, and then she smiled feebly at Knollis and moved his arm from her shoulders. "I'll be all right now, thank you. It—it was such a shock. I still can't quite believe it."

"You did write the letter in Thorpe's name?" Knollis asked gently.

She lowered her head. "Yes," she whispered. "It was the only way I could think of. Thorpe wrote me a nasty letter, and it had got to the point where it didn't matter whether the money came through me or direct from Paul, providing Thorpe got it."

"Look," said Knollis, squaring round on the settee so that he could see her face; "what *have* you done with all the money you've had from Murray?"

A contemptuous smile came to her bloodless lips. "Oh, I know what you all think about me! You think I'm just a loose woman, don't you?"

"No, I don't," said Knollis. "I think you've been a desperate woman fighting for your son—even if you've used some queer methods to get a square deal for him."

She nodded towards the bureau. "In there are receipts for documents in safe deposit at the bank. Out of what Paul gave me I kept back enough to live on, and the rest has been invested for David. He can't touch it, and nobody else can touch it, until he's eighteen. That's where Paul's money has gone to!"

"Why on earth didn't you tell him the truth?" demanded Barnard.

She looked up. "He's dead now? Honestly dead?"

"Yes," said Barnard. "What's that got to do with it?"

"It doesn't matter what I say if he's dead!"

"Then let's have it," snapped Barnard.

"If he'd known about David he'd have murdered Brenda years ago to get the money."

"You think he was capable of murder?" Knollis said.

She looked down at her hands, clasped nervously together in her lap. "Yes," she said. "Yes, Paul was capable of murder. I know he murdered Dennis Palmer so he could marry Brenda and get the money that way. He thought she'd be easier to handle than she was. She looked all feminine and soft on top, but she was hard as iron underneath, and once she found out what he was really like—with her, I mean!—she got tough with him. I know he murdered Dennis Palmer. He once talked, you know!"

"I know," said Knollis. "Now about that story you've written for Mr. Jennings. How much of it was true?"

She shrugged. "Not all of it. Mr. Jennings said Paul was bound to hang for Brenda's murder, and where would I be then? A girl had to look after herself and her boy. If I'd write the story for him, he'd tell me what to put in to make it get the readers, and he'd pull in enough money for me to enable me to move to another part of the country and start all over again—and I'd be able to have David with me for always."

She shook her head. "Mr. Jennings didn't like Paul, you know, and it was really him who put the idea into my head about telling Paul about David. He said a father was entitled to know he had a son, and entitled to keep him. He said that was a father's privilege, and I must let him know the truth. . . ."

"So you wrote the letter, making it look as if the news was coming from Thorpe?"

"Yes," said Gloria. "Mr. Jennings said if I did it that way it wouldn't look so bad as if I'd tried to upset him when he had enough on already. I posted it down the street at nine this morning—yesterday morning," she corrected herself as she glanced at the clock.

"Are you at all interested in Mr. Roy Palmer?" Knollis asked cautiously.

"He seems very nice," she said simply.

Knollis patted her shoulder, and rose. "I think that is all. Go back to bed and don't worry. You've probably seen the last of Inspector Barnard and myself. We'll let ourselves out."

Sergeant Richardson had Roy Palmer waiting at the office for them, but Knollis decided to let him stew in suspense until they had interviewed Thorpe. Gloria Dickinson's story was sufficiently straightforward to be satisfactory, but it would be better to hear whatever Thorpe had to tell.

Scroggey returned with him half an hour later, and he was shown straight into Barnard's office, where Knollis sat behind the table-desk like a magistrate, his lean features disconcertingly bland.

Thorpe was a little man with baggy eyes and large ears, dressed in a sports jacket and grey flannel trousers. He had a grey-and-white checked scarf tied round his neck, and an empty briar pipe was hanging from his mouth.

"You are the foster-father of David Murray," said Knollis.

"Yes, sir. That's right."

"You wrote to his mother a few days ago asking for the money due for his upkeep and whatever she has been paying you for looking after him?"

"Er—yes, sir."

"You haven't officially adopted him?"

"Well, no, he's sort of lodging with us until his mother can have him."

"He knows his mother, and knows you are only temporary parents?"

"That's right, sir."

"How did you get to know who was his father?"

Thorpe hesitated. "I had to get to know. She was slipping on the money, and I can't afford to keep him on my money, so when the last election was on, I got a job in the local Labour Committee Rooms—part-time, and I managed to dig all the Murrays from the register. Then I whittled 'em down. I was going to tell him, if she didn't come up with the cash."

"Yes," Knollis said grimly, "and the rest!"

Thorpe shifted his weight, and looked uncomfortable under the direct gaze of Knollis's eyes. "Er—well, when I twigged it was his father that was going to be hanged—"

"He was not going to be hanged," said Knollis.

"Well, I sort of thought, you see. . . ."

"That you'd better make the picking while it was there?" said Knollis. "So you wrote a threatening letter to the mother. Tell me, Mr. Thorpe, who had the boy's photograph taken?"

"Me—but his mother paid for 'em."

"How many copies did she have?"

"Her? Only one, sir. She daren't have any more in case he got hold and wanted to know who it was."

"That's all," said Knollis, dismissing him. "The sooner the boy's out of your hands the better—and in the meantime, be very careful, Mr. Thorpe! People who write and send threatening letters often finish up in prison!"

Thorpe was taken out for a cup of tea before being run home again. Roy Palmer was sent for, and came into the office looking both sleepy and puzzled. Knollis waved to a chair.

"'The time has come, the Walrus said, to talk of many things,'" Knollis quoted; "'of shoes and boots and kippers, and your visit to Paul Murray last evening!'"

Palmer started, and made no reply.

Knollis took the crumpled cheque from his pocket and threw it on the table. "That help your memory?"

"Well, there was nothing wrong in going round, was there?" Palmer demanded. "It was half-past six. I went straight there from the office. I'd thought it out and wanted to be straight with him and tell him everything that was said when I saw Brenda last Friday. I also took the three hundred in notes back. Truth is, I've done a lot of thinking since Brenda died, and I saw what had to be done to square things."

"He accepted the money?"

Palmer shook his head. "No, sir. He shook me. He was very decent. He said it was Brenda's money, she had given it to me of her own free will, for a good cause, and he would be happy thinking it would be spent in giving my mother a few more years of life. He was in a bitter mood, and said he didn't know why anybody wanted to live longer than they need. Life wasn't much to look forward to."

"And the cheque?"

"It was useless. I gave it back to him, and he threw it in the hearth."

"What time did you leave the house?"

"Shortly after seven, sir."

"And where did you go?"

"I went round to see Peter Fairfax and tell him what I'd done. Earlier we'd made a compact to get Murray for Brenda's murder—whether he'd done it or not, and to square off Dennis's death. After I saw Murray last night I felt so dam' sorry for him that all the hate went out of me. The man was a wreck! I told Peter he'd had enough, and I was pulling out." His mouth twisted ironically. "Trouble is that he still thinks I killed Brenda! That is, he pretends he does, and if he turns the heat off Murray, he's just as likely to start the story rolling round town that it was me!"

"And you think it was—?" said Knollis.

Palmer hesitated.

"Well?" coaxed Knollis.

"Well," Palmer said reluctantly, "I think it was Fairfax! I honestly went straight home that night. Fairfax has admitted that he was there after I left, and so, who else could it be? He's always been waiting for the chance to pay Dennis's score, saying that Dennis was once one of his men, and he always saw to it that any man under his command got a square deal! Can he prove where he was that night, sir?"

"He can't," Knollis said frankly. "At what time did you leave Fairfax?"

"He walked into town with me, we had a drink to settle the bargain to call the dogs off Murray—with apologies to you and Inspector Barnard!—and he left me to go home about half-past eight."

"Miss Dickinson," said Knollis; "what do you think about her?"

"I'm sorry for her," replied Palmer. "I think she's had a dirty deal and a rotten break!"

"You're probably going to see her again?"

Palmer nodded firmly. "Yes, I am!"

"You—er—know she had a son by Murray, a son who is farmed out with a working-class family in Westerby?"

Palmer blinked the sleep from his eyes. "She has? I didn't know. It makes no difference. I'm—yes, I'm going to ask her to marry me."

Knollis looked over Palmer's head to Barnard, and sighed. "Think you can take another shock, Mr. Palmer?"

"About—her?"

"Murray," said Knollis. "He was found shot in his house a few hours ago. To all appearances he committed suicide."

Palmer took a deep breath and expelled it in one long expression of relief. "The first decent thing he's done—apart from letting me have the money for my mother. He left it all a bit late."

"I said, to all appearances he committed suicide," Knollis remarked casually. "He was murdered, Mr. Palmer; very neatly murdered so that it almost looked like suicide!"

Palmer sprang from his chair and bent over the table. "Paul Murray murdered! Brenda *and* Paul!"

"That's it, Mr. Palmer. You'll see now why I sent for you at this unearthly hour of the night. He was coshed with the butt of a revolver, and then the barrel was pushed into his mouth and the trigger pulled, thus blowing away the top of his head and the marks of the coshing!"

Palmer found his chair, clasped his hands between his knees, and stared at the floor, his brow creased in thought.

"He must have gone straight there!" he whispered. "He must have done! Knowing I wasn't going to help him any more. He's squared the whole of Dennis's account!"

Knollis signalled to Scroggey. "Please fetch Fairfax and his wife in, Sergeant. On your way through the outer office, ask them to get Mr. Jennings out of bed and on the 'phone."

Palmer sat watching Knollis as they waited for the telephone buzzer. Knollis went into an ante-room, and came back with a large tray, its contents hidden under a large square of baize.

The buzzer sounded in the silent office. Knollis picked up the hand-set. "Knollis here. That Mr. Jennings? Like to be in at the finish? You would? Then come down here straight away. If you can bring your wife, I'll be obliged—with apologies for disturbing her rest. You see, she holds vital evidence. Hm? Seeing Fairfax in the Avenue? I can't discuss that over the 'phone! You'll be down then."

He replaced the receiver and turned to Barnard, leaning on a filing cabinet, with a puzzled expression on his face. "Think we could have a cup of tea each, old man?"

CHAPTER XVII
THE CONFIDENCE OF
MRS. JENNINGS

FOR THE NEXT HALF-HOUR there was a restrained atmosphere in Barnard's office. Knollis, clad in his usual sober grey suit, sipping his way through four cups of tea and occasionally running his hand through his badly ruffled greying hair as he stared vaguely at the fleeting pictures moving across the screen of his mind. Barnard, uncomfortable and uncertain, glancing from Palmer to Knollis, and trying to understand what conclusion Knollis had reached, and how he had reached it; his cheeks were flushed with weariness and the heat of the room, and he was having the utmost difficulty in keeping awake. Palmer, completely out of his depth in such surroundings, three times drained an already empty cup in his nervousness, and muttered his thanks as Scroggey took it from his hand and refilled it from a family-size teapot standing on a dingy tray, which advertised the products of the East Courtney Brewery Company.

Scroggey had been to the Fairfax home and knocked up Peter and Nancy from their sleep. Having given them the news that Palmer was now at the police-station, and suggesting that he was under arrest, he had ensured their appearance in accordance with Knollis's orders, and was now ambling about the office smoking cigarette after cigarette and wondering, like Barnard, what the Scotland Yard man had up his sleeve.

"Open a window, Scroggey," Barnard said somewhat irritably. "The place stinks like a public bar at ten on a Saturday night!"

Sergeant Richardson appeared in the doorway. "Mr. and Mrs. Fairfax, sir," he said, stepping aside.

Peter and Nancy Fairfax came cautiously into the office, Nancy clinging tightly to her husband's arm. Her manner was uncertain and suspicious. She kept looking anxiously into Peter's black-browed and black-moustached features, on which rested a blasé and non-committal expression. "Mornin' all!" he nodded. "Rum time for a social call, isn't it?"

"Very rum," said Knollis, rising. "If you and your wife will sit over there against the wall. . . ."

"Pleasure," replied Fairfax. As he went past Palmer he laid a hand on his shoulder. "It'll be all right, old man!"

The silence descended on the room once more, and Knollis was probably the only person present who was at his ease. A light, almost cynical, smile had appeared on his lips, and he looked down his long nose at the baize-covered tray that lay before him on the table. Beneath it lay the sack, the bean-tin, and the cracked plate found in the hut on the waste land at the bottom of Brandon Avenue.

The Jennings arrived, Frank Jennings briskly professional, with his usual array of pencils and pens sticking from his breast pocket. His greatcoat was flying open, and his hands were deep in the pockets. His wife, bewildered, walked behind him in the respectful manner of a squaw, her gloved hands clasped before her.

Jennings looked at Palmer and then at the Fairfax's ranged against the wall like sitters-out at a ball. He smiled at Barnard, nodded to Knollis, and seemed highly satisfied with life. "This is it, then?" he said brightly.

"This is it," said Knollis shortly. "Find pews, please. This won't be a long session, but we may as well be comfortable while it lasts."

He scribbled a note and handed it to Scroggey. The sergeant read it, disappeared for a few minutes, and came back leading the bloodhound, which appeared to be as surly as anyone else at being disturbed from his sleep.

"The dog may also be seated," Knollis said humorously.

The bloodhound slid heavily to the floor, and sank his dewlaps on his great paws.

"The assembly is complete," said Knollis. He sat with a back like a ramrod, his fingers interlaced, and his hands resting lightly on the edge of the table. He reminded Barnard of the president of a military court, and it was in light but crisp tones that he gave a *résumé* of the known facts of the case, and then went on:

"The murder of Mrs. Brenda Murray was a pre-meditated one. That fact is a very obvious one. The branch with which she was tripped into the pool was taken from a refuse heap behind Mr. Jennings's house. The cat was lured by a trail of scent laid from the back door of the house to a point in the field. It was caught, taken away, and confined for an indeterminate time. It was given a meal of raw fish to induce a contented mood, being kept in the derelict hut at the bottom of Brandon Avenue. The murderer kept watch on the house, brought the cat to the rear of it, and on Mrs. Murray's appearance misused it so that it screamed. She rushed to find it in the darkness . . ."

He paused to look round the room. "It was a very neat and very simple murder, but from a purely academic point of view, the murder of her husband last night—"

Nancy Fairfax started from her chair. "Paul dead as well!"

"Mr. Murray was found shot last night, Mrs. Fairfax," said Knollis. "Didn't you know, Mrs. Fairfax?"

Jennings waved a hand to attract attention. "This true, Inspector? It isn't a—a kind of trick?"

"We can assure you that Paul Murray is dead, and that he was murdered, Mr. Jennings," Knollis said gravely.

"Lord," said Jennings. "Lord, in my own avenue, and I went to bed and knew nothing about it!"

"Did you know?" Knollis asked Fairfax blandly.

Fairfax shook his black head. "Shock to me as well, Inspector. I thought he might shoot himself, but to be murdered—well, I don't like it."

"You hoped he would commit suicide," Knollis corrected him. "You've been trying to drive him to it all the way through the case since you understood we had no intention of hanging him for his wife's murder!"

"Then that would be what I heard last night!" interposed Mrs. Jennings. "I thought it was a car back-firing in the Avenue again."

Knollis cocked an eye at her. "At what time was this, please?"

"I'm not sure," she said slowly. "I knitted until twenty-past eight, and got both sleeves of Frank's pullover finished. Then I read my library book. I'd say it was no earlier than half-past eight, and no later than a quarter to nine, Inspector."

Knollis looked across the room at Palmer. "You told us you went to see Murray at six-thirty. You left him shortly after seven and went to see Mr. Fairfax. You walked into town together, had a drink or so to seal a bargain, and parted at half-past eight. It is a twenty-minute walk from town to Brandon Avenue, but a deal quicker on the bus."

He turned to Fairfax. "Where did you go when you left Mr. Palmer last night, Mr. Fairfax?"

Fairfax gasped, and his wife reached out a hand and took tight hold of his sleeve. "I went straight home, Inspector."

"Exactly as Murray is supposed to have done on the night of the murder of his wife?"

"Er—yes!"

Knollis smiled. "It puts a different complexion on the matter when you find yourself in the same situation, doesn't it?"

Fairfax looked puzzled, and drew his black brows over his eyes. "The same situation?"

"At what time did your husband reach home last night, Mrs. Fairfax?"

"Shortly before nine," she said, almost too quickly to be convincing.

"Your wife would naturally provide you with an alibi, Mr. Fairfax," said Knollis. "Brenda Murray was murdered between half-past eight and nine, while her husband was walking home. Paul Murray was murdered between half-past eight and a *quarter to* nine, while you were allegedly walking home. Did you meet anyone you knew, Mr. Fairfax? Did you speak to anyone who could vouch for you between half-past eight and a quarter to nine? Did you?"

Fairfax looked at his wife, and slowly looked back to Knollis. "I see-e," he said. "So Paul Murray might have been innocent all the time!"

"He was innocent," said Knollis firmly. "So far as we were concerned he was the most innocent and least-suspected man in East Courtney, while yourself and Mr. Palmer were stalking round the house, listening at windows, hiding behind garages, and jumping hedges."

"But I've explained—" Fairfax began to say.

His wife shook his arm. "Don't darling!"

"I want to say—"

"I think the Inspector would rather you didn't say," she replied. "I see what he's driving at."

"Then you're way ahead of me. What are you trying to do, Inspector? Pin both murders on to me because I knew Murray was a murderer and a damned rat!"

"I'm seeking the truth," said Knollis. "Did you have your car out last night?"

"No—and that is the truth!"

"Mr. Palmer?"

"I haven't one," replied Roy Palmer. "Can't afford to run one."

Knollis scribbled another note and handed it to Scroggey. Scroggey left the office, and was gone a long while.

Knollis looked at his notes, and then, still straight-backed, faced his audience again. "The sycamore branch was taken from Mr. Jennings's refuse heap, and the point arises that the murderer of Brenda Murray might have collected his other materials from the same or a similar local source. I inquired of Murray, and he was able to assure me that his wife had bought no fish for several days. As the branch came from Mr. Jennings's house, perhaps I may ask Mrs. Jennings when she last bought fish, and what was done with the scraps?"

Mrs. Jennings reflected for a moment. "Why, it would be Tuesday. I bought a pound of halibut from the van-man."

"The scraps?" murmured Knollis.

"I put them in the dustbin."

"You're sure of those two points, Mrs. Jennings?" said Knollis. "You bought fish on Tuesday, and put the scraps in the dustbin?"

"Positive, Inspector."

"Beans," said Knollis; "when did you last open a can of beans?"

She frowned. "Beans? See, we had baked beans on toast for supper on Wednesday."

"And the dustbin was emptied—when?"

"Early Tuesday mornings, always."

"Thank you," said Knollis. "That is all I wanted to know. It proves my point, that the killer gathered his materials locally, thereby saving himself a lot of work—"

A loud report like a shot, coming from the court-yard below, interrupted his explanation.

"What was that?" exclaimed Jennings.

"It sounded like a shot," said Knollis.

"It was several noises like that I heard last night," said Mrs. Jennings quickly.

"It would be," said Knollis quietly. He turned to Peter Fairfax. "Can I see your key, please?"

Fairfax fished in his pocket and held up a latch-lock key.

"Mr. Palmer?"

"The house is never locked, Inspector. Either my father or myself are awake through the night, and we never bother to lock the doors."

Scroggey re-entered the office, accompanied by a man in brown overalls. They waited inside the door-way.

Knollis picked up a pen and drew four vertical lines on his blotting-pad, and then four horizontal ones across them, forming a grill. He began to loop the ends together.

"All the houses in Brandon Avenue are built from the same plan, with left and right variations, so that the front door and stairs are on the right in one case, and on the left in neighbouring houses. Such building schemes as Brandon Avenue were planned on a contract basis, so that all the doors and windows were bought from one source, all the bricks from another, and all the fittings such as locks, door-knobs, and letter-boxes from another—naturally so, since such a system of buying is the only sensible one. The only variation to be found is with the latch-locks on the front doors, which are made so that no one key will undo any lock other than the one it is cut for. This does not apply to the back doors, and the Brandon Avenue back-door locks will be found to be similar. The murderer of Paul Murray obtained entrance to the house by knocking in the normal manner and was admitted by Murray. He killed Murray, took the latch-key from his pocket—unnecessarily—took the key from the back door and laid it with the other on the sideboard, and then went out, locked the back door with the key of his own house, and went home. He further confused the issue—Scroggey!"

"This gentleman is a motor mechanic, sir," said Scroggey. "He has examined the car, and is prepared to state that the engine has been tampered with so that when a too-rich mixture is introduced into the cylinders the engine backfires. It is a simple operation."

Jennings looked up apologetically. "You'll excuse me for a minute, please? I'll be straight back!"

Knollis smiled, and nodded. He waited until Jennings had left the office, and then threw back the baize cover. He handed the sack to Barnard, who held it before Mrs. Jennings. "Have you seen this before?"

"It *looks* like one we keep in the shed in the yard for storing salvage," she said in a puzzled tone.

"And this plate?" said Knollis.

"How on earth did you get hold of that?" she demanded. "It's the odd one from my dinner service."

"You didn't put it in the dustbin because it was cracked?" asked Knollis.

"Good gracious, no! It was always at the bottom of the—"

She suddenly broke off, to stare with wide eyes at the mask-like face of Knollis. She licked her lips and looked round the office—at the surprised Barnard, the startled Fairfax couple, the bemazed Palmer. Scroggey was not there. At a signal from Knollis he had followed Jennings.

"Not—not—my God, it can't be *Frank*." she screamed.

"It was Frank!" came Scroggey's tough voice from the doorway, and he came in again, holding a struggling Jennings by the collar of his coat.

"Yes, it was Frank," agreed Knollis. "Frank was a very clever man. Frank Jennings knew all about crime—he studied it and even wrote books about it! He knew that all murderers make at least one mistake. He was too clever! He was not murdering with hate, or passion, or greed in his heart. He was the coldly academic murderer, proving to himself and to us that a perfect murder could be committed!"

"Let me go!" shouted Jennings. "This is an outrage! I'll see my solicitor in the morning—"

"That's true!" said Knollis. "Friend Jennings was in a fortunate position. He could wander about town at any time of the day or night, knowing that the general public look on newsmen as something different from ordinary men and women. He was in a position to keep check on every move we made. He could pump all the witnesses and suspects, and even his next victim. He learned the inside stories of the lives of all the people concerned. He watched and waited for the psychological moment—and then he struck, knowing there was such a tangle of possible motives that everyone but himself would be suspected. He didn't even bother to provide himself with an alibi, because he knew that we could not attribute to him any of the motives we usually seek!"

"It's a rotten, lying frame-up!" said Jennings. "If this is a trick to make the real culprit confess, then get it over. I'm not in favour of this kind of play-acting. It's—it's unnerving!"

Knollis got up and came round his table. "Everyone back to the wall, please!"

He cleared the floor-space, and then took a pair of gloves from his pocket, laid them in the centre of the floor, and looked up.

"We know that Fairfax handled the kippers, because he has admitted it," he said. "Now, Mr. Frank Jennings, if we trail these across the floor and out into the corridor, and down the passage, and then give the hound a kipper to smell at, and he starts from the centre of the floor, and goes out into the corridor, and down the passage . . ."

Jennings licked his lips.

"Open the door, Scroggey," said Knollis. "We must prove it to him!"

Scroggey obeyed, and stood back. Jennings didn't wait for the test. He took one bound forward and vanished through the open doorway, his feet pounding along the tiled corridor.

Knollis made no move. With an apologetic glance at the weeping Mrs. Jennings he said: "He may as well make his own way to the charge-room. They're waiting for him, aren't they, Scroggey?"

"As per your note, sir," said Scroggey.

Barnard came forward.

"You know when you exchanged cases in the Brandon Club? His gloves were lying on top of his case."

"Well?" said Knollis.

"I asked you if you'd knocked them off, and you said yes!"

"That's correct," said Knollis. "You don't mind me descending to the vernacular now and again, do you? I did knock 'em off!"

THE END

Made in the USA
Monee, IL
17 February 2022

91381977R00115